She'd always been good

But what about the empty place inside Ann? That place where her woman's heart beat? That place that needed to connect; that needed to be held, stroked?

Hell, what about that place that could use some good, raunchy sex?

"Oh, my," she muttered, sure that everyone within a fifty-mile radius—including her son sitting only a few feet away—could hear her X-rated thoughts.

But when Eddy Winters, with his mane of hair draped over his broad shoulders, told her she was beautiful and brushed his lips across hers with well-honed skill, he'd stirred her deepest desires. Ann knew he had to be an operator, used to getting his way with a smile and a kiss, but that didn't mean she couldn't enjoy it. When would she ever be swept off her feet by a modern-day pirate again? Only she'd have to remember he'd surely swashbuckle his way out of her life as easily as he had stolen his way in.

Dear Reader,

Sometimes becoming a family takes years. But for three unlikely couples, it happens in an instant—in the new SUDDENLY...A FAMILY miniseries!

As any single parent can tell you, courtship with kids is anything but slow and easy. But three popular American Romance authors show you how much fun it can be to be caught in a "family affair."

Join Nikki Rivers for the snowy tale of a single mother's fantasy-come-true. The gorgeous hunk of a guy who's winking in her direction sure beats spending another evening alone with her mug of hot chocolate and a sitcom.

We hope you've enjoyed all the books in the SUDDENLY...A FAMILY miniseries! Be on the lookout for more in the months ahead.

Regards,

Debra Matteucci
Senior Editor & Editorial Coordinator
Harlequin Books
300 East 42nd Street
New York, NY 10017

Nikki Rivers

ROMANCING ANNIE

Harlequin Books

TORONTO • NEW YORK • LONDON
AMSTERDAM • PARIS • SYDNEY • HAMBURG
STOCKHOLM • ATHENS • TOKYO • MILAN
MADRID • WARSAW • BUDAPEST • AUCKLAND

To one of my very favorite women, my daring and outrageous daughter Jennifer, whose '81 Olds started the whole thing.

ISBN 0-373-16664-8

ROMANCING ANNIE

Chapter One

Eddy Winters paced to the wall of glass overlooking the eerie, lunarlike landscape and stared out into the night. His brooding image stared back at him.

Right about now he should have been cozily ensconced in a luxurious A-frame in the mountains of Vermont with a long-legged blonde named Ingrid. And he would have been—if Hank Lewis hadn't interfered.

"Lighten up, Winters," he mumbled to himself. "This is no ski chateau, but there's plenty of snow."

Unfortunately, there would be no willing female to warm his bed—that is, *if* he ever made it to his bed.

Wisconsin, after two blizzards in as many weeks, was frozen and forbidding as an uncharted planet in the throes of an ice age. The snow had finally tapered off, but the clearing skies had plunged temperatures to well below freezing. Cabs not stuck in snowbanks or tangled in fender benders were crippled with frozen batteries. Every rental car in town still running had been snapped up long before Eddy's plane touched down on the frozen runway at Mitchell International Airport in Milwaukee.

He turned away from the window and wound his way through crying babies, rambunctious children, irritated parents and snoring businessmen.

"Any cabs yet?" he asked the young woman behind the airline counter.

She didn't even bother looking up from her computer. "Not yet, sir."

Eddy sighed. "What about rentals? Any luck there?"

"Sorry," she answered automatically, "nothing yet."

It was the same answer he'd gotten every twenty minutes since he'd landed.

He made his way to the empty patch of carpet in front of the windows and watched the heavy equipment trying to move the snow from the runways. Behind him, the sound of disgruntled humanity was interrupted regularly with static-laced, disembodied announcements of canceled flights and late arrivals.

With a short, sharp sound that wasn't quite a laugh, Eddy remembered Hank telling him that this job would be an easy one for a pro like Eddy. Hank predicted it would go so fast Eddy wouldn't even have to unpack his luggage.

"Well, Hank was right on that one," Eddy murmured with a rueful twist of his mouth. Eddy wouldn't have to unpack his luggage because he *had* no luggage.

His suitcases, managing to make connections ordinarily too complicated for a mere human, were on their way to Tahiti. Eddy pictured his suits and shirts, his jeans and sweaters, whiling away the tropical days under a palm tree like a scene from *The Invisible Man* and fervently wished he could follow.

For several minutes he watched a plow dig into another foot of snow on the runway, then looked at his watch. The Northcott Inn had promised to send a limo to pick him up over two hours ago. Frustrated, he decided to head to a pay phone to try to call the inn again. But when Eddy swung around he ran smack into a hooded creature carrying a very hot cup of coffee.

"Oops! Sorry!" she said, then yanked his doused sweat-shirt away from his chest, pursed her lips and started to blow.

"Uh...what are you doing?" Eddy asked.

Her head came up, her lips still pursed. "I'm trying to cool you off before you get burned."

Eddy got a quick glimpse of a quirky little nose sprinkled with brown freckles and a small but lusciously full mouth before she dipped her head again and resumed blowing on his soaked sweatshirt.

A current shot through him, and he stirred, shifting his weight a little. If she thought she could cool a man down by pursing her soft, full mouth and blowing, then there was definitely something wrong with the men in Milwaukee, Wisconsin.

Or maybe he had just spent a far too long, far too frustrating day. Either way, now was not the time to explore those...possibilities.

As if on automatic pilot, he lifted her chin with his thumb and forefinger. "Uh, I think you'd better stop now."

Her eyes were the color of warm brandy. At least he thought they were. Not only did her oversize fur-trimmed hood shield half her face, but her gaze also skittered away from his so fast that it was hard to tell.

She began to rummage in a huge shoulder bag, then pulled out a wad of paper napkins.

"Here, let me see if I can—"

Eddy looked at the mittened hand dabbing at his sweatshirt, then to her bent head. She seemed tall, but it was hard to tell much else about her. Her bottle-green anorak provided enough padding to send her out to scrimmage with the Green Bay Packers, the oversize hood giving her a strange, quirky anonymity. The phantom of the airport, he thought whimsically.

A phantom that was wreaking just a little too much havoc on his libido.

He placed his hand over hers, stilling its restless movement. "Look, it's all right—really. Besides," he added teasingly, "it's the nicest thing that's happened to me all day."

Her head jerked up again, and he thought he glimpsed surprise—or was it confusion—on the phantom's face before she quickly looked away again.

"Well . . . sorry, again," she stammered before shuffling off, leaving a trail of napkins in her wake, one damp one stuck to the heel of an aggressively furry boot.

Eddy shook his head. Phantom or not, she wasn't anything like the women Eddy was usually attracted to. His taste invariably ran to beautifully poised, elegantly turned out women. Women who didn't bump, didn't spill—and didn't surprise. Just the kind of woman Eddy would be with right now if he wasn't stuck in an airport on the first leg of Hank Lewis's wild-goose chase.

Eddy shook his head. Hell, maybe he owed Hank yet again. Forfeiting the prospect of endless days in a ski chateau with the beautiful but predictable Ingrid suddenly didn't seem like much of a loss. No—he wouldn't be exactly missing Ingrid. But he *was* missing *something*. There was a restlessness inside Eddy—a slight dissatisfaction he couldn't quite name. His life was as he'd made it, as he'd wanted it. And yet . . .

Automatically his gaze swung to the spot where the phantom with the freckles had disappeared. There was no sign of her. Too bad, Eddy thought. He wouldn't mind a little diversion in the form of finding out what was under that oversize hood. Whatever it was, he'd be willing to bet that it'd be a surprise.

He had just thrown himself into one of the torture devices the Mitchell International Airport used for chairs when he was paged. Threading his way to the information desk, he asked, "You paged me? Edmund Winters?"

"Yes, Mr.—"

Before the woman could finish, a vaguely familiar voice at his side said, "*You're* Edmund Winters?"

Eddy turned and found himself staring at that freckled nose and ripe mouth again. "The phantom of the airport," he murmured, wondering if maybe he was going to find out what was under that hood, after all.

"I'm from the Northcott Inn," the phantom said.

Eddy grinned. He was. Indeed, he was.

HE WAS NOTHING like she'd expected. The Northcott Inn generally attracted two types of people—elderly couples who'd been coming to the inn since the beginning of time to celebrate birthdays, anniversaries, holidays or for a quick shopping trip to the stores on Wisconsin Avenue, or the brand of businessman who wore a conservative three-piece, pinstripe suit five years short of being in style and had short, graying hair. The kind of man who was so much a creature of habit that even though the fading, aged Northcott Inn wasn't what it used to be—like a lizard following the same muddy track to its watering hole throughout its life—he kept coming back.

This guy didn't look like a creature of any kind of habit—unless it was something vaguely illicit. True, his dark hair was heavily streaked with silver, but it waved to nearly his shoulders—his very *broad* shoulders—and flowed from a high, unseasonably tanned forehead. A skier, Ann thought with a touch of envy as she pictured sunny slopes, mulled wine, beautiful people.

She stuck out her hand. "I'm Ann Madison, your chauffeur for the evening." Too late she realized she still had her bulky green mitten on, soggy with cooling coffee. Ann wrinkled her nose. "Sorry about that."

"No problem," he said, "I can use the caffeine."

Ann started to laugh, wringing out the soggy end of her mitten onto the snow-wet carpet. But when she looked up, she immediately sobered. Lord, the man was a hunk—a good six feet of heart-stopping hunkiness. And all she'd managed to do so far was keep him externally supplied with badly brewed airport coffee.

Nice first impression, she thought, wishing she'd worn her other boots. Heck, if she'd known she was picking up a guy who could easily fill out a beefcake centerfold, she'd have worn her other coat, as well. She squirmed under her hood. No way to look professional with polyester fur in her face and on her feet. But, then, Edmund Winters wasn't exactly dressed for success himself. Instead of boring, out-of-style business clothes, he was wearing faded blue jeans with a battered leather bomber jacket over a faded black sweatshirt.

Ann let her gaze run over him. Okay—so he was making a pretty good success out of the way those jeans fit him. And the bomber jacket looked soft as butter as it spread itself around his shoulders and down admirably filled-out arms. But the guy was going to wish he was wearing something a little less sexy and a lot more practical as soon as the frigid air hit his backside.

When her gaze traveled past his fleece-ensconced chest and to his face, she read the amusement in his eyes. Eyes that turned down slightly at the corners and radiated the kind of crinkles that came from laughter and the great outdoors.

"Will I do?" he asked, those eyes glittering.

Oh, he'd do, all right—and for something far more interesting than delivering him to the Northcott Inn. Ann buried the thought somewhere in the back of her brain to be taken out and fantasized over on some cold, lonely night, and answered, "I was just thinking that it's pretty cold out there and you're not exactly dressed for it."

He thrust his chin up, his hair flowing back, his eyes dancing like he carried his own private disco ball inside his head. "Ah," he said. "I see. I did pack warmer clothes, but they decided to skip Milwaukee and head for Tahiti."

"Smart shirts," she quipped.

He grinned. "That's what the lady told me when I bought them."

Ann started to laugh, but looking at that grin seemed to wipe her brain clean. She broke her gaze from his, searching for something to bring her feet back to ground level and ended up studying the signs above the escalator as if English was a language she had yet to master. It was a whole lot easier to get words out when she wasn't looking at him. "Would you like some hot coffee for the trip?" she asked him with an air of distraction.

"I've had some, thanks."

Ann quit trying to figure out what down escalator meant, her eyes going back to his face as if they just couldn't stay away. He was grinning again and it took her a long moment to recover. "Oh...uh, yeah, I guess you have," she stammered then headed for the escalator. "I'm parked right out in front," she said over her shoulder, "in a tow-away zone."

"A tow-away zone?" he asked, a touch of a groan in his voice.

She saw no point in turning around to offer an apology. Besides, if she had to keep looking into his face, they'd never get out of there. Anyway, no one who owned a tow truck was going to be hanging around airports on a night like this to hassle people who were only hoping to save a few steps with their luggage—not when the real money was out on the streets.

She led him down the escalator and out into the night, shuffling through the snow to her rusted, battered Oldsmobile.

"Wait a minute," came the incredulous voice behind her.

Ann looked back. Edmund Winters was perched atop the snowbank lining the curb like an angry conqueror who'd found himself in the middle of the wrong movie.

It was all she could do to tear her mind from his stance, his widely braced, muscular legs.

"Something wrong?" she asked mildly.

"*This* is the Northcott Inn's airport limo?"

Ann refused to apologize again. "The limo wouldn't start."

His eyebrows shot up. "And *this* would?"

"It's here, isn't it?" she answered, instantly regretting the sarcastic bite to her words.

She watched him give the Olds the once-over. Okay, so maybe it didn't exactly *look* reliable. But it was. Much more reliable than the inn's limo—or just about anything else at the Northcott Inn these days.

But let Edmund Winters discover that for himself. Shivering, she unlocked the driver's door. He was still on top of the snowbank. She held the door open, but he didn't seem to take the hint. "Mr. Winters, if you don't mind, it's freezing out here. Could we go?" she asked, her patience starting to plummet with the windchill.

As graceful as a latter-day Errol Flynn, he jumped from the snowbank, landing with a soft thud, then walked to the passenger door and tugged. "It's locked," he stated flatly.

"No, it's not. It just—"

"Ann," he said softly, with exaggerated calm, as he continued to tug at the door, "this door definitely *is* locked."

"If you will let me finish, Mr. Winters," she replied, a saccharine sheen to her words. "The door isn't locked, it just doesn't open. You'll have to get in on this side."

He stared at her for a second before murmuring, "Unbelievable."

Ann watched her passenger swagger—a mite slowly, considering the weather, she thought—to her side of the car. As he bent to peer into the car Ann suddenly wished she'd taken the time to clear out the evidence of Jason's last fast-food meal. So maybe she had a habit of throwing candy wrappers on the floor and leaving half-empty foam coffee cups on the dash, but it's not like she'd been planning to chauffeur the elite around town. Besides, Mr. Edmund Winters might have a classy-sounding name, but in faded denim, distressed leather and an old sweatshirt, he hardly looked the part.

"Climb in, Mr. Winters. Or are you afraid you'll get your sweatshirt dirty?"

The words were out before she could stop them. Not at all the way she should speak to a guest of the inn, but she'd be damned if she was going to apologize. Just because a man was gorgeous didn't give him the right to be difficult when the windchill was forty below.

Edmund Winters straightened and turned to face her. He propped one elbow on the car roof, his narrowed eyes glittered at her like fire reflected in blue ice. His full, soft mouth curved into the gentle ghost of a grin.

And Ann's stomach did a somersault.

Such a face. He had a large, straight nose, high cheekbones, a strong chin sporting rakish, dark stubble. A gust of Arctic wind whipped silver-streaked hair across his face. When he pulled it back with a strong, blunt-fingered hand, the twinkle of an earring glinted from his left ear.

A modern-day pirate.

Ann conjured a brief picture of him on the ski slopes as he dug his poles into deep powder, avoiding avalanches, effortlessly ravishing snow bunnies along the way.

Okay, so he was a charmer. So all he had to do was move that mouth a certain way and he could probably get away with being as difficult as hell—in any kind of weather.

But Ann wasn't in the mood to be charmed. She was in the mood to get warm.

Sighing, she thrust her hands deeper into her pockets. "Look," she said, "if you want to take a chance on a taxi or a rental, you're welcome to. But if you're coming with

me, would you mind getting in before I freeze my fanny
off?''

EDDY CLIMBED into the front seat and slid over, wondering
just what kind of fanny Ann the chauffeur had to freeze off.
She'd surprised him with that sassy comeback out of her
sweet mouth. Maybe once in the car she'd pull back her
hood so he could see her eyes and her hair. He was in-
trigued—and more than mildly curious. The women he
knew drove Porsches, BMWs or, at the very least, Toyotas.
If they'd had to ride in a jalopy like this one, they'd pout for
a week. And they'd certainly never get behind the wheel.

Eddy watched Ann climb in and turn the key in the igni-
tion. The engine started right up—loud but steady. Another surprise. "I'm impressed," he admitted with a shake
of his head. "What's your secret?"

"I bake cookies for my mechanic," she said blithely.

"Really?" he drawled.

"Chocolate chip."

"Well, then," Eddy stated as if that explained the matter
entirely.

Ann pulled away from the curb, gunning the engine
through a ridge of snow left by the plows. The car jerked
over it, and the door of the glove compartment fell open,
hitting Eddy smartly on the knee.

As he rubbed his knee with one hand, he shut the compartment door with the other. It promptly fell open again,
hitting his hand this time.

"Sorry about that," Ann murmured.

"Maybe if you made the guy a chocolate cake—" Eddy
began, but then she swung the Olds into the road and Eddy
was too busy bracing himself against the door to finish the
sentence. Another surprise—Ann the chauffeur was not
only capable of the snappy comeback of a New York cabby,
she also drove like one.

"Uh, Ann? Aren't you going a little fast for road conditions?"

"Don't worry, I'm used to this Wisconsin weather. Besides," she added breezily as she passed a city bus, "there's hardly any traffic out here."

She swung in front of the bus, sending the glove compartment door smacking against his knee again. By the time Eddy looked at the road, they were barreling down on what appeared to be two very stationary brake lights. "Uh...that car ahead seems to be stalled—"

Ann whizzed around it, and Eddy ended up with half a cup of cold coffee in his lap.

They looked at each other. "I know," he said, "you're sorry. Just turn up the heater, okay?"

She bit her lip. "It is up."

Eddy groaned as he grabbed a wad of napkins from the littered floor and tried to dry himself off. "What's the matter—run out of chocolate chips?"

She shot him a look, her hood jerking back just far enough for him to catch the flash in her eyes. "If you'd worn the appropriate clothes you wouldn't be so damn cold—no matter what fell in your lap! Honestly, you'd think you were going on a picnic or something."

Stifling a grin, Eddy picked up a half-eaten chocolate bar from the seat beside him. "Guess I'm a little confused since you seem to have brought the food and beverages. On the other hand," he added sarcastically, "if you didn't drive like a maniac, I wouldn't be wearing half the refreshments."

She gave him another look, but her hood had slipped into place again, and he could only imagine the flash in her brandy eyes. For the first time in the long, tedious day, Eddy felt his mouth curve into a broad, genuine smile. "I can't offer you chocolate-chip cookies, Annie," he drawled, "but if you get me to the Northcott Inn in one piece, I'll share my candy with you.''

MY, OH, MY—the pirate had a voice on him, too. Low, teasing. You'd swear he was offering to share more than a candy bar.

Yeah, right, Ann. What modern-day pirate wouldn't fall for a woman in polyester fur and a car that gave him all the luxuries of a vending machine gone insane?

Get your mind back on the road, Ann, where it belongs on a night like this.

As if responding to some divine cue, a car suddenly appeared out of nowhere, sliding through the intersection against the light. Ann whipped the steering wheel to the right, sending the Olds into a skid. They missed the other car by mere inches. Ann started to let out her breath in relief, but it turned into a high-pitched, ''Yikes!'' when she saw they were careening straight for a light post.

''Hang on!'' she yelled, suddenly certain she was never going to taste chocolate again—Edmund Winters's or anyone else's.

She pumped the brakes like a madwoman and turned into the skid. The car missed the post by a foot and plowed into a three-foot snowdrift with a sickening thud, sending a spurt of the icy powder across the windshield.

The night was suddenly too quiet, the sky as black as coal. Eerie halos surrounded streetlights and traffic signals blinked to an empty road. The runaway car was nowhere in sight.

''Oh, my,'' Ann murmured, laying her forehead against the steering wheel. When Edmund Winters touched her arm, she jumped and gave a little cry.

''Are you all right?'' he asked softly.

She put her hand on her chest and stared at him for several jumpy heartbeats, then nodded. ''You—you just startled me. Guess I'm a little shaky.''

"Here, maybe a little chocolate will help."

She looked at the bar he held out and into his eyes. "But I--I haven't exactly gotten you to the inn in one piece yet."

The pirate grinned, and her heart stopped jumping. In fact, it seemed to have stopped beating altogether. The only sound in the cold, silent car was a snap as he broke off a piece of candy before holding it to her lips.

What could she do? She opened her mouth, felt his fingers against her lips, tasted cool, hard chocolate on her tongue.

"Better?" he asked gently.

She nodded mutely as the chocolate started to dissolve in her mouth, watching him raise the candy to his lips and bite off a hunk with strong, white teeth.

She watched him chew and thought, *Lord, I almost wish I needed mouth-to-mouth.*

She blinked. What was she thinking? That the touch of his mouth on hers would be worth a near-death experience? *Get a grip, Ann. You've got a kid to go home to and a car to get out of the snow. And if the only way you'd ever get to feel the lips of a Viking pirate against your own is to be near death, then you can live without it. Literally.*

Shoving open the door as far as it would go, she wiggled out. Edmund Winters slid over and followed.

"Let's find a phone," he said.

"What for?"

"To call a tow."

Shaking her head, she answered emphatically, "Nothing doing. I haven't got the money for a tow."

The pirate shrugged. "So put it on your card. The inn will reimburse you."

"The way things are going at that place," she muttered, "there is a better chance of spring coming early than there is of me getting reimbursed."

The pirate looked at her sharply. And why not? Employees should know better than to bad-mouth an establishment to a paying guest. "Look, on a night like this," she thought it prudent to add, "a tow could take forever." She drew the fur of her hood closer around her face and wiped the water running from her eyes with a still damp mitten. "We'd have our choice between freezing to death or dying of carbon monoxide poisoning."

Eddy took a look around. True, they weren't exactly in a rural area, but every business within walking distance was dark and appeared to be deserted. No doubt because of the weather. "Okay," he said, "what do you suggest?"

"I suggest we get to work and get the car out ourselves."

Eddy plowed through the snow to the front of the Olds. "The damn thing's suspended in snow. There's no way this car is going anywhere without a tow."

"Defeatist," he heard her mutter as she got in the car again. The engine started right up, but when she put it in drive and stepped on the gas, the wheels spun, sending snow flying to hit Eddy square in the face.

He heard her muffled giggle as he wiped his eyes. But he had the last laugh. The car wasn't going anywhere. "Guess I was right," he drawled as he watched her climb out of the driver's seat.

"We'll see about that," she muttered.

He watched her trudge through the snow, open the trunk of the car and haul out what looked like a miniature snow shovel.

Eddy shook his head and gave a snort of laughter. "What do you think you're going to do with that little thing?"

She thrust up her chin and straightened her back. "I'm going to shovel us out of that drift."

Eddy snorted again. "Right. You and what munchkin?"

Ann gave him a look, then gave the shovel handle a pull. "Presto! A full-size shovel." She grinned at it with pride. "Jason gave it to me for Christmas."

Eddy lifted a brow. "Your mechanic?"

"My son," she corrected shortly. "Now get out of the way so I can get us out of here."

He shook his head. "You wait in the car." He held out his hand. "Give me that thing and I'll get started."

"Don't be so chauvinistic," she huffed. "We'll take turns. Me first."

So Eddy leaned against the car and watched the phantom of the airport with the unflagging spirit dig into the snow.

After five minutes, he was beginning to see the wisdom of grabbing the first shift. He was freezing. He tucked his hands under his arms for warmth and began to walk back and forth along the length of the Olds.

"You can wait in the car if you'd like," she said sweetly.

The sound of her voice reached him in the cold air, and he could tell by her tone that she was amused at his discomfort. Well, he'd be damned if he'd sit in the car while a woman did all the work.

He stalked over to the phantom and held out his hand. "Give me that shovel—*you* wait in the car."

The phantom slapped the shovel in his hand. "*I'm* not cold."

She wouldn't be, thought Eddy, as he started to dig. Not dressed like that. And neither would he if his gear wasn't winging its way to the tropics.

The wind blew his hair into his eyes. His ears felt like they were about to crack and fall off. Maybe her hood was ridiculous, but Eddy was beginning to wish he had one just like it.

After five minutes of watching him, Ann figured she could probably manage to get the car out, but what the heck, she'd let him suffer just a little longer. Teach him a lesson on how to dress for a Wisconsin winter.

Besides, watching him do physical labor was pretty entertaining. His long, leanly muscled legs braced and dipped. His bomber jacket rode up with every shovelful of snow, revealing slim hips and a nice, tight backside. Occasionally, a gust of biting wind blew the hair from his clean profile and the glitter of his earring.

Ann sighed. Much as she was enjoying herself, it was time she called a halt to the show. Edmund the pirate was looking athletic but frozen.

"That should do it," she called over the wind. "Stand aside and watch an old pro at work."

His bark of laughter rang out into the crisp dark night. "It'll never happen!"

Ann climbed into the car and rolled the window down. "Care to make a little wager?"

He shook his head, his eyes dancing with that disco ball again. "I never take advantage of a woman."

"I'll just bet," Ann muttered and started the engine.

She threw it into reverse and gunned it. The wheels spun uselessly.

"Told you," he yelled over the engine.

Ignoring him, Ann just smiled serenely, drove forward, then back, forward and back, rocking the car till it bounced free. She backed up several feet, threw it into drive and pulled alongside an astonished-looking Mr. Edmund Winters.

"Need a lift?" she asked sweetly.

He grinned and shook his head. "Quit gloating and let me in before I freeze to death."

Ann laughed heartily and did just that.

Half an hour later, she pulled the Olds into the Northcott Inn's parking lot.

"We're here," she announced with satisfaction.

"Safe and sound," he agreed, grinning at her. "Where did you learn to handle a car in the snow like that?"

She shrugged. "You live in Wisconsin long enough, you learn. Don't you have snow where you come from?"

"New York has plenty of snow. I've just never owned a car of my own."

She looked at him and thought, *Of course you haven't. You probably have a couple dozen Barbie doll girlfriends who drive Corvettes or Jaguars and are only too happy to pick you up and pick up the tab.*

"I guess I owe you another bite of my candy," he said with a gentle rumble, amusement sparkling in his eyes as they traveled over her face.

He turned toward her, leaned forward and raised his hand to push back her hood. She gulped, her eyes widening as her hair came tumbling out across the back of his hand. The car was cold enough to show the cloud of their breath mingling between them, but Ann felt suddenly too hot inside her anorak. One hand still tangled in her hair, his other brought the chocolate bar to her mouth. She looked into his eyes, about to refuse. But who could refuse a pirate with eyes of ice and fire? Her lips parted, and he slid the chocolate between them.

Hershey had never tasted so good.

While it melted on her tongue, she watched him raise the bar to his lips, his strong teeth severing a morsel with the precision of a Viking pirate gripping a blade.

She watched his mouth as it made quick work of the chocolate, wondering what other tasks those wide, firm lips were capable of performing with such precision and ease. Just as her imagination was beginning to enter embarrassing realms, those lips quirked into a grin and the pirate started to slide over the front seat toward her.

"Wha—what are you doing?" she stammered.

The grin deepened. "I have to get out your door, remember?"

"Oh—yes, of course."

What had she been thinking? she wondered as she opened the car door. Did she think a man who looked like Edmund Winters was suddenly overcome with desire for a thirty-five-year-old mother who drove a broken-down heap, wore furry, braid-trimmed boots and was a good ten—okay,

okay, fifteen—pounds overweight? A woman who kept him soaked in coffee—hot or cold? Did she think he was so overcome with the wonder of her winter driving skills that he was prepared to sweep her off her feet?

Did she think she might let him?

Before she could ponder that little question, she got out of the car, waiting for him to follow. He stepped out beside her, the cold wind catching his silver hair, blowing it straight back from his strong, bronzed forehead. His earring winked, his frosty blue eyes glittered. A Viking pirate.

Not a man for good old practical Ann Madison.

Definitely not.

And certainly not a man who, by any stretch of the imagination, could be possible father material for Jason.

Definitely not.

And the sooner she deposited him safely at the hotel and bid him good-night, the sooner she could stop all these crazy fantasies and get home to her son.

Chapter Two

"The hotel's around the corner," Ann told him briskly. "Just follow me."

Eddy was happy to. The converted gaslights that lined the street were dark, the power probably knocked out by the storm, but the snow illuminated the darkness enough to see Ann's hair bounce on her shoulders with each quick, energetic step she took. She was a surprise in more ways than one. And it wasn't just that she was clumsy enough to douse him in coffee, gutsy enough to save his life and resourceful enough to get a car out of a small mountain of snow.

When he'd pushed her hood back and that confusion of chestnut hair tumbled out, he'd nearly lost his breath. And her eyes—warmed brandy, tilted down at the corners under quirky little brows that always seemed confused and questioning. Despite the cold, Ann had a warmth a man could sink into—and a mouth on her that could hold her own. Not a phantom at all, but a provocative combination of damsel and wench. They rounded the corner and an icy breath caught in his throat. His thoughts couldn't have been more appropriate.

He'd seen it before, of course. The last time had been too many years ago to count, and it'd been summer, a long, lazy, sweet summer. On this night, many years and assorted experiences later, The Northcott Inn rose from the sidewalk like an ice mansion, its turret and arched windows frosted in new snow, its wide stone staircase leading to its massive, elaborately carved wooden door nearly buried in powder.

He had the crazy sudden urge to sweep sweet Ann into his arms and carry her to the castle.

He also had the feeling that she'd fight him every inch of the way. And he had a feeling he'd enjoy it.

But she'd already started up the stairs, so he let her go, pausing a moment to picture her in long, white ermine, moonlight playing in her hair.

He shook himself. The night was getting to him. The night—and the long, frustrating day. And memories. Memories of a sweeter time, an innocent time. And, oh, yes, Ann was definitely getting to him. He took the broad stairs two at a time to catch up with her.

The door creaked when Ann opened it. He followed her inside.

The place was lit only by firelight. The glow flickered over a massive pink marble fireplace, warming the floral chintz sofas and rose-colored wing chairs scattered around the lobby. It looked homey, inviting, and memories washed over him anew—he knew those sofas, knew what it felt like to curl up on them. Unbidden, Eddy's mind put Ann on one of those sofas with him—necking in the firelight, his hands buried in that thick mass of hair. That would be something new. He'd never necked on the sofas at the inn. Life as Eddy the boy had known it had fallen apart long before he was old enough to know that pleasure.

"There you are!" Came a voice from the darkness. "I thought you'd never get back! The power's out because of the storm, and the inmates are wailing. I've been running around with candles for the last two hours!"

Eddy turned to find a young woman with short, slick blond hair charging down the sweeping open staircase with a candelabra held in one hand, the wax from the candles guttering dangerously, the wavering flames blinking off the multitude of earrings dangling from her ears.

"I'm sorry, Lara, but it's wicked out there. If you'll check Mr. Winters in, I'll take over with the rest of the guests."

Lara skidded to a halt at the foot of the stairs, the firelight sparking off the metallic silver combat boots on her tiny feet. "Mr. Winters?" she asked with a gulp.

"Mr. Winters," Ann repeated. "You know," she prodded while Lara stood staring, "the guy I was picking up at the airport?"

Lara screwed up her face. "Uh-oh."

"Uh-oh? What do you mean, uh-oh?"

Lara lifted her shoulders. "We're full."

"Full?" Ann shook her head. "Impossible. We're never full."

"We are tonight. We've got the overflow from the Pfister, the Hilton and the Park East. The whole city is closed on account of weather, Ann. You just came from the airport—you should know that."

Eddy squeezed his eyes shut briefly. "Don't tell me, Lara. Please don't tell me," he pleaded.

Lara screwed up her face again. "Uh—I gave away your room."

Eddy opened his eyes. "I asked you not to tell me that, Lara."

She lifted her shoulders again, her earrings casting a weird shadow across her cheek. "Sorry. Power's off—no computer. Guess in all the confusion I forgot you were coming."

"Well, one of you two ladies is going to have to find me a bed to lay my weary body on—even if you have to take me home with you to do it."

"Hey, Mr. Winters, that'd be fine by me, but I don't think my boyfriend would like it. Besides, I'm on duty all night."

"Lara!"

"Well, he brought it up," Lara said defensively. "Hey, wait a minute! There is one place left!"

Eddy thought he knew that place, and there was no way he wanted to stay there. Wouldn't that just feed into Hank's little scheme? In fact, he was beginning to wonder if Hank had engineered this whole thing.

"Surely, you have one room left. Anything will do— anything at all. A closet, a storage room—"

"A penthouse?" Lara interrupted brightly.

Eddy closed his eyes and groaned inwardly. Just what he needed. A few days in the Northcott Inn's penthouse, and there was no way he'd be able to remain detached.

"Look, I'd rather not pay for a penthouse," he began, grasping at the first excuse he could think of.

"Of course not," Ann agreed. "Since it's our fault, Mr. Winters, we'll give you the penthouse for the same rate as a regular room."

Ann was already moving behind the desk, plucking a key from a drawer.

"No, really—" he started to protest.

"We insist. Besides, the penthouse is usually kept for the owners of the hotel and their families—we aren't expecting a visit from any of them any time soon."

Right, he thought wryly.

The penthouse was the last place he wanted to stay. But what could he do? In order to do the job Hank hired him for, he had to stay at the Northcott Inn. That is, if there really was a job to do and this wasn't just some new scheme of Hank's to get Eddy to do what Hank thought was the right thing to do. Besides, he was beat. He needed a bed.

He sighed, his weary bones urging him to give in and give them a place to rest. "All right," he finally said. "Guess the penthouse it'll be."

Ann's smile was almost worth the concession. The vibrant turning up of her lush mouth was almost enough to make up for what he knew awaited him in the penthouse—longings for impossible things, long-ago days.

"Great!" Lara said, pushing a red leather book his way. "Sign here."

By the light of the flickering candelabra she still held, Eddy signed his name.

"Okay," she said after blowing on the signature and shutting the book with a flourish, "I'm off to the café to start pots and pots of coffee. Thank goodness the stoves are all gas!"

ANN GULPED down panic. "Aren't you going to show Mr. Winters to the penthouse?"

Lara flapped a hand. "You do it—I've been up and down those stairs a hundred times. I must have lost five pounds," she said, patting the flat tummy showing itself off in a tight, black mini-skirt. Lara, who was about five foot two and must have weighed all of one hundred pounds, didn't need to lose an ounce, while Ann could certainly stand to lose a few. But escorting a Viking pirate by candlelight to his sleep chamber wasn't how she would have chosen to do it.

"Here." Lara thrust the candelabra at Ann. "Take this. I've got a flashlight somewhere." She rummaged under the desk. "Eureka! Here it is. Pleasant dreams, Mr. Winters, I'm off to find some caffeine."

"Lara!" Ann tried to call her back, but it was too late. She'd already disappeared.

"Let me take that," the deep voice of Edmund Winters said. "You lead the way."

Ann placed the flickering candelabra in his waiting hand. The glow played across the planes of his face, sending his cheekbones into harsh relief, lighting his glacier-blue eyes to an icy flame. She turned from him, determined to make it up the five flights of stairs without falling at the man's feet. But as she turned she glimpsed his shadow thrown across the wall. His long, tangled hair fell to the outline of his broad shoulders. His profile was still and majestic—a long, fine nose, a hard, determined chin. To see him this way, without the way his eyes could sometimes tease or his mouth could sometimes soften, sent a chill down her spine. He could easily be from another time. A Viking. A pirate. Maybe it was not mere chance that Edmund Winters would be spending the night in the penthouse.

She turned away from his shadow and looked into his face. "They say it's haunted, you know," she blurted, wincing at her unexpected words. With the candlelight on her she must look and sound like one of those jumpy heroines in an old, not very good, black-and-white movie.

Amusement danced in the candlelight glowing in his eyes. "Do they?" he asked, a deep, sardonic lilt to his voice. "Then lead the way. I'd like to meet my hosts for the night."

"DO YOU BELIEVE the place is really haunted, Ann?"

His voice, coming from behind her, sounded normal enough. It was the first he'd spoken in the five flights they'd climbed, and she was relieved to find that he hadn't transformed into some sort of spirit along the way.

"There's a legend," she told him as they reached the door to the penthouse. "The couple who once owned the inn died in a fiery car crash when they were only in their fifties. If spirits walk, I suppose theirs might. But I have no personal knowledge of it."

"Spoken like a true diplomat," he murmured, leaning slightly closer to her, far too close for Ann's comfort. "And are they rumored to be the friendly kind of ghosts or are they out to get anyone who dares cross their threshold?"

"Oh, friendly, I think," she answered, bending to fit the key into the ancient lock. "It's said that—oops, I dropped the key!"

They knelt in unison, their hair brushing, tangling, their fingers colliding as they reached for the key at the same time. From just a breath away, she looked at him. There was a stillness in his face, an impossible-to-read look in his crystal blue eyes.

"Maybe you'd better let me open it," he said softly.

She nodded mutely. The candlelight turned the strands of chestnut and silver into magical threads, slowly untangling as they drew apart and rose. Ann stepped back, scarcely breathing as he unlocked the door and it creaked open.

He gave a little bow. "Damsels first."

The man was way too perfect for the night, thought Ann. And the place. He could be the hero, escaped from the pages of a dusty old book to haunt the night. She tore her gaze away from him and stepped over the threshold with the odd feeling that she might be entering another dimension, that she might really be going back in time.

If she was, then it must be spring.

"Can you smell that?" she whispered.

"Lilacs," he murmured.

"Yes," she said softly. "Lilacs."

She watched him stroll to the fireplace, a miniature of the pink marble one in the lobby, and gaze at the portrait in oil above it. "Our ghosts?" he whispered.

Ann came up beside him. "Yes. Nathan and Hattie. She was the daughter of a wealthy beer baron. He was charming but penniless. They say both families were against the union, but they loved each other enough to defy anything that stood in their way." She sighed. "It's said that it was lucky they died together, because they could never have lived apart."

He raised the candelabra higher, casting long shadows against the pale, yellow striped silk wallpaper. "She's wearing lilacs in her hair."

"They say she wore them often."

He turned to her, the flickering candlelight playing over his face, the now familiar amusement dancing in his eyes. "Then the scent—"

She stared at him, licking suddenly dry lips with her tongue. "You—you don't think—" she stammered.

He raised a brow. "I'm not wearing lilacs, Ann. Are you?"

She swallowed hard, then turned briskly away, busily checking out the room, smoothing a ruffle here, a cushion there. "It's a well-known rumor that someone here at the inn keeps the place smelling like that. Someone who's been here long enough to remember."

Edmund Winters laughed softly, the sound rolling around the room like a presence of its own. "But, as you said, only a rumor."

She straightened and turned, thrusting her hands into the pockets of her anorak. "I don't believe in ghosts, Mr. Winters," she stated briskly. "Do you?"

"I don't know," he answered, his voice soft and low, his wide mouth twisting, taunting as he left the fireplace and started to walk toward her. "Ask me again in the morning. If there really are ghosts haunting these rooms it should make for an interesting night." He was close to her now, his voice dropping even lower. "And I'm all for interesting nights. Aren't you, Ann?"

Ann gulped. It'd been a long time since she'd had the kind of interesting night this Viking pirate put her in mind of. A long, *long* time.

Shadows wavered, as if in some unfelt gust of wind. The scent of lilacs bloomed sweeter, overwhelming—as was the slow, sweet curve of the Viking pirate's mouth and the icy glimmer of his eye. She felt herself swaying closer to him, reaching out for him—

"Ann! Ann!"

Her heart gave a little jump and she pulled back as the sound of Lara's voice pulled her back to reality. "Uh—that's Lara calling me. I better go."

She started to turn, but he stopped her with a hand on her arm. She looked into that face again, wondering if he could hear the beat of her heart.

"Better take this," he said, removing a candle and handing her the candelabra. "You'll get lost in the dark."

Yeah, she thought, taking it from his hand. She felt pretty lost already.

"Good night, Mr. Winters."

"Good night, Ann. Sweet dreams."

EDDY ROLLED OVER and reached for her. She wasn't there. His eyes flew open. It took him a moment to remember where he was—the penthouse apartment on the fifth floor of the Northcott Inn.

Hattie and Nathan's bed was soft, sumptuous, the natural Egyptian cotton sheets Hattie always favored reflected in the elaborate brass headboard. The creamy cashmere blanket was soft and warm against his skin, an inviting contrast to the cool, smooth slither of the champagne-colored silk jacquard coverlet spread over the high, soft bed.

Eddy was naked beneath it, his body a hell of a lot more awake than his mind.

The place was haunted, all right. But it wasn't Nathan's or Hattie's ghost that lurked in the dim corners of the bedroom. It was a brandy-eyed, wild-haired woman with freckles and furry boots that wouldn't let him be.

Had he dreamt of her? Languidly, he let his palm travel over his chest and down to the lower part of his body, cradled in the cashmere. He grinned. Yeah, he'd dreamt of her, all right. He searched his memory, but the dream was elusive, already lost. To his mind, that was. His body was obviously going to need a cold shower to forget.

Ann, he mused. No, *Annie.* Yeah, she was an Annie, all right. And as different from the brightly polished women he knew as you could get. And maybe that was why he'd woken up wanting her. Nothing more than that. Nothing more than the fact that she was a surprise and he was in the mood to be surprised.

He threw back the fine bed linen and stood, then strode naked to one of the tall windows that looked out on the Milwaukee skyline. Pulling open the heavy drapes, he was hit with blue sky and sunshine and a world suddenly come alive again after a frozen, restless sleep. It was obvious from the pattern of smoke billowing out of distant smokestacks that it was still January, but the sun had seemingly warmed the air to above freezing, the pristine, new snow throwing back its brilliance with a blinding energy. And Eddy felt that energy in his bones.

He also felt it in his stomach. He was starving. Still naked, his black silk robe somewhere over the Pacific, he headed for the phone in the sitting room.

"Room service, please."

"Sorry, Mr. Winters," answered a voice that Eddy thought might be Lara's, "the Northcott Inn has no room service."

Eddy ran his hand through his tangled hair. "Since when?"

"Almost a year. Breakfast is served in the restaurant off the lobby."

Eddy hung up the phone. The Northcott's room-service breakfast had been legendary. The cart draped with snowy linen, fresh flowers in a crystal vase, a morning paper, an assortment of fresh rolls baked on the premises, a tub of sweet Wisconsin butter and fresh-squeezed juice—a whole pitcher of it. Hattie and Nathan had always partaken of it themselves, including Eddy in the ritual when he'd come for his summer visits. Staring at the phone, Eddy wondered when—and why—it had been discontinued. It had been one of the few things he'd been looking forward to on this trip—and now it was gone.

And so was the scent of lilacs, he mused as he walked through the rooms. He paused at the door of the other, smaller bedroom, hesitating a moment before pushing the door open gently with the palm of his hand. The quilt on the bed had been changed, but other than that the room was as he remembered it. He had the urge to enter, fling himself on the bed and stare out over the treetops just as Eddy the boy had done.

Damn Hank. He must have known that coming to this place would open the door to a lot of conflicting memories.

Eddy set his lips together in a firm, grim line. Of course Hank knew it. He was counting on it.

Eddy shut the door with a solid click. He'd spent half a lifetime not playing into their hands. He wasn't about to begin now.

The big, bright, eat-in kitchen across the hall from the bedroom would only make matters worse, so Eddy skipped it altogether.

He went to the sitting room and scanned the floor-to-ceiling bookshelves on the far wall. He already knew nearly every title they held. But one book caught his eye. A tall, thin, leather-bound book in an unusual, for a book anyway, shade of lilac. He slipped it out of its place on the shelves and flipped it open.

It was a journal—Hattie's journal. He snapped it shut. The memories were already too strong.

The sitting room was the same as he remembered. Still bright, still comfortable, still full of the warmth of the woman who'd decorated it—still the closest thing to a real home he'd ever had.

The only thing that had changed was the smell of lilacs. It was gone.

Eddy moved to the fireplace. Logs were laid, a paper fan lying on top, ready for a match. He looked at the portrait of Hattie and Nathan, wondering how many fires they'd shared sitting on the flowered sofa. Hattie was as he'd remembered her, soft, feminine, yet with a spark of mischief and defiance in her dark eyes and fire in her auburn hair.

Nathan was handsome, sterner, yet with a deep kindness in his eyes and an abiding love for the woman at his side shining out of his face.

"What about it, you two?" Eddy murmured softly. "Is it true? Do you really haunt this place?"

Something in the place was haunting him—feeding into those restless feelings he'd had of late, making him wonder if all the boyhood memories assaulting his senses were true, after all. Did love like Hattie and Nathan seemed to have shared really exist? Or did it only exist in the imaginings of a boy who had long since grown up to face reality?

Eddy turned away from the portrait, wishing they were still here, right here in this sitting room, the room-service cart between them, Hattie lightly buttering a bran muffin for Nathan while Nathan gruffly insisted on a Danish.

Eddy shook his head as if he could shake loose the memory. "You're losing it, pal," he muttered. "What you need to do is grab a nice hot shower, get dressed and get on with it." The sooner he got busy, the sooner he could get out of there. Yeah—first a shower, then breakfast. And then he'd start checking out the Northcott Inn. After all, that's what he was there for.

And that was all he was there for. When this job was over, he was heading to New York where he belonged.

In the bedroom, he realized he still held the journal in his hand. Maybe he'd have a look at it someday. But not now. He tossed it onto the window seat and headed for the shower.

"Ann, sweetie, I'd love to help you out—you know how much I adore Jason—but it's my weekly lunch with the girls. I was just heading out to do a little shopping before I meet them at Watt's Tea Room."

Ann's upstairs neighbor, Estelle Kowalski, had been meeting the women she'd worked with at the telephone company for lunch for years. They were all well into their sixties, but she always referred to them as the girls.

"Oh, that's right. I forgot that this was your day for the tearoom."

She watched Estelle's tiny form hurry around her living room, collecting handbag—a Chanel knockoff, but a good one—gloves—fine leather—and coat—a silver fox that she'd bought herself to celebrate her retirement a few years ago. She slipped into the coat and tied a chiffon scarf around her champagne-colored cotton-candy hair. "Sorry, sweetie, but I've really got to run. Wish I could help you out."

"Don't give it another thought. It won't kill Jason to spend a snow day at the inn. He'll gripe and grouse but he'll end up being content to have the extra time on the computer."

She followed Estelle down the stairs, marveling at her gracefulness in three-inch heels covered with old-fashioned galoshes.

"Have a good lunch," she called after her before letting herself into her first-floor flat.

Jason did grouse, wasting precious moments fighting the notion of having to spend the unexpected school vacation day cooped up at the inn. By the time she'd gotten him out the door she was really running late. It was nearly nine-thirty when Ann rushed into the lobby, Jason, earphones fastened to his head, bopping to the beat of the music ahead of her. She could blame her son for making her late. But she couldn't blame him for the feeling of befuddlement that seemed to have followed her to work. Nor could she blame the fact that it was a Monday. Not when she knew who the real culprit was—damn his winking earring and streaming hair.

For the first time in years—oh, hell, for the first time in her life—Ann had met a man tempting enough to invade her dreams.

Edmund Winters was the reason she'd slept badly. Edmund Winters was the reason she'd felt sluggish and out of sorts when the alarm went off that morning. Edmund Winters. With any luck, the alleged ghosts of Nathan and Hattie had kept him up all night, and he'd checked out early. Workdays at the inn were unpredictable enough without a Viking pirate invading her days. The image of him invading her nights was quite enough of a challenge, thank you.

"Hey, Lara! Cool earrings! Mom—"

"No, you can't," Ann automatically answered, never missing a step.

"Aw, Mom," Jason groaned, "you don't even know what I was gonna ask."

"You were going to ask—again," Ann said over her shoulder, "if you could get your ear pierced."

Jason plopped his books on a table next to a wing chair, where they teetered dangerously close to the edge. "How does she *do* that?" he asked Lara in a plaintive wail.

Lara shrugged. "She's a mom, Jase. It's her job."

"Yeah, well, I don't see why Lara can have about a hundred holes in her ears and I can't even have one!"

Ann sighed heavily. She'd been through this before. "How old is Lara, Jason?"

"Aww—"

"How old?" she insisted.

"Twenty-two," he conceded grudgingly.

"And how old are you?"

"Aw, gee, Mom—you know I'm ten."

"I rest my case."

"But I bet when Lara has a kid, it'll have its ear pierced at birth."

"And its nose and its belly button," Ann muttered.

Lara laughed. "You might be right, at that. When and if I decide to procreate, you can give me a baby nose ring for a shower gift."

Jason kicked his feet against the worn carpet. "Aw, life isn't fair."

"Rarely," Ann agreed dryly. "Now why don't you get over to the café and get some breakfast. Tell Maria I said to let you have whatever you want."

As always, Jason brightened at the thought of food. "Cool. I'm starved!"

"Except ice cream. No ice cream, Jason!"

"Yeah, yeah," he said over his shoulder on his way to the inn's café.

"You might want to pay a little visit to the café yourself, Ann," Lara ventured cautiously.

Ann shook her head. "I'm fine. I had toast and coffee while I waited for Jason this morning."

"Well, I wasn't exactly thinking about your breakfast, Ann."

Ann looked up from the precarious pile of Jason's books she'd been trying to straighten. "Uh—oh. What now?"

"It seems the chef is freaking out—and we've got a houseful to feed."

"Damian? He's a sweetie," Ann said, shrugging out of her coat and skirting the registration desk to reach the tiny office behind.

Lara rolled her eyes. "Sure he's a sweetie, but even sweeties can freak. He says he can't *create* when his endive is on the missing greens list and his lamb is gross."

Ann wrinkled her nose. "Gross?"

Lara shrugged. "Well, too fat, or something. He's still ticked that we changed suppliers."

"Yeah, well, it's a mystery to me, too, considering this new one charges even more. But who can figure New York out?" Ann sighed, wondering for the hundredth time what the home office in New York was thinking of to insist on all these cuts.

The Northcott Inn was losing its reputation—fast. When Ann had started working there, it had been old but venerable, a distinguished elderly lady whose class more than made up for her eccentricities. But in the past year, the old lady's hair and teeth were falling out, and nobody seemed to care enough to do anything about it.

"I guess we should just be grateful that with business off New York doesn't tell us that we don't even need a chef. I would not look forward to firing Damian, that's for sure. " Damian was a great chef, but he had a penchant for dramatics and could be pretty unpredictable.

"Well, at least you don't have to worry about having to fire Austin anymore. Have you heard the news?"

"What news?"

"He got his scholarship to Yale. He'll be leaving at the end of summer."

"You're kidding? Austin? Yale?" Austin Patrick could barely handle the job of part-time desk clerk. Somehow Ann couldn't see him managing to navigate the hallowed halls of an Ivy League institution.

Lara nodded. "Hard to fathom, isn't it?" Then she shrugged. "Maybe he's one of those absentminded geniuses. You know, a bust at everyday life, but still managing to come up with a cure for the common cold?"

Ann laughed. "Guess you can't judge a genius by his messed-up hotel reservations." She bent to the computer on her desk and scrolled the screen.

"My, what a lovely sight. Just look at all of last night's check ins. Wouldn't it be great if we could say that every morning?"

Lara flicked a hand through her short hair. "Awesome but doubtful. Not when our lamb is gross and the bedspreads on the third floor have enough holes to let your toes out for fresh air."

"I've got a requisition in for new bedspreads, but as usual—"

"As usual," Lara finished for her, "the heads are blind, deaf and dumb to anything that doesn't net them at least a million."

"Exactly," Ann agreed. She checked out a few more things on the computer, then asked Lara hopefully, "Are you by any chance sticking around this morning?"

"Yeah, I figured I'd catch up with the auditing now that the power is back on. Besides, you're going need help with all those check outs while you're busy trying to calm Damian down."

Ann grinned. "Lara, you are truly a sweetheart."

Lara grimaced. "Yeah—don't let it get around."

"They'll have to pierce my nose to get it out of me," she said over her shoulder as she crossed the lobby and pushed her way through the double French doors that led to Café Northcott.

The place was bustling. The dozen and a half white-clothed tables, usually empty this time of day, were scattered with customers. The lone morning waitress, Maria— it'd been months since they'd needed two—scurried back and forth with steaming, fragrant plates.

"Ain't this great?" she called to Ann as she whizzed past.

"This is fantastic," Ann answered, wishing that this was the scene they faced every morning. All too often, the room was empty. Maria, who'd been at the inn for years, was threatening to quit. No customers, no tips. The nearly full restaurant was the best sight Ann had seen in months—well, except maybe for a certain Viking pirate.

Maria whizzed by again and Ann asked, "Are you going to need some help? Should I call a temp agency?"

"No way! I'm not sharing a dime of these tips!"

Ann laughed and pushed open the kitchen door.

"Miz Madison! What am I to do? My lamb is nasty! My endive is missing!"

Letting the door swing shut behind her, Ann wondered how on earth she was going to keep Café Northcott's handsome, temperamental chef happy enough to keep him from defecting.

Chapter Three

Eddy decided to take the stairs. That way, he could arrive in the lobby unheard—and, with any luck, unseen, as well. Experience had taught him that if you moved quietly and quickly enough to make yourself nearly invisible, you could sometimes manage to pick up the most important information of any job.

The front desk was deserted, the lobby empty. In quick silence, Eddy moved to the registration desk. He could see the computer on the desk in the office behind. Scanning the lobby, he stood quietly for a moment, just listening, then, walking backward, his eyes and ears alert to the slightest change, he skirted the registration desk and slipped into the office.

The computer was on, the cursor winking. He hit a couple of keys. Twenty-five check ins last night. Twenty-one check outs scheduled this morning. His fingers moved quickly, searching for the location of the rooms that would remain occupied, committing them to memory. He'd learned long ago that keeping track of where all the players were was essential to the success of any job.

He fiddled with the keys some more and checked out the reservations for the rest of the week. The place would be nearly empty, just as Hank had promised. Bad news for the inn. Good news for Eddy. The less people around, the easier this job would be to complete. But still, it surprised him. Maybe Hank hadn't been singing the same old tune when he'd told Eddy that something was going wrong at the inn.

He stepped to the door, scanned the lobby again and listened with a stillness and concentration he'd honed over the years. Nothing. He stepped to the desk and hit some more keys, looking for financial records.

"Ah, this looks promising," he muttered, and was about to choose a file when he stopped, stepping back and smoothly leaving the office, thrusting his hands in his pockets and turning toward the elevator just as the doors swished open.

Lara stepped out, still wearing the miniskirt and boots from the night before.

"Good morning, Mr. Winters. Something I can do for you?"

"I was wondering if the manager was available."

"Something wrong with the accommodations?" she asked, a hint of mischief in her heavily made-up eyes. "Our resident ghosts didn't pull any funny stuff last night, did they?"

Eddy gave her an answering grin. "No—afraid not. I was just wondering if it would be possible to move to another room some time today."

Lara looked surprised. "You don't like the penthouse?"

"Well, uh, it's just that I heard you say that the place was kept ready for the owners, so I thought—"

Lara flapped a hand at him. "Oh, don't worry about that. It's not like the old days. The place is run by a big corporation now. And heaven knows, they never show their faces. The place was supposed to be left to a grandson, and he could care less. As far as I know, he's *never* been here."

Eddy's neck moved a little uncomfortably against the collar of his sweatshirt. "Really?" he asked mildly.

"Not as an adult, anyway. They say he doesn't want anything to do with the place even though he practically grew up here. That's probably why the place is falling to rack and ruin—" Lara stopped speaking and suddenly looked up, chagrined. "Oh," she said in a stage whisper, "I guess I shouldn't be telling you this."

"Don't worry, Lara" he said easily. "Your secret is safe with me." Indeed, he hoped, given the sentiments she had expressed about the grandson, that his secret would be just as safe.

Lara looked relieved. "Thanks. I can change your room for you if you like, but it'll have to wait until the house-keeping staff gets going."

It was essential that Eddy meet the manager, get a measure on the man. Especially if, as Lara said, the place was really falling to rack and ruin. Hell, had Hank been speaking the truth, after all? "I'd really like to speak to the manager. Convey my thanks for the use of the suite last night."

Lara shrugged. "Sure. The manager should be back any minute, if you'd care to wait."

"I was just on my way to breakfast. I'll check back when I'm finished."

Eddy headed for the café and was immediately shown to a table. He was trying to decide between the omelet and the Belgian waffle when he felt someone watching him.

"Did that hurt?"

Eddy looked up from his menu and into the round, brown eyes of a boy. "Excuse me?"

"That—your ear. Did it hurt when you got it pierced?"

Eddy set down his menu. "Not really—no."

The boy wrinkled his nose. "Did you have to ask your mom?"

Eddy laughed. "No—I was a little old for that."

"How old?" the boy prodded, a serious look in his eyes.

"Eighteen—and if you're going to interrogate me," Eddy said, nodding toward the empty chair next to him, "why don't you sit down."

"Okay," he said with a shrug.

Eddy watched him pull out the chair and throw himself into it. He wore a long T-shirt over baggy jeans, a huge jacket over that and gigantic athletic shoes, the laces untied. His mahogany hair was shaved to within a quarter-inch of his scalp up the sides and back, the rest of it falling straight to the tops of his ears and parted slightly off-center.

"Your mom won't let you get your ear pierced, huh?"

"Nah."

"Well, she let you get a pretty cool haircut. Maybe she'll change her mind."

The boy shrugged again and stared at the table. "I doubt it." Then he looked up and brightened. "Is that a real diamond?"

Eddy laughed again. "Yup—real diamond."

"Cool."

The waitress came for his order. "Want anything?" he asked the boy after he'd ordered the omelet.

"I guess I could eat another stack of cakes."

The waitress grinned at him. "And chocolate milk, right?"

The boy gave her a sudden, brilliant smile, and Eddy could see the girls were going to have their hands full in another couple of years.

"You must be a regular here," Eddy said, once the waitress had gone.

"Kind of," he said, scrunching his nose.

"How come you're not in school?"

"Snow day. How come you're not at work?"

"'Cause I have to go shopping."

The boy made a face. "Yuck."

Eddy laughed. "Yeah, yuck. Can't be helped, though. My luggage ended up in Tahiti, and this sweatshirt is on its second day."

"Whoa—my mom would never let me get away with *that.*"

"Neither would mine," Eddy said ruefully, thinking it was really his grandmother who would have objected. His mother had generally left that kind of thing to the servants.

The waitress came and set steaming plates of food in front of them. They ate in silence for a while, Eddy marveling at what short work the boy could make of a stack of pancakes.

Suddenly, his breakfast guest stopped eating, letting his fork clatter to his plate. "Hey, you ought to ask my mom to take you shopping. She loves to shop, man."

"Really?"

"Oh, yeah." The boy nodded. "She's like the Power Ranger of shopping. She's real good at picking out guys' stuff."

"For your dad, I suppose," Eddy said around a mouthful of omelet.

"Nah—we're divorced," he answered matter-of-factly.

"Oh—sorry." Eddy knew all about divorces and what they could put a kid through.

Again, the kid shrugged. "It's cool. He wasn't around much, anyway. Mom always buys my stuff, though. 'Course, I usually go with her—just to make sure. Why don't you ask her?"

Eddy squeezed his eyes shut. He was lost—the boy was too fast for him. "Ask her what?" he questioned when he'd opened his eyes again.

"Ask her to take you shopping—I'll come along, too. It'd sure beat hanging around here all day."

Eddy laughed. "I don't even know your mother. I'm sure she wouldn't want to—"

"Yeah, she will! I'll go ask her."

The boy started to get up. "Maybe you should finish your milk first," Eddy said.

The boy grinned and grabbed his glass. "Oh, yeah," he said, then gulped half the glass down at one go. Then, before Eddy could stop him, he went running from the restaurant.

Maybe you should finish your milk first? Where the heck had that come from? Eddy wasn't used to being around kids—and he was certain he'd never admonished one to finish anything before.

He was still musing over it when he saw the boy come running back in, disappearing just as quickly again, through a door that Eddy figured led to the kitchen.

He came out moments later, dragging behind him— *Annie.* Eddy grinned and stood, waiting for the boy to drag her over to his table, catching a good long look at everything he'd missed the night before. She wore a dark green turtleneck tucked into tailored trousers of the same color. The sweater clung to her lush curves. The dip of her waist flared out into abundantly curved hips. He let his gaze travel over her, stopping for an extra heartbeat on her ankles. No polyester fur encasing her feet today, just trim ankles shown off by the black flats she wore.

Nice. Very nice.

"Here he is, Mom. This is the guy who needs some clothes. I said we'd take him shopping. Can we? Come on, Mom. It'd be cool."

"Good morning, Annie," he said, managing to finally get his gaze off the surprise of her luscious body and onto her face. "How's my favorite chauffeur?"

ANN DECIDED right then and there that she was going to kill Jason. She'd make him do his homework first, of course. Then she'd slay him slowly, feeding him Brussels sprouts and calves' liver while she did it.

Trying to buy a little time, she attempted to stop at Mr. and Mrs. Albert's table, two regulars who'd remained loyal to the inn. But the most she got out was a hurried good-morning and half a smile while Jason dragged her to the next table.

"Good morning, Mr. Winters," she replied with what she hoped sounded like a normal tone of voice. It wasn't easy having to face the object of a long, hot dream from the night before.

"Eddy," the dream man said.

"What?" she asked, her mind not tracking properly.

"My friends call me Eddy."

"Oh, yes, of course. Eddy."

Jason was looking from one to the other of them, his nose scrunched up in question. "You guys know each other?"

Ann cast what she hoped was a sweet, patient look at her son. "This is the man I picked up at the airport last night, Jason."

Jason's eyes grew round. "Wow! The guy staying in the haunted penthouse? Cool!"

"That's me," Eddy said.

"Awesome," Jason breathed with just the proper note. "Now we *gotta* take him, Mom. I want to find out if he saw Hattie and Nathan last night."

Maybe she'd make him eat some dried fruit—apricots and prunes—too, just for good measure.

"Jason, would you get lost for a minute so I can talk to Mr. Winters alone?" she said sweetly.

"Eddy, Mom. His friends call him Eddy."

"Go!" she said.

"Oh, all right," Jason said, sulking, and started to shuffle away. Then he turned, his face brightening. "Hey, I'll go ask Lara and Max to cover for you!"

Ann opened her mouth to tell him not to, but Jason was too quick. He was across the café before she'd formed the first word. She could choose between raising her voice or chasing after him—and with the Viking pirate's cool blue gaze on her there was no way she was doing either.

When she turned to Eddy Winters, there was laughter in those blue eyes and an enigmatic smile curving his soft, full mouth.

She smiled ruefully. "My son gets a little excited sometimes. I'm sorry if he was bothering you."

"No bother, Annie. I enjoyed his company." His smile
deepened. "I should warn you, though, he seems very fond
of my diamond earring."

Ann raised her eyes to the ceiling. "Oh, great—between
you and Lara, looks like I'm in for another siege in the *I-
want-a-pierced-ear* wars."

Eddy laughed. "When can you be ready to take me?"

"Take you?" Despite the fact that her son might be tearing into the café any minute, the phrase was conjuring up
images best left in the pages of a historical romance novel.

"Shopping," Eddy said and it took her a moment to rec-
ognize the word.

"Oh—I'm afraid that won't be possible."

"Do you have to pick another guest up at the airport?"

"No, but, I—"

"Jason says you're the Power Ranger of shoppers." He
tilted his head to the side, the look in his eyes sliding into
mock soberness. "Come on, Annie," he cajoled in a voice
that said he knew how to get his own way. "Help me out,
here. My clothes are on their way to French Polynesia and I
haven't got a thing to wear."

Her gaze went unbidden to his crotch. Oh, my. Did that
mean he wasn't wearing any underwear? She felt her cheeks
go hot and shot her gaze to safer ground. He was wearing
the same sweatshirt he'd worn the night before, minus the
bomber jacket. His shoulders filled it out with enthusiasm.
The stubble on his face was darker. Apparently, his razor
had ended up in Tahiti along with everything else.

The amusement in his eyes, when she met them again, had
gone deeper, sending crinkles cascading across those incredible cheekbones, causing his eyes to turn down even
more at the corners.

Was she nuts? The Viking pirate was practically begging
her to take him shopping. She, along with half the women

in the world, should be more than happy to take him anywhere he wanted to go.

The problem was that she wasn't nuts enough. 'Cause it'd be far crazier to take this man anywhere at all. If she didn't watch herself, she'd be nursing a broken heart and a fond memory for the rest of the winter. And winters in Wisconsin could be long, indeed.

The door burst open again. "Mom!" Jason yelled, obviously not caring that he'd claimed the attention of every diner in the café. "They said yes! We can go!"

Eddy was looking at her, eyebrow raised, sweet smile on his lips. "So, Annie, are you going to make two men happy, or what?"

"Mom—?" Jason cajoled, in a manner that was too close to the Viking pirate's for comfort.

She looked at her son, at the bright expectation in his face. How could she resist two men who were so charmingly bent on getting what they wanted? She sighed. "I guess I'm going to make two men happy."

"All right, Mom!"

"Okay, big mouth, let's let Mr. Winters finish his breakfast." She took Jason's shoulders and turned him toward the door, giving him a little push. "We'll meet you in the lobby in about a half hour," she said to Eddy as she started after Jason.

"I'll look forward to it," he murmured in the kind of voice that had her doing a double take. The kind of voice that didn't sound at all as though all he was looking forward to was a shopping trip with an ordinary woman and her overly zealous son. The kind of voice that had her stumbling backward right into Mr. and Mrs. Albert's breakfast table, sending a coffee cup rattling in its saucer, sloshing coffee over the edge and onto the tablecloth.

"Oh! Sorry!" she said, still backing away.

"Think nothing of it, my dear," said Mrs. Albert, patting her tight, gray curls. "And enjoy your shopping trip."

Ann stopped dead as Ada Albert winked one pale green eye at her. She looked at Harold Albert. His eyes were twinkling merrily, and he was giving her a jaunty little wave with his fingers.

Lord—did everyone in the hotel know what she was thinking? What she was *feeling?* Her face felt hot as a poker—and it was probably just as red. Was the Viking still watching her? She turned and started walking as fast as her legs of jelly would carry her toward the exit, because she just did not want to know.

"DOESN'T THE INN have valet parking?" Eddy Winters asked as they walked side by side to the parking lot.

Ann shook her head. "Not anymore. Which is a shame considering the parking lot is around the corner."

He grunted. "No room service anymore, either."

Ann looked at him sharply. What was he? Some kind of hotel spy? Was this shopping trip just a pretense to get her to talk about the Northcott Inn's shortcomings? She watched him out of the corner of her eye. He definitely didn't look like the kind of man who would be happy whiling away the hours in an old-world inn like the Northcott. Maybe he was with one of those rating services—or with a guidebook, out scouting for the best places to stay in the Midwest. The Northcott Inn would hardly qualify, she thought ruefully. Not anymore.

In the two years she'd been at the inn, Ann had come to love the place, and had a lot of ideas to get it going again, make it profitable. But her letters to the New York headquarters either went unanswered or were rejected outright. The corporation obviously had bigger fish to fry. Northcott Hotels had become Northcott Enterprises. It wasn't just a family business anymore. In any case, she'd heard that there wasn't much family left to care. A few Northcott cousins—and, of course, the grandson who'd inherited the Northcott Inn. And, according to Doris in housekeeping, he was reported to be an irresponsible playboy with absolutely no interest in the place. The inn was run by an executor, or something.

All Ann knew for sure was that it was being run badly, and if she could get her hands on that rake of a grandson, she'd be only too glad to give him a piece of her mind. Hattie and Nathan must be restless in their graves, indeed, knowing they'd given their pride and joy to someone who just didn't give a damn.

They'd reached the car, and Eddy held the door for her. Jason had run ahead and was already in the back seat, ubiquitous headphones covering his ears, his head moving to a beat only he could hear.

The Viking was staring at her again. "Uh, you have to get in first, remember?" she told him.

His face made the same transformation it had the night before. That same slow, gentle grin, his glacier-blue eyes glittering with amusement.

"Ah, yes. How could I forget."

It took a moment for Ann to recover and climb in after him. If somebody had sent Eddy Winters to spy, they'd chosen well. He was damned disarming.

"What kind of shopping do you have to do?" she asked him briskly, hoping to get her mind to the business at hand.

"Everything," he drawled.

She resisted the urge to study his crotch again. "How much do you want to spend?"

"Well, I haven't much cash, but—"

"Well, if you don't mind a short trip on the freeway," she quickly interrupted, eager to spare him any needless discomfort discussing his finances, "I know of an outlet store that carries brand-name stuff at incredible prices."

He grinned again. "Do you?"

She nodded vigorously, hoping she hadn't offended him. Old clothes, no car, little cash—and last night he had all but said he couldn't afford the penthouse. "It'll save you a lot of money since you need—uh—everything."

He touched her cheek lightly with a fingertip, and she sucked her breath in and held it. "Okay, Annie," he said softly, deeply, "a trip on the freeway it is."

She'd scoffed about it when she'd read it in books, but damned if she wasn't getting lost in his eyes.

"Where are we going?" screamed Jason from the back-seat.

Ann jumped about a foot, the breath gushing out of her. Talk about coming back to earth with a vengeance.

"Jase, take off those phones," she said, tearing her gaze away from the pull of the Viking pirate's and getting on the mommy track.

"What?" he screamed.

"I said, take off those phones so you can hear what's going on!"

"Huh?"

Eddy started to laugh.

She rolled her eyes and shook her head. "I said, take off—"

Jason dragged the headphones from his ears. "What did you say, Mom? I can't hear you with these phones on."

Ann jerked the car into reverse and started to back out of her parking space. "Gee, Jase, I never would have thought of that."

Eddy was still laughing when she pulled out into the street.

EVEN IN THE DAYLIGHT, with traffic all around them, Annie still drove like a New York cabby. In fifteen minutes they'd made their way to the suburbs and pulled into the nearly empty lot of an outlet store. Eddy waited for her to get out then followed, holding the seat so Jason could scurry out. The kid seemed to do everything in hyper motion. A ball of energy. Now that Eddy knew he was Annie's son, he saw the resemblance in the color of his hair and in the freckles on his upturned nose. Jason barreled ahead, holding the door for them long before they'd reached it. Eddy followed Annie into the store, taking the cart she'd selected from her hands and trailing her to the menswear section.

She was wearing a wool coat this morning, camel colored and slightly fitted at the waist. She had a cute walk, her abundantly flared hips keeping time to some silent, energetic music as she moved, her lush blaze of hair bouncing on her shoulders. He was so busy watching that he almost ran into her when she stopped.

"Shirts?" she asked him.

Reluctantly, he got his mind back on business. "A few."

"Jeans? Trousers, maybe?"

"I don't know, Annie," he asked her teasingly. "Which do you recommend?"

"Well..." He saw her take a deep breath, a faint blush rising in her cheeks. "Are you here on business?" she finally asked. "Do you have meetings and such?"

Eddy looked into that flushed, ingenuous face and wondered if she knew something. Was she feeling him out? Was she suspicious? Or did she really have his wardrobe in mind? He shook his head, trying to shake off his suspicion. "No—no meetings. Mostly, uh, research."

"Then jeans will go farther. I mean, you can wear them longer without washing them."

Eddy relaxed. Apparently, shopping was serious business to the lady. And, looking at her wide brandy eyes full of the innocent question, he'd be willing to bet that suspicion was the furthest thing from her mind.

"You can listen to my mom," Jason piped up. "She knows all about that kind of stuff."

"Then who am I to argue? Jeans it is."

Eddy propped himself against a pillar and watched her sort through the racks like an expert. Clearly, she was used to shopping this way. Eddy usually frequented the same

stores in New York, and by now the salespeople knew what
he liked and wanted. He hadn't had a woman help him shop
since his mother stopped doing it when he'd turned twelve.

She eyed his lower body, a blush staining her cheeks.

"You're probably a thirty-two, right?" she asked, looking quickly away. "Maybe a thirty-four inseam?"

He grinned. The lady was good. "Right on target, Annie," he said.

She pulled out a couple of pairs. "What do you think?"

Because she seemed to expect it, he studied them for a
moment. "I like the black ones."

"So do I, and they're Calvin Klein. Nineteen ninety-
nine," she added proudly.

"What'd I tell ya," Jason hooted. "The power shopper
hasn't even been in the store ten minutes and she's found her
first bargain."

Eddy's mouth cocked, and he slowly shook his head.
"Can't argue with you, Jason. Calvin Klein for nineteen
ninety-nine? I can see I've been shopping in all the wrong
places."

Annie's big, brandy eyes widened in shock. "Don't tell
me you've been paying full price? Never, *never* pay full
price!"

She threw the jeans in the cart and started toward the
shirts at a rapid enough pace to leave Eddy and Jason behind.

Eddy grinned after her, shaking his head. "Is your mom
this single-minded about everything she does?"

Jason screwed up his nose—just like his mother. "What's
single-minded mean?"

"You know—focused. Sticking with something to the
exclusion of all else until she's satisfied."

"You mean like a dog who won't let go of a bone till all
the meat's off of it?"

Eddy laughed. "Beautifully put, Jason. That's exactly
what I mean."

Jason nodded. "Yeah, that's Mom all right. Single-minded."

Good for shopping, thought Eddy. Bad for the job he was here to do. Good thing Annie was only the chauffeur. He wouldn't want her getting in the way of what he'd come here to accomplish.

When Jason and Eddy reached the shirt department, Annie was pawing through a rack of long-sleeved Oxford-cloth shirts with the speed of a seasoned inspector, only to proclaim them too expensive. She headed for the clearance rack.

By this time, Jason had the headphones on his ears and was busy trying to master a moonwalk down the main aisle.

Eddy loved it. He'd never associated the words "fun" and "family" with each other—at least not since that long-ago last summer spent at the Northcott Inn. Something shot through him, through his heart, or maybe his soul, when he watched these two—the nonstop energy of the kid, the honest enthusiasm of the mother. In his line of work, he didn't often get to deal with honest people. It was a trait that he valued. One he practiced as often as he could.

When he'd told Annie he didn't have much cash, he hadn't really intended to lie. He really didn't have much cash on him. But she'd interrupted him before he'd had the chance to tell her that he had plenty of plastic. Now he was finding that he rather liked her assumption that he didn't have much money. It put him in a position he'd never been in before. The women he knew expected their trinkets and such, and it was easy enough to oblige them. Hank had said he'd wanted the best in the business for this job. And Eddy was the best. But Annie didn't know how he made his living—or what a good living it had turned out to be. He was starting to think it would be interesting to see how a woman would react to him as an ordinary guy, without much cash, with no family connections.

He watched her mining a mountain of shirts on clearance like she was hoping to unearth a champagne-colored diamond.

"Wow, look at this! A Perry Ellis for ten bucks!" She gasped. "This thing's worth at least forty! Medium, right?"

She was looking at him so eagerly all he could do was nod. He'd never seen a woman so excited over a shirt before.

"Pearl gray. It's gonna look great on you. And look at this—a Guess sweater for twenty-two ninety-five!" Her face sobered for a brief moment. "That's not too much, is it?" she asked solemnly.

He let out a small, soft laugh. "No—it's not too much, Annie."

"I mean, it's worth about a hundred."

Eddy knew exactly what the sweater was worth—he had a black one just like it in his apartment in New York. This one was cream. It looked softer, more sensual. Or was it just because it was loosely held in Annie's white, freckled hands? He ran his fingers over the fabric, letting his thumb brush the back of her hand. "I like it," he said, looking into her brandy eyes instead of at the sweater. "I like it very much," he added softly.

She turned quickly away, but not before he saw sweet color rising in her cheeks.

"Good, then let's take it," she said briskly, throwing it into the cart, then leading him on a brisk tour of the rest of the store. They found a few more shirts and a pair of leather gloves for an obscenely low price.

"Let's see, what else?" Annie asked.

Eddy stopped near a bin of after-shaves and colognes. "Hey, they've got my brand."

"*That's* what you wear?" Annie asked in surprise.

He hefted a bottle of very expensive cologne, then looked at her questioning brows. "Um . . . well, uh, everyone needs some of life's little luxuries."

She nodded. "Why don't we pick out something different? Something a little less, uh—"

"Expensive?" he finished for her, grinning at the war she was obviously having between being helpful and being offensive.

"Well," she drawled.

"Tell you what, Annie, you choose something for me."

He watched her opening bottles and sniffing, always checking the price tags first.

"Mmm, this is fantastic!" She splashed a little in her hand and brought it up to his face. "What do you think?"

He took her wrist, bringing her hand closer still, and inhaled deeply. "I think you have excellent taste." He moved his palm over hers, transferring the after-shave to his hand, leaving their flesh pressed together several heart-beats longer than necessary. The scent seemed to come alive with the heat generated between them. He looked into those confused brandy eyes and wondered just how fast, how far, a man could fall.

"Hey, Mom! Look what I found! Can I have them, huh?"

Annie blinked, cleared her throat and pulled her hand from his.

Jason was holding up a pair of Mickey Mouse suspenders. Annie was looking at them, but Eddy wasn't sure she was seeing them. She seemed in a daze. He knew just how she felt.

"Put them in the cart, Jason," Eddy said. "My treat."

"Cool! Thanks!"

Jason popped the phones back on and took off again.

"You—you didn't have to do that," Annie stammered.

He touched her cheek. "I know. I wanted to. He's a great kid, Annie," he told her, meaning it. He never thought he'd enjoy a kid so much—or be so content in the company of that kid's mother. Was this what was missing from his life? A life that, given his background, he'd carefully constructed to keep away all the pain he associated with the word family? Had he been wrong all these years?

"Thanks," Annie murmured. "Uh, what else?" she asked in a more normal voice, suddenly busying herself with carefully placing the bottle of after-shave in the cart.

"Underwear," Eddy answered.

Her head shot up abruptly, her gaze going low, then quickly traveling to his face. He tried to keep from smiling.

"I like string bikinis," he said, emphasizing the word *string* a little, just to see if he could make her blush again.

She blinked and then turned away and marched to the proper aisle. "Um, here they, um, are. While you're doing this, I'll just go and—"

He stepped in front of her before she could take off, bringing her to a halt just inches from him. "Aw, Annie," he breathed in a mockingly desperate whisper, "you're not going to leave me here with all these piles of underwear, are you? I'll never find what I'm looking for." Because he was enjoying teasing her so much, enjoying seeing her get flustered, he decided to push it. Placing two fingers beneath her chin, he brought her face up until she had no choice but to look at him. "Come on, Annie," he pleaded gently, "help me."

Lord, the woman could blush. She was about as sweet as anything he'd ever seen. But as he watched, her confused, shy brown eyes transformed into the flash of brandy being warmed by a flame.

She cleared her throat. "Tell me, Mr. Winters," she said, a little edge to her voice, a little lift to her brow, "do you often get strange women to help you buy your underwear?"

He laughed softly, liking it when she got a little mouthy as much today as he had the night before. "Nothing strange about you, Annie, my sweet. Nothing at all."

Because he couldn't help himself—because he didn't want to help himself—he lowered his mouth to hers and brushed her lips once, twice. The softness drew him like a down comforter on a cold night. He knew that's how she would be. Sweet Annie would fill a man up with pure golden warmth. She'd fill his heart and soul while he filled her body.

"Annie, my sweet," he murmured, brushing his thumb across her lower lip, "unless you want something really embarrassing to happen between us right here in the underwear aisle at T. J. Maxx, you'd better get going and let me find those string bikinis all by myself."

Chapter Four

Ann figured she must be out of her mind, letting him kiss her like that. Jason might have seen, for heaven's sake! And what did she really know about the man? He was from New York City. He was gorgeous. But he was also a pirate—and pirates were always up to no good, weren't they? Practical Ann Madison had no business letting a pirate kiss her—in T. J. Maxx or anywhere else! She was a mother, not some sophisticated woman of the world who went around buying underwear for strange men and kissing them in public!

But, oh, she silently told a ceramic cat in the household clearance aisle, it sure felt good. Heat all the way to her toes. Heat every damn place she hadn't thought about for a long, long time—and shouldn't be thinking about now.

The ceramic cat just stared, a knowing Mona Lisa smile on its calico face. Ann moved on to a lamp with a brass cherub sticking out of the top of its shade. Bikinis, she conveyed mutely. *String* bikinis.

Was it possible to shiver with heat? Because she was hot—and she was shivering.

Have mercy.

"Hey, Mom, where's Eddy?"

Her heart hit her throat with record speed, accompanied by enough guilt to make her choke. Good thing Jason couldn't read minds "Uh, he's, uh, picking out some, uh, underwear," she finally stammered.

"Cool," Jason said. "I'll go help him."

She watched Jason run off. "Better you than me," she muttered, fanning her face with a Chinese fan that had two ribs missing, and they were still asking five dollars for it. Criminal, she thought. There ought to be a law.

Yeah—and there ought to be a law against men as potent as Eddy Winters.

"Time for a reality check," she muttered to a pensive marble gargoyle. Eddy Winters would be gone in a few days, leaving only the memory of one—well, maybe actually two—little kisses behind. *He'll forget all about you,* she told herself, *and when you're sixty-five and playing bridge with the girls, you'll tell them all about that brief shining moment when a Viking pirate blew in with a snowstorm and swept you off your feet—okay, okay, a little tiny sweep—in the underwear section of T. J. Maxx.*

ON THE TRIP back to the hotel, Eddy struggled to keep his hands to himself. The winter sun sparked off Annie's hair like it had nothing better to do with its day. Her freckles danced in it. Every once in a while, she glanced at him to find him watching her and her tongue would dart out of her mouth and she'd nervously run it over her top lip, her cheeks turning as crimson as the sun in her hair.

He glanced at Jason to see if he was safely plugged into his Walkman, deaf to what was going on in the car. He was.

Eddy laid his arm across the car seat, letting his fingers play in the ends of Annie's hair. "Do you know how beautiful you are?" he murmured.

She shot him a look of such undisguised astonishment that he had to laugh. "You don't, do you?"

"If you'll look to your left, Mr. Winters," she said crisply, "you'll notice we're passing one of the oldest churches in the area, built in—"

"Are you changing the subject?"

"I'm doing what every good chauffeur does—giving you a little tour of the city. Here, on the right, we have Cathedral Square ice rink. It's particularly lovely after dark when the trees are lit with fairy lights and—"

"Take me there."

"What?" she asked, glancing at him nervously.

"Tonight. Come ice-skating with me, Annie." He leaned in a little closer, adding softly, "I'll twirl you under the fairy lights."

"I don't skate," she stated emphatically.

"I'll teach you."

"Hey, Mom, take him up on it!" Jason piped up from the backseat. "She really is an awful skater, Eddy."

"Jason, put the headphones on," Annie ordered.

Ignoring her, Jason scooted up and leaned over the car seat between them. "Come on, Mom, let's go skating with Eddy tonight."

Eddy twisted a strand of chestnut hair around his finger. "Yeah, Mom—come on," he cajoled. "What time do you get off tonight? I'll meet you in the lobby."

"Not till eight—and that's too late," she said firmly. "It's a school night."

"Aw, Mom," grumbled Jason, "I'll get all my homework done! Come on—it's not like one night is gonna destroy my academic record or something."

"Say yes, Annie," Eddy murmured, surprised at the tightening in his lower gut, surprised at just how much he wanted Annie's warm hand in his out on the cold ice—even more surprised that he wanted Jason there with them.

Annie sighed, but her glance at him this time was much softer. She was going to give in. "Okay," she said, "but I warn you, I'm lousy on skates."

"Put yourself into my hands, Annie, I'm a he—heck of a teacher."

She laughed out loud, and it was deep, throaty—another incongruity in a woman of surprises and contradictions.

"Yeah," she said, shooting him a look, her eyes flashing with mischief. "I just bet you are."

Jason was slouched in the backseat, tunelessly singing along to something that sounded like a Hootie and the Blowfish number, when they pulled into the Northcott Inn's parking lot. Eddy waited for Annie to slide out of the Olds, then followed, once again holding the seat forward for Jason.

"Hey, Mom, can I work on the computer?" Jason asked, hopping from one foot to the other.

"You know the rules. History homework first."

"Aw—" Jason kicked up a small cloud of snow with his toe.

"You're wasting time. The sooner you get started, the sooner you'll hit that keyboard."

The boy hooted and tore off in the direction of the inn.

"Is he always so full of energy?" Eddy asked, watching Jason scoot through the snow.

Annie nodded. "Always. Wears me out sometimes."

"It must be tough, being a single parent."

When she looked at him, there was surprise in her eyes.

"Jason told me you were divorced."

"Oh." She looked away.

Fingers under her chin, he turned her head to face him again. "Hey, you didn't think I went around kissing married women in outlet stores, did you?"

Her grin was a little uncertain. "Tell you the truth, Eddy, I don't know what to think of you." She batted his hand away and went to open the trunk. "Are you happy with everything?" she asked him, after he'd retrieved his packages and she'd closed the trunk.

"No," he answered.

That stopped her. She faced him again, her brows rising in surprise. "No?"

He backed her up against the car, wishing his hands weren't full of packages, and breathed in the scent of her. A field of flowers bending in a fresh breeze. Innocent. Sweet. Warm. As if she carried a ray of summer sunshine in the blaze of her hair.

He moved his head close to hers, his lips within touching distance, his gaze taking in the lush sweep of dark lashes making a secret of her eyes, her quirky little nose and finally resting on her full, heavenly mouth. "I wish I'd kissed you one more time," he murmured.

Her lips parted, and he felt the sweet breath of her surprise. How could a grown woman not know how much a man could want her?

"I—I meant the clothes," she finally stammered.

He grinned. "Ah, yes. The clothes. Yes, Annie, I'm happy with the clothes. Thanks for taking me. I don't think I've ever enjoyed a shopping trip quite so much."

"Me, either," she murmured.

A faint flush stung her cheeks, and he savored it. He liked the way he was getting to her, because the lady was getting to him. She surely was.

He shifted his body a little, letting it press lightly into hers, his mouth barely grazing her chin, barely skimming her cheek—teasing her. Teasing himself. "I guess I have to let you go, huh?" he whispered along her pale skin. He was so close, he could feel her swallow.

"I—uh—I think you'd better," she answered, her voice a husky murmur.

Eddy knew what he wanted, and it wasn't to let her go. He wanted the taste of her mouth, the feel of her breath mingling with his. But there were all kinds of dangers in her innocent eyes. *Annie, Annie,* he thought, *am I ready for you?*

He pushed himself away from her. "Come on, Annie," he said, "I'll walk you to work."

After leaving Annie in the lobby with a promise to meet him there at eight, Eddy took the elevator up to the fifth floor. It was time he checked in with Hank.

He let himself into the penthouse, grabbed the phone and punched out Hank's number.

"Lewis," Hank rasped into the phone.

"I'm here, Hank, and I'm *still* not buying it."

"Eddy! Heard they had a big blizzard out that way. How's it going?"

"It's not. The only thing moving on this job so far is my luggage—all the way to Tahiti. The files you gave me and my laptop went with it."

Hank laughed. "Tahiti," he said, "damn good taste your luggage has. I could use some of that sunshine myself right about now."

"And what I could use is my head examined. I must be crazy to have let you talk me into this bogus investigation."

Hank snorted. "That mean you haven't found anything?"

"That means I haven't bothered looking, because there's nothing to find. You think I don't know why you talked me into this job, Hank? You've been trying to get me to accept my inheritance for years."

"Look, Eddy, you're right about that, but I also believe that there really is something going on out there. The place is going to hell fast—and it doesn't make much sense from this end."

Eddy didn't believe a word of it. "Right, Hank," he drawled.

"Really, pal," Hank insisted. "Hey, I'd be out there myself if I didn't have to get ready to do battle with the board later this week. Your cousin Clifford is supposed to be helping me convince them to give the inn more time, but he seems to be about as effective with that as he is with everything else. Damn shame you never went into the business, Eddy," Hank grumbled. "Damn shame."

Eddy raised his eyes ceilingward and dragged a hand through his hair. "Here we go again."

"Aw, forget I said anything, pal. Just find out what's going on out there. Give me something to give the board—anything that'll help keep the place open. Pick up a new computer, and I'll express copies of the files to you. What room are you in?"

"This'll really get you, Hank. I'm in the penthouse. Because of the storm last night, it was the only room left."

Hank chuckled over that for several seconds—just as Eddy knew he would. "That's priceless, Eddy. I couldn't have done it better if I planned it myself."

"Are you sure you didn't?" Eddy asked.

"Huh! I can do a lot of things, pal, but so far I haven't been able to control the weather. Now, I really have to go—got a meeting."

"Hank!" Eddy barked before his old friend could hang up. "It would help if I knew what I was supposed to be looking for."

"That's the hell of it, pal. I don't know. Occupancy is down, business is lousy, but expenses are up. They're spending money hand over fist out there, and it doesn't seem to be doing much good."

Hank paused, and Eddy could hear him say something to someone in the office. "Look," he said when he got back on, "I gotta run. Keep in touch."

Eddy stared at the receiver for a moment, then hung it up. Damned if Hank didn't actually sound worried. He prowled the sitting room, restless. Was there something to find? If it was true that management at the inn was blowing money, he'd like to know what they were blowing it on. He'd already found out that room service and valet parking had been cut. The lobby and the café had barely changed at all since Hattie and Nathan's day and were looking more than a little worn.

Hank made no bones about what side he was on. From the time the first rumblings came from the board about going to court to nullify Hattie and Nathan's will, Hank had made it clear he wanted the will upheld. From the start, Eddy had figured Hank was using a ruse to get him out here, banking on Eddy falling in love with the place once he'd seen it again. Banking on Eddy finally claiming it—which would take the issue of the will and the future of the inn out of the board's hands. But doing what his grandparents wanted came with the kind of strings Eddy had spent his adulthood trying to avoid. To claim the place, he'd have to live in it.

Eddy walked to the windows, thrusting restless hands through his hair. There was no way he was living in this penthouse. Not with the memories that haunted the place. Not that they were bad memories. Just the opposite. And that was the problem. Life like the one he lived when he'd spent those golden summers here didn't really exist. Love like he'd seen between Hattie and Nathan didn't really exist. His parents and their assorted marriages and divorces had proven that to him. And the boy Eddy had always gotten lost in the shuffle. No way was Eddy going to be responsible for doing that to a kid.

But that's what he needed to claim the inheritance—a wife and a kid—a family of his own to make their home in the penthouse. Knowing that their only son—Nathan, Jr., Eddy's father—didn't care about the inn and would have torn it down in a heartbeat if he thought there was a profit to be made, Eddy's grandparents had left it to the boy who'd loved it as much as they had. But the emotional price was too high and he wanted none of it.

"Yeah?" he muttered, his warm breath clouding the cold pane of glass before him. "Then why are you here? What are you doing here if you're so sure this isn't where you want to be?"

He turned from the window, shot a look at his grandparents over the mantel and just as quickly looked away again. Enough reminiscing. It was time he got to work and got it over with. If there was something to find, he'd find it. If there wasn't, he'd prove it—and get back to New York where he belonged.

He picked up the phone again. While he waited for those files, he could have a little talk with the manager. You never knew what kind of information you could glean if your questions were clever enough.

"Front desk," replied a male voice.

"Is this the manager?" Eddy asked.

"No, sir. This is Austin, desk clerk on duty. The manager's not here right now. Try back in half an hour."

"Thanks."

Eddy hung up the phone. If the place was in bad shape, it was no wonder. Whoever was managing the place was making himself scarce. Bad for business, good for Eddy's job. The less the brass were around, the better. He should be using the waiting time to check out the other floors, but damned if that floral chintz sofa wasn't beckoning him. Eddy walked over and sank onto it with a sigh. Hattie and Nathan had liked their comfort.

His eyes were just starting to close when it hit him.

Lilacs.

The room smelled like lilacs again.

His eyes flew open, and he found himself staring into the laughing face of his grandmother. She'd been more vivacious than pretty, and the artist had done a good job of capturing her personality.

Annie had said legend had it that it was a good thing they'd died together—because they couldn't have lived apart. That was true, Eddy knew. But it hadn't kept his heart from breaking when he'd heard the news. He hadn't bothered to come to the funeral—but he'd mourned. Mourned not only their passing but all the wasted years, the years after his parents divorced when his mother, bitter about the divorce settlement, forbade him to visit his grandparents.

After the divorce, he'd spent summers in New York with his father, Nathan, Jr. Or that's how the story went. Mostly, he'd spent the time with his father's right-hand man, Hank Lewis. Hank was the closest thing to a real father Eddy ever had. Nathan, Jr., wasn't exactly daddy material. Nor was he much of a businessman. He kept an office at Northcott Enterprises, but he usually only checked in in the morning on his way to the golf course or the yacht club. He'd take Eddy along and dump him on Hank. Hank spent as much time as he could with him. Eddy had always craved more.

By his teen years, he was more than ready for rebellion. It was Hank who'd caught him trying to burglarize rooms in the New York Northcott.

"You lookin' for adventure, pal? Then you look for it on the right side of the law," Hank had told him gruffly while dragging him by the scruff of the neck all the way to his office. Then he'd called a friend of his, and Eddy found himself spending the next few summers of his life learning from one of the best private investigators in the business. When he was old enough, he'd gone into business for himself, specializing in jobs for insurance companies and corporations.

For years he'd been content to make New York his home. The work was exciting and lucrative enough to allow him to work sporadically enough to keep him from feeling tied down. He spent his free time on women, sports, travel—or at least that's how he *had* spent his time. But lately, maybe for the past year or so, he was feeling restless, itchy for something he couldn't quite name.

He looked at Hattie and Nathan. Was it what they had had that he finally wanted, finally missed? Hattie's hair glowed in the sun with nearly the same fire as Annie's. Eddy settled deeper into the sofa, letting the heady scent of lilacs wash over him, remembering the soft touch of Annie's mouth against his own, remembering the feel of her hair in his hands. If she was beside him right now, he would light a fire, put on some music, pour some wine and just drift with her. Just *be*. Just like Hattie and Nathan had probably done on cold winter afternoons long ago.

Swearing between his teeth, Eddy sprang to his feet. The damn room was seducing him as much as Annie was. Before he knew it, he'd get out a Ouija board and ask the ghostly couple questions about how to tell if you were really falling in love.

True, he couldn't make any big plans until he got those files from New York. But he could quit mooning about a woman he barely knew, quit remembering things that no longer mattered.

He'd begin by talking to the employees. He'd have to watch his step, but anything would be better than sitting around thinking about the ghosts of the past and smelling lilacs in winter.

THE ELEVATOR gave its customary whomp, and Ann's heart raced. It was impossible not to look.

"Oh, good evening, Mr. Peters." She tried to keep the disappointment from her voice as she greeted one of the members of the *old-timers'* club, as Lara always referred to them. The *club* consisted of a few dozen businessmen who'd remained loyal to the Northcott Inn despite the fact that there were no phones in the bathrooms and no CNN on the televisions.

"Mrs. Madison." The man nodded. "I see our little man is hitting the books again." Mr. Peters paused long enough at Jason's chair to ruffle the boy's hair. "Good lad."

Ann sent one of her best *don't you dare* looks Jason's way, but it was too late—he was already sticking out his tongue. He hated having his hair ruffled or being called *little man*. Fortunately, he was as quick as he was insolent. By the time Mr. Peters looked into the boy's face again, Jason was smiling angelically, his tongue safely in his mouth. Mr. Peters hadn't even known he'd been insulted as he made his ponderous way to the Café Northcott.

"That will get you twenty minutes docked from computer time, Jase."

Jason groaned. "Aww, Mom—"

Ann pointed a finger at the history book in his lap. "Get back to it. You're losing computer time even as we speak." Jason hated history, and Ann had finally hit on the perfect bribe to get him to do the dreaded homework. He wasn't allowed to touch the Northcott Inn's computer until he'd finished. With Jason, who'd taken to his school's computer like he was born with a microchip in his brain, it was a potent bribe, and it usually worked.

Jason slumped farther down in his chair, kicking his feet out in front of him. His enormous athletic shoes seemed to take up a good part of the lobby. "Gee whiz—aren't you supposed to be doing your homework, too, Mom? Some example—all you're doin' is fidgeting with your hair and watchin' the elevator."

Ann became still, her hand buried in her hair. Uh-oh. Jason was right. She'd been primping and watching, watching and primping like a high school girl getting ready for a little lunch hour seduction. You'd think she'd never been kissed before.

She made an effort to get her mind off the elevator and onto the paperwork before her. After fifteen minutes of shuffling papers and not comprehending a word she read, she finally gave up and strolled around the lobby, stopping at one of the tall, arched windows that looked out on the street.

It was the favorite time of day for Ann, that magic hour in the winter when the sun hadn't quite gone down and the moon hadn't quite come up. The hour when the snow was bathed in blue and the sky was streaked with pink. The hour almost anything seemed possible.

Even the kiss of a Viking pirate.

Well, it hadn't really been a kiss. But somehow, the quick brush of Eddy Winters's lips had wreaked more havoc than if he'd stuck his tongue down her throat.

"Oh, my," she murmured. "What a thought."

Yeah, what a thought!

And now that she'd thunk it, she couldn't get the idea out of her mind. Yeah…Eddy Winters and that nice hard, long body pressed against hers, that full, sensual mouth devouring her. Maybe just one night—and then, of course, he would leave and she'd never see him again. But so what? Maybe she wouldn't mind having a few nice, hot memories to warm her on cold, lonely nights.

She'd never had an affair. She didn't believe in them— wasn't the type. Vows were vows, and she'd taken hers seriously. She'd married young and she'd been a virgin. Despite problems in the marriage, she'd remained faithful. But as soon as she'd found out that Al Madison hadn't, she realized that the marriage had been over for a long time—she just hadn't wanted to notice. Now her ex-husband was selling cars somewhere in California, letting his tan and his new Ferrari feed his mid-life crisis. Ann had always figured good riddance—except for Jason, of course. Jason seldom heard from his father. The checks were always late, the birthdays always forgotten. Jason deserved better. But Al had been a lousy, emotionally absent father when they'd all been living under the same roof, so what could you expect when he was a couple of thousand miles away?

Jason had learned to expect nothing, and Ann hoped she was compensating well enough for the empty place in Jason's world.

But what about the empty place inside Ann? That place where her woman's heart beat? That place that needed to connect, that needed to be held, stroked?

Hell, what about that place that could use some good, raunchy sex?

Ann's head whipped up as if she'd actually spoken the uncharacteristic thought aloud and the entire population of her life had unexpectedly shown up in the lobby just in time to hear it. Cautiously, she looked over her shoulder, relieved to see that only Jason sat there, head still bent over his book, oblivious to his mother's X-rated thoughts.

With a long sigh, she sank her chin onto her fist, leaned against the wide windowsill and settled into a nice, sizzling replay of that afternoon's kiss on the movie screen of her mind.

Mmm.

Then she switched the sound on and heard that low, masculine murmur asking her if she knew how beautiful she was.

Well, Ann knew she wasn't beautiful. My goodness, of course she did. But it was a treat to have a Viking pirate tell you you were anyway. Sure, maybe he was an operator, used to getting his way with a smile and a kiss, but that didn't mean she couldn't enjoy it. Just as long as she knew that it ended along with Eddy Winters's reservation.

"I'm done!"

Startled, Ann whirled. "What?"

Jason slammed his history book on the front desk with an air of triumph. "Done. Finito. My history is history."

Ann stared for a second, trying to get her mind off Viking pirates and on to the American settlers. She left the window and walked over to her son, holding out an unsteady hand. "Let's see it."

Jason flung his head sideways. "Aw—"

She wiggled her fingers. "Come on. Hand it over."

Jason whipped a paper out of the book and thrust it at her. Everything looked in order, as far as Ann's fevered mind could tell.

Jason squinted at her. "Somethin' wrong, Mom? You look kind of hot. You sick?"

Ann shook her head and shoved the hair from her face. "No, I'm fine."

"Danny's mom is going through somethin' his dad calls the change. She gets hot all the time. Maybe you—"

Ann quickly gave him his history paper. "I am *not* going through any change. I'm not old enough," she added primly.

Jason peered at her, wrinkling his short, freckled nose. "I don't know, Mom, you're pretty old."

"Gee, thanks, kid. I really needed that. Now, you're gonna have to give me a great big kiss just to make me feel better." He tried to duck out of the way, but she was quicker. She grabbed him and gave him a good smack on the cheek.

"Mom—you know I hate that!" he squealed, but the grin on his face gave him away.

"You'll live. Now, if you want any time at all on the computer tonight, you better hit that keyboard."

Jason happily sauntered to the back office, leaving Ann to ponder the recent change that had come over her body. It was hormonal, all right. But it had absolutely nothing to do with menopause. A few sweet brushes of Eddy Winters's mouth on hers, and her body had come out of years of hibernation.

EDDY TOOK the last flight of stairs slowly, quietly. The lobby was lit softly from an assortment of shaded lamps and the fire in the hearth. The sweeping, open staircase afforded enough cover so that if he just leaned over the banister a little he could scan the area with no one seeing him unless they had their eyes trained on the staircase.

Annie was in the office behind the registration desk, showing something on the computer to Jason. Her head was bent, her hair falling forward, the curls burnished from the lamp on the desk. He almost felt its softness in the tingling of his fingertips.

An older man was looking over her shoulder—fairly short, wide of girth, gray-haired. The elusive manager? Eddy intended to find out just as soon as he returned.

He descended the rest of the staircase, the worn carpet absorbing his footfalls enough not to alert the trio in the office, and made it out the front door with no one at all taking notice.

Outside, the night had nearly descended, the sky a dark, rich blue. Thrusting his hands into the gloves Annie had found for him, he sauntered down the wide steps of the hotel, pausing on the sidewalk to look at the facade. The place looked magical. A miniature castle. A horse-drawn carriage clip-clopped along the narrow street of red brick, the horse's braided mane gleaming in the light from a converted gas street lamp.

The Northcott Inn should have been reigning over the old-world charm of the street. It should be drawing in honeymoon couples and yuppies on getaway weekends. Apparently, it wasn't. Was Hank telling the truth? Was the place struggling to stay alive? And if so, why? From what Hank had said, there was no shortage of funds going out to maintain it. And yet the place clearly needed to be maintained. The inn was getting pretty worn around the edges, with almost no amenities in sight. The glory days Hattie and Nathan had reigned over were gone. But were they gone forever?

His gaze moved to the turret rising with Gothic splendor against the last pink rays of the day streaking the sky.

The glow emanating from the frost-laced windows drew his gaze, and he imagined what Annie would look like framed in one of them, her hair aflame, waiting for him to return from the cold winter night.

He shook his head and laughed softly into the cold air. "Face it, Eddy, the old place is doing a number on you."

Yeah, he thought, the old place and a certain sweet lady and her wide-eyed boy.

Turning up the collar of his bomber jacket against the cold, he shoved his hands into his pockets. Was it too late to turn the inn into the kind of place where dreams could still come true? Right now it looked as though it might be the kind of place where they could be lost forever. Fleetingly, he told himself that he was more than glad Annie was only the chauffeur. If Hank was right, if there really was something funny going on, then by the time Eddy was through, someone was going to get hurt. He didn't want it to be Annie.

People passed behind him on the street. Cars honked. The night fell. Eddy shivered. Time to move on. Time to get to work. He turned away from the inn, angling across the street on the way to the computer store on Wisconsin Avenue.

Chapter Five

Max chuckled, the smoke from the cigar wedged between his teeth drifting upward in little puffs. "Jason, you must be some kinda genius," he said around the cigar. "I can't even figure out how to turn one of those contraptions on, let alone make it do all that stuff you do. What are ya up to now, boy?"

"I'm trying to work up a bar graph, Max."

"Whatcha gonna do with it when you're done?"

"I'm gonna enter in all my grades from this year so far then use it to try to convince Mom that even though I do lousy in history, she spawned a genius."

Ann, filing invoices at the file cabinet across the room, laughed. "I guess if you can use words like spawned maybe you really *are* a genius."

"Hey," Jason said, hooting, "I've been tellin' ya!"

Shaking his head, Max ambled out of the office behind Ann, bringing along the scent of cheap cigars that always clung to him. He sat in a wing chair near the front desk, plopping one short pudgy leg across the other.

"He's a bright one, Ann. You oughta be proud."

"Oh, I am," she answered softly, sinking into the chair opposite Max and opening the file she'd been working on earlier.

"What ya workin' on there?"

She shuffled some papers and sighed. "I'm trying to figure out a way to increase occupancy, Max. I noticed that some of the other hotels downtown are offering weekend packages over the winter months to generate business. I thought we might do the same."

"They got a lot more going for them than we do, Ann," Max said sadly.

She sighed. "I know. But we have to do something or I'm really afraid this place is going to fold." She looked at Max. "I got another one of those corporate newsletters from Northcott Enterprises," she said grimly. "There was a nice big editorial aiming at all the reasons the chain should give up the inn. Apparently they're trying to convince the rest of the stockholders to go to court to have some sort of stipulation in Hattie Northcott's will nullified." She shook her head. "I don't understand the ins and outs of it. But you were here when she died, weren't you, Max? Do you know what they're talking about?"

Max chuckled deeply, the folds of age on his face vibrating slightly with the movement. "Oh, I've always been here, girlie. Nearly from the beginning." He puffed on his cigar for a moment before going on. "You already know the place was left to the grandson. There were rumors at the time that there was something else in the will—something that made him stay away. I only know I ain't seen hide nor hair of him since he was a young boy." Again, Max pulled on the cigar, his sagging cheeks puffing in and out with the effort. "He was a nice enough lad," he said, expelling the words with a puff of smoke. "Hattie doted on him—but apparently he turned out to be as worthless as his father, Nathan, Jr." Max snorted. "All that man cared about was money. If he was still alive, there's no way he'd be holding on to this place— not if he could find a way to get rid of it. I guess Hattie and Nathan knew that, that's why they left the place to Nathan III."

Ann leaned forward in her chair, almost beseechingly. "Sometimes, Max, I feel as if someone *is* trying to find a way to get rid of it. The head office has no interest in our problems at all. What I've asked for isn't unreasonable, yet they keep turning me down, making even more cuts in staff." She shook her head and settled back in her chair again. "I don't get it. Why would anyone want to go against what Hattie and Nathan wanted and shut the place down? The Inn would still be making money if only New York would give me the funds to run it the way it should be run. I've let them know there's a possibility that the new stadium will be built nearby. You'd think they'd be eager to spruce up the place to handle that possibility." She was silent for a moment, thinking. "If only," she mused softly, "I had the help of someone who had some clout."

Max snorted. "Huh—the only one left to put up a fight is that grandson, and that ain't likely to happen. He's too busy trottin' the globe or doing whatever the rich and worthless do these days." Max shook his head sadly. "Poor sweet Hattie must have turned over in her grave when he refused his inheritance."

Ann sat up straighter, her brows going up. "*Refused* it?"

Max nodded and blew a ring of smoke toward the ceiling. "That's the story. Didn't want no part of it." Max took the cigar out of his mouth and stood, straightening his uniform jacket over his girth. "Well, better get back to work. The Alberts been clamoring for someone to take a look at their thermostat."

"Uh-oh—do you think we need a repairman, Max?" Ann asked, envisioning endless requisitions and countless stall tactics from New York.

"Nah." He flapped a thick, weathered hand. "What we need's a new heating system. I'll fiddle with it a little, we'll all cluck about how the place has gone downhill since the old days, and they'll be satisfied for a while."

Ann shifted the pages she'd been working on, biting her lip and wrinkling her nose, trying to find some answer in the pencil scrawls. The heating system wasn't the only problem. The plumbing needed work, as did the wiring. It was only a matter of time before the roof started to leak.

She crammed the papers into the file folder with disgust and leaned her head against the rose-colored chair. If a huge corporation like Northcott Enterprises couldn't keep this place going, what could possibly come of her secret dream to buy the inn and restore it to what it once was?

"If only I could get enough money together before they decide to sell it," she muttered.

"Ya love the place, don't ya?"

Ann looked up to find Max still standing there, fondly smiling at her. "I really do, Max," she answered earnestly. "I think I know exactly how Hattie and Nathan felt about it, why they chose to live here when they had much grander hotels in the chain." Her gaze swept the lobby. It was careworn and slightly shabby, but it still had a quality that a newer, grander place would have a hard time duplicating. She sighed. "It must have been pure magic back then."

"That it was, that it was." He shook his head. "Seems a long time ago," he murmured. "So many years—and I been here through every one of 'em." He snorted impatiently. "But nothin' lasts. You best learn that, girlie, if you're gonna survive."

Ann watched Max amble off, thinking that she wanted to more than survive. She wanted to *live*. She wanted this place to live.

If only she had that grandson, Nathan III, here right now. She'd give him an earful that he wouldn't soon forget. He was probably the one trying to close the place down. Probably needed the money for women, or gambling, or—or something even worse, she brooded, picturing him to be as worthless as Max had said he was. He had to be, or he'd never be able to stay away with the place failing like it was.

The elevator door opened, and her heart leaped again, her body coming alive, her breasts yearning with something between pleasure and pain. But it was only old Mr. and Mrs. Albert, who tottered off when the doors slid open, their matching raccoon coats held tight against their withered necks with long striped mufflers—Ada's blue, Harold's red.

"Good evening, Mrs. Madison," Ada said.

"We're off for our evening walk," added Harold, "while Max does something about our heat."

Ann stood. "I'm sorry you haven't been comfortable."

"Oh, think nothing of it, my dear," Harold hurried to say. "Max will have it to rights in no time."

"My, yes," agreed Ada. "Besides, we wouldn't think of staying anywhere else, would we, Harold?"

"No, indeed."

"I can't tell you how much it means to me to hear you say that," Ann said, feeling a tight lump of emotion rise in her throat. That's all she'd need, to start babbling in front of this sweet couple. Ada would probably get out her smelling salts. She stood up straighter and cleared her throat. "Well, you certainly have a beautiful night for your walk. Be careful on the stairs."

"Oh, we'll be fine, my dear. We bought each other new boots for Christmas, and they're quite the thing," Harold said proudly, sticking out a foot for Ann to admire.

There, beneath the fur of a raccoon long dead, protruded the latest in hiking boots. Ann thought she'd seen some just like them in a Land's End catalogue. She grinned. "They look wonderful."

"Yes, indeed." Harold beamed as they headed toward the door.

Harold and Ada Albert had been coming to the Northcott Inn since the days of Hattie and Nathan. Ann couldn't even begin to guess how old they were. She only knew that they were still very much in love—in love enough to make a bi-monthly pilgrimage to the inn where they'd spent their honeymoon. Ann sat down and picked up her file with renewed determination. If she didn't come up with a plan soon, Ada and Harold would have no place at all to go.

THE LOBBY was quiet when Eddy returned. A fire burned in the hearth. A male guest sat in a wing chair rustling the *Wall Street Journal*. An old couple, the same one who'd had the table next to his at breakfast, were seated on a love seat near the fireplace. There was no sign of Annie. He glanced at his watch. Not quite eight. He'd just have enough time to check out the manager before meeting Annie and Jason for their ice-skating date.

He walked to the registration desk and rang the bell.

Lara stuck her blond head out of the office.

"Hi, Mr. Winters," she said brightly. "What can I do for you?"

"Is the manager around?"

"Sorry—just left."

Eddy closed his eyes briefly and shook his head. Right now he was beginning to believe more in the existence of the ghosts that supposedly haunted the penthouse than in the existence of this manager.

"Left for the day?" he asked.

"Yeah—afraid so. Anything I can do to help?"

Eddy shook his head. "No—it'll wait."

"If you still want to change rooms, there are plenty to chose from."

Eddy hesitated, surprised to realize that he really didn't want to give up the penthouse. "I think I'll stay where I am," he said.

Lara shrugged, sending a myriad of hoop earrings in graduating sizes swinging. "Great."

Lara's blond head disappeared again, and Eddy moved over to a love seat opposite a little old couple and sank down into it. The fire felt good. He laid his head back, closed his eyes. He didn't know if he dozed off—or for how long. He only knew that when he opened his eyes again, Annie was standing before him.

She must have gone home and changed into warmer clothes, because she was back in her green anorak, with the hood down this time, the firelight blazing in her hair, her cheeks flushed from the cold, her small, full mouth red with it. Kissing red.

"I must be dreaming," he murmured.

"If you're still planning on taking me ice-skating," she said with a shake of the head and a lopsided grin, "then I think the word nightmare is more appropriate."

Eddy grinned and patted the space beside him. "Come...sit."

She shook her head, more emphatically this time. "I thought you wanted to skate?"

He caught her hand in his. "Let's do a little necking first." He tugged but she held fast.

"Fat chance, Winters," she muttered. "Not with Mr. Peters and Mr. and Mrs. Albert nearby."

"Oh, we don't mind, dear," piped up the reedy voice of Ada Albert. "You two go right ahead."

Ann's mouth dropped open.

Eddy grinned. "It seems I have an ally," he whispered, giving her hand a harder tug.

"You're forgetting one thing. Jason. He's outside waiting for us. He's counting on seeing the great Eddy Winters on blades—and nothing else will do." She grinned and tilted her head. "Unless of course you were just blowing your charm around. Maybe your ankles are as weak as mine?"

"I'm a laser on blades."

She nodded. "Right. You're a chicken on feet," she quipped, twisting her hand out of his grip and clucking all the way to the door. With a laugh, Eddy gave a beaming Ada Albert a wink before he jumped to his feet to follow.

"Where's your car?" Eddy asked when he'd joined Jason and Ann on the wide stone steps of the inn.

"Mom made us walk here after we changed into warmer stuff. She thinks walkin' in the cold is good for you," Jason said with the air of a child who thought his parent might be just this side of crazy.

"If it's not too cold to skate, it's not too cold to walk," Ann insisted. "Besides, Cathedral Square is only a few blocks away. There is absolutely no chance that you'll need the services of a Saint Bernard to rescue you before we get there."

"Aw," Jason moaned, but Ann could tell he wasn't really put out. How could he be on a night like this?

Bells from nearby Saint John's Cathedral chimed out the hour of eight. They walked in silence, Jason running ahead as usual, his skates hanging over his shoulder. Traffic lights winked around them, pedestrians passed, and snow started to softly fall.

"Perfect," murmured Ann.

"I'm glad you like it," Eddy said softly. "I ordered it just for you."

Ann gave him a long, sideways look. "Lines like that work in New York, huh?"

Eddy laughed and skipped ahead of her, turning around so he faced her, his body stopping hers mid-stride. "Hell with New York. Do they work here?"

Her heart was pounding, but she gave him an emphatic answer. "No way."

"Then, how about," he drawled, lifting her chin with his finger, "I just wanted to see how snowflakes would look melting on your gorgeous lashes and tumbling into your beautiful hair?"

His voice was light, teasing. But the look in his eyes sent her pulse into double time. "Better," she whispered. "Much better."

He lowered his head, and she watched his eyes travel over her face. "Aw, Annie, Annie, you keep looking at me like that and we're not gonna make it to that ice rink."

"Then I think I'll keep looking at you like that," she whispered around the lump rising in her throat.

He laughed softly, the sound running through her veins like hot sweet chocolate. Then he lowered his head closer to hers. She closed her eyes and waited for the warmth of his mouth.

"Hey, come on, you guys!" Jason shouted. "The rink closes in an hour!"

The soft breath of his laugh warmed where his kiss should have been. "Our chaperon," he whispered.

She opened her eyes and groaned. "I guess I really have to skate now, huh?"

"I guess so. Come on." He took her hand and ran with her around the corner.

Ann was totally unprepared for the sight that greeted them as they turned into North Jefferson Street. She'd seen it before, of course. The ice-skating rink at Cathedral Square had become a fixture of Milwaukee's long, cold winter. But she'd never before seen it while a Viking pirate held her hand in his.

Thousands of fairy lights lit the bare branches of trees surrounding the rink. Skaters gracefully moved to music that seemed to cascade from the sky along with the huge, lazy flakes of snow. They waited on the curb for a carriage to pass, the clip-clop of the horses' hooves making her feel like she'd felt the night before when she'd climbed the stairs with Eddy in the dark. It was like entering another time. It was as if magic was at work—magic made only for them.

As they walked hand in hand beneath the trees, Ann looked up through the thousands of lights to the black sky, the snow dropping like stars into her outstretched hand. The air was cold, crisp, like sparkling wine as it filled her lungs. It was a night made for romance, and she was sharing it with a Viking pirate who could set any maiden's heart aflutter. And he thought she was beautiful. And he'd wanted to kiss her. And while the night cradled them and the music played on, while the snow fell and her heart yearned, he spoke the five most frightening words she'd ever heard.

"Let's go rent some skates."

Jason leaped into the air and hooted, running ahead while Ann tried to protest. But Eddy just kept pulling her toward the tent that housed the skate rentals. The tent was bright, heated and filled with one of the biggest enemies of her childhood.

Skates—in a numerous array of sizes—lined a wall.

"What size?" Eddy wanted to know.

"Um . . ." She stalled. "Look, they probably don't have my size. I'll just watch."

"They've got your size, Annie." He swung an arm wide. "Just look at all these skates!"

Yeah, look, she thought, swallowing hard. There they all were, their sharp little blades threatening her, their tongues hanging out to taunt her. Already she could feel her ankles starting to ache.

"What size?" the college hunk behind the counter asked.

What—did every man in Wisconsin suddenly need to know her shoe size?

Eddy, already clutching a pair of sinister-looking black skates, was watching her with amusement dancing in his blue eyes, a brow raised in challenge. She sighed, giving in to the enemy, offering herself up for torture. "Size eight," she said.

She took the skates, sat on a wooden bench next to Jason to put them on, fiddling with the laces as long as possible.

Jason jumped to his feet. "Aw—you old guys take too long. I'm going out on the ice."

"Be careful!" Ann called after him.

He turned and gave her a look. "Gee whiz, Mom, I been skatin' since I was a little kid," he huffed, before disappearing through the doorway to the ice rink.

He looked confident enough. Obviously he didn't get his skating prowess from his mother. She bent and started reorking her laces, giving Eddy a sideways glance to see if he oticed.

He did.

"You're stalling, Annie."

"Who, me?" she asked innocently.

He held out a hand to her. "Come on, you can't be that ad."

"Care to make a bet?"

He grinned. "I told you last night that I never take ad-antage of a woman." He grabbed her hand and pulled her o her feet. "Just hang on, I won't let you fall."

And she did hang on, tottering gracelessly behind him cross the wooden floor, through the strips of plastic cur-ain in the doorway that led to the rink.

"Okay," she said, taking in a gulp of icy air, "I'm out ere—now can we go?"

Eddy laughed. "You really can't skate, huh?"

"Eddy," she said patiently, "women lie about their age, heir weight and maybe about the store-bought cake they erve for dessert, claiming to have made it themselves. But vomen do *not* lie about whether they can ice-skate or not."

"I'm pretty good—"

She didn't doubt it.

"I'll give you a lesson."

She shook her head. "Waste of time. I'm a lost cause."

"Never—anyone who moves like you do off the ice can urely learn to skate on it."

She looked at him through her lashes. "You like the way move?" she asked him timidly, wrinkling her nose.

He pulled her forward, and she glided smoothly into his rms. "Very much," he murmured. "That sweet backside f yours moves to a beat all its own. Just hold tight, Annie, nd you'll be moving to the music in no time."

He kept his hands at her waist, skating backward, mov-ng her along with him. She tried to follow his movements, ried to keep her feet synchronized with his. But when she looked up to find him grinning at her, she faltered, missed a beat and found herself prone on the ice—with Eddy Winters prone right on top of her.

"I told you I was a lost cause," she muttered against his shoulder.

He raised himself on his elbow and looked at her, his eyes crinkling, his mouth giving her that soft grin she'd come to crave in such a short time. "You know," he murmured, "I think I like this position even better than the one that had us on our feet."

She did, too. Oh, infinitely better. But not necessarily with an audience. "Very funny, Mr. Winters. Now get off me— there are children present, including my son."

At that moment, she saw Jason whiz by like he was born on blades. She said a silent prayer that he didn't see them. But it was useless. It took him only seconds to double back and come to a quick, elaborate stop next to them.

With his fists on his hips, he shook his head in disgust. "What did I tell ya, Eddy. Is she hopeless, or what?"

Eddy looked at her, enough heat in his eyes to make her forget the heat of his body—almost. "Oh, I don't know, Jason," he said. "I think she has possibilities."

Before he could go into what those possibilities were, Ann gave him a shove that sent him sprawling on his back.

"Hey," Jason said, "you two are embarrassing me—I'm outta here."

Jason skated off with the precision of an Olympian. Eddy lay there laughing for a moment more, then jumped gracefully to his feet, hoisting Ann alongside of him.

"Come on, sweet Annie, let's show him what we can do."

"But the *I* in *we* can't do anything," she wailed as he started to pull her along.

"Sure you can—I'll skate backward, you just follow me."

"You won't let go?"

"I won't let go, Annie, I promise," he answered softly. "Don't look at your feet, sugar, look here, into my eyes."

How could she resist? Staring into his bright baby blues would be the easy part. Staying on her feet was another matter.

"Lighten up a little, Annie. You're gripping my hands like you expect to fall."

"I do!"

"Aw, I won't let you fall, I promise."

"That's what you said the first time," she told him dryly. "I'm beginning to think you don't keep your promises, Mr. Winters."

"Have a little faith, sweet Annie."

Faith in men was something she'd had in very short supply ever since her divorce. But what the heck—this wasn't real life. This was a magical ice rink with a magical Viking pirate. If she could ever do the impossible, it would be on this night with this man.

"Come on," he coaxed, while she tried her best to keep from falling. "Let your body float a little. That's it, Annie—just keep coming to me."

He zigzagged backward, carrying her along with him. His eyes held hers, and she felt her body grow a little weightless as she glided along. They went around the entire rink, and she was still on her feet.

She grinned. It felt wonderful.

"Aw, Annie, that smile could keep us both floating."

"Sweet talker," she said, telling herself it was just the cold making her tremble a little, just the cold. She needed her mittens.

Like hell. Her hands in his vibrated with the warmth of his blood. Between that and his soft, broad smile, she could easily have shed her coat without risking hypothermia.

Suddenly the music changed from a light rock beat to something slow. Violins on ice. Eddy brought them to a stop, let go of her hands and gave a little bow. "Will the damsel honor me with this dance?" he asked.

She knew better than to try to curtsy. "Only if you give me back your hands," she said nervously.

"I'll do better than that, my lady. I'll give you my whole body."

Oh, my, she thought. And wouldn't she just love to take him up on *that* offer? But if the only way she could get his body on hers was to fall flat on her back on the ice once more, she would just as soon skip it.

Before she could say anything, he pulled her into position and started to move with the music.

"Eddy," she started to protest, "I don't know if—"

"Shh, Annie, just follow my lead—you'll do just fine."

And she did. Her eyes fixed on his like they were the shore and she was a ship searching for a port. And he never looked away, that sweet, slight grin on his mouth, his silver-frosted hair blowing behind him. Cold wind stung her cheeks. Fairy lights were a dizzy blur above them. It was magic.

The music stopped, and she automatically let go of one of his hands, moving alongside him to swish backward and dig 'n her blades, coming to a stop with a flourish and a spray of ice.

Eddy threw back his head and laughed at the moon.

"You were wonderful!" he shouted. "I knew you could do it!"

Hands at her waist, he picked her up as he spoke, twirling in a circle, her skates dangling a foot off the ice.

She laughed with him, feeling younger, giddier than she had in ages.

"I did do it, didn't I?" she said into his face, just inches below hers. "I really did it!"

He stopped twirling, holding her aloft, his face shining, his white teeth flashing. "You bet you did it, sugar!" His hands still at her waist, she slid down his body until her feet touched the ice.

"Thank you, Eddy," she whispered.

"My pleasure," he whispered back.

He was so close that she felt the warmth of his breath on her mouth, felt the hardness of his body pressing into hers. She wanted the touch of his mouth again, but it couldn't be here, couldn't be now. Once more Jason was beside them, his mouth open, his eyes like a couple of moon-pies ready to be eaten.

"Awesome," was all he said.

Ann grinned at him. "Thanks, Jase," she told him simply, knowing that that one word was high praise from him indeed. Then she turned to Eddy before she could embarrass her son by grabbing him and giving him a mighty hug— because that's just what she felt like doing. "Why don't you and Jason go do figure eights or something?" she suggested, still a little breathless.

"You come, too, Mom."

She shook her head. "I've had my thrill for the night. I'm not about to push my luck."

Jason shrugged. "Okay. Come on, Eddy."

"I'm right beside you, kid," Eddy said, giving Ann a long look and an ice-melting smile as he skated off, Jason keeping pace with him effortlessly.

For the next half hour, she stood in the cold and watched Eddy skate with her son. Jason was obviously nuts about him—and Eddy seemed to take to Jason, as well. Ann laughed at their antics until cold tears froze on her cheeks.

When the rink closed, Eddy walked them home, holding her hand, Jason carrying on about how he'd never seen his mother look so good on the ice before.

"Wow—it was so cool! I never thought I'd see Mom skate like that! Eddy, you must be some kind of funky wizard!"

"Nah," Eddy answered. "Your mom's just a very special lady."

Jason ducked his head as if embarrassed, but Ann could see he was pleased—pleased that such a cool guy liked his mom.

"Yeah, she's okay," he finally said. Jason walked beside them in silence for only a moment and then his head came up again, his usual grin in place. "Give me the keys, Mom, I'll run ahead and unlock the door."

Ann fished the keys out of her pocket, and Jason was off like a bolt of lightning, running past the two remaining houses and up the walk of the white Milwaukee bungalow where Ann rented the downstairs flat.

When she and Eddy paused in front of it, she found herself wondering what he thought of it. Eddy Winters didn't appear to have much money, and she hadn't a clue as to what he did for a living, but he had a certain casual elegance about him, a certain mystery that spoke of no ordinary life. What would he think of the life she'd tried to put together for Jason and herself?

And would he be around long enough to think about it at all?

"Hey, Mom!" Jason called from the front porch that ran the length of the house. "Can Eddy come in and have hot chocolate?"

"What about it, Mom?" Eddy asked with soft amusement. "Can Eddy come in?"

The snow had frosted the silver in his hair, his earring winked in mischief. His eyes gleamed, his mouth curved in a smile that would shatter any woman's resistance. But she wasn't ready to have a Viking pirate invade her home—because he was already invading her heart.

She shook her head. "It's late. I'll never get him to bed if you're there."

He looked away from her, into the sky, and she heard his sigh of regret, then he grinned again and called to Jason, "Sorry, kid. It's late. Another time."

"Aw—" Jason started to grouse, then immediately brightened. "Hey, how about tomorrow? Can Eddy eat over, Mom? Isn't tomorrow meat loaf night? Mom makes great meat loaf, Eddy."

"How about it, Mom?" Eddy asked, that same soft amusement in the words. "I love meat loaf."

"I'll just bet you do," she answered ruefully.

"Can he, Mom?" Jason hollered, impatiently bopping around on the front porch.

"Want to?" she asked Eddy softly.

"Very much."

"Yes," she called to Jason, her eyes still locked with Eddy's, "he can."

"All right!" Jason hollered, leaping a foot off the porch floor before disappearing into the house, the storm door slamming behind him, leaving her out in the snow with the Viking pirate.

He laughed softly and shook his head.

"What?" she asked.

"It's just that I feel like a high school kid, prolonging the moment when we have to say good-night—working up enough courage to steal a kiss—only this time, instead of being afraid of my girl's parents catching me, I'm afraid her kid is spying on us."

My girl. How casually he said it. She laughed, and it sounded nervous, young. "You make me feel about seventeen," she said.

His eyes were suddenly sober on hers. "You look about seventeen."

She started to answer, to make some light remark, to laugh off the compliment, but she was caught by his eyes, suddenly serious, suddenly moving closer, suddenly robbing her senses of all but the need to feel him against her, to have his mouth on hers.

And then—suddenly—it was.

His lips parted, his sweet, hot breath pulling her in, sending a river of flame running through her veins. And then his mouth left hers in a rush, and she felt it, quick and wet, against her throat before he moved on, gently pulling on her earlobe with his teeth, then burying his face in her hair.

"Annie, Annie." The words were a breathless, muffled whisper. "I don't know what's happening here." He pulled back, holding her at arm's length, staring into her face, then pulling her roughly to him again, taking her mouth once more with a violent energy that stole every last ounce of hers, then gentling the kiss till it brought tears to her eyes.

And then he just held her—held her tight for long moments before murmuring into her hair, "I better go."

They parted slowly, reluctantly, and he stayed to watch her climb the stairs and open the door. He was still standing on the sidewalk in the frosty darkness when she went in and closed the door behind her.

Chapter Six

Eddy tumbled Annie down into the long grass. Her hair, warmed by the sun, brushed his face like threads of burnished silk. Her mouth tasted like spring, warm, seductive, new. The scent of lilacs drifted with the breeze—heady, consuming. In the distance, across the meadow, a bell was tolling. No, ringing—

Eddy opened his eyes. The only things left of the dream were the humming of desire in his body and the ringing of the telephone.

Rolling over, he pushed himself up on an elbow and snagged the receiver.

"Yeah?" he grunted into the phone, his voice rough with sleep.

"Eddy, pal, wake up—we got problems."

Eddy pushed the hair out of his face. "Hank?" he muttered. "What time is it?"

"Nine New York time, which makes it eight Milwaukee time. And I got bad news, Eddy. The meeting was pushed up. The entire board of Northcott Enterprises is meeting this afternoon." Hank sighed wearily. "Eddy, boy, if I'm going to convince them to stay out of court and keep the inn open, you gotta give me something to go on. Why is the Northcott Inn losing money?"

Eddy sat up and swung his legs over the side of the bed. A few days ago, he wouldn't have cared, but since coming to the inn again he found himself liking the prospect of the inn closing down less and less. "You've got to stall them, Hank."

"Stall them? Haven't you found anything? This job should be a cinch for a pro like you. What the heck's been going on out there?"

What was going on was he'd been busy falling in love. He cleared his throat. "There have been . . . complications."

Hank gave a bark of laughter. "Right, pal," he said. "What's her name?"

Eddy laughed and got to his feet. "You think you know me so well—"

"Huh—tell me about it. Look, pal, I don't even want to know her name, I just want you to get on with it out there."

Naked, Eddy paced to a cream brocade boudoir chair and sank into it. He supposed he *had* been dragging his feet, but he hadn't really believed there was anything to find. From the beginning, he'd been certain this trip was just a ruse to get him to visit the Northcott Inn again—to make him come under its spell as he had as a child.

And maybe he *was* falling under its spell—just a little. He only wished he had more to give Hank. But he did have a theory.

"The personnel files and payroll records haven't gotten here yet, Hank, but there are suspiciously few employees wandering around. According to the waitress and the housekeeper, a lot of people have gone out the door since new management came in two years ago."

"Fired?" Hank asked.

"Fired," Eddy confirmed. "And another thing, the room service has been cut along with the valet parking. Guests have to haul their own luggage from the lot around the corner."

Hank grunted, and Eddy could hear the shuffle of papers. "That makes no damn sense. I've got the inn's records right here in front of me, and according to them, those cuts never happened. In fact, the parking valets got a raise just months ago."

"What about the firings?" Eddy asked, getting out of the chair and taking the phone with him to pace around the room, his bare feet warmed by the worn yet still beautiful Persian rug that covered the floor.

Again, the rustle of papers, then, "That information should be here, but I don't see it. I'll have to look into it."

"Do that."

"Meanwhile, you got any ideas at all?"

"After I talked to the housekeeper yesterday, I started thinking about this case I had back when I started out."

"Yeah?" Hank grunted.

"An Italian family," Eddy went on. "Calmeri or Carmaleta—something like that. Family owned a couple of grocery stores in Brooklyn. The old man was retired and the son was running things."

"Listen, Eddy," Hank interrupted, "I'd love to talk over old times with you. But the clock is ticking. What does this have to do with—"

"I'm getting to that. The kid resented the fact that the old man still held the purse strings, made all the decisions while the kid did all the work. Turned out the son had fired everybody that wasn't family but the old man was still paying their salaries—right into the kid's pocket."

Hank grunted approvingly. "Neat little scam," he muttered.

"The neatest," Eddy agreed.

"But it'd be a hard scam to run on something as big as a hotel chain."

"But not something as small as a twenty-five-room inn where all the job titles seem to overlap. Don't forget, this place isn't run like the rest of the hotels in the Northcott chain."

Hank grunted again. "How could I forget, pal. It's because of *you* I'm still administrator of the trust that's keeping it alive."

Eddy shook his head, one corner of his mouth lifting ruefully. "All right, Hank. I'm finally starting to feel guilty about that." Laughing softly, he added, "I almost expect to see Hattie coming around the corner any minute and letting me have it."

"Good. Then as soon as you get back here, you know what you can do."

"We'll see, Hank. We'll see."

Hank chuckled. "I knew the place would get to you."

Eddy smiled and shook his head. "Yeah, Hank you were right," he said resignedly, "the place is getting to me. And I'm beginning to think you were right about something else, too. It looks like there really could be something strange going on out here."

"Foul play?" Hank asked, an edge of childlike enthusiasm in his gruff voice.

Eddy squeezed his eyes shut and chuckled. "Yeah, Hank. Foul play. And don't sound so tickled about it. You're the one who should have been the PI—not me. Sometimes I think you only pushed me toward it because you felt you couldn't get it for yourself."

"Hey—don't forget, pal, I rescued your butt. Put you on the right side of the law." Hank was silent a moment, then said, "But you're right. I would have loved it. Only your old man needed me more, Eddy. He never could have hung on to the business if I hadn't been there for him."

Eddy knew that. Hank had been a rough cut when Nathan, Sr., had taken him on. But he'd quickly moved up to chief assistant. Nathan, Jr., Eddy's father, had inherited Hank—and it was a damn good thing for the business that he had. "He was lucky to have you, Hank," Eddy said. "And so am I."

Hank went silent a moment, then cleared his throat. "Well, now I need you, pal. This afternoon, the board is going to push to go to court to nullify the will. And the way things are going out there, the courts just might agree."

"I'd say someone on this end is determined to see that that happens. From the senseless changes I've seen, it's almost as if someone is deliberately setting out to ruin the place."

Hank grunted. "That's a little farfetched, pal. I'd be more willing to believe it was a scam like the one in Brooklyn. Someone's lining their pockets the easiest way they know how. Obvious place to start checking it out would be the manager. Express oughta have those files to you any time now, but you better get yourself a computer with a modem to replace the one vacationing in Tahiti. We can't be waitin' for FedEx to get information to you."

"Already done, Hank. Just waiting for the delivery. Meanwhile, do me a favor. Look up the manager's name. I've been trying to get a meeting but the guy is making himself scarce, almost as if he suspects something's going down. Thought I'd snoop around and check out where—and how—he lives, but I need a name and address."

"Sure, Eddy. Hold on a second."

Carrying the phone to the window, Eddy pulled back the heavy silk drapes. Last night's snow had blanketed everything with a new coat of white, and the sun was out in full brilliance, making it shimmer like the blood in his veins when he thought of the feel of Annie under his mouth and in his arms. He was looking forward to the meat loaf she was going to feed him tonight as if it was the food of the gods. He grinned at the crazy thought that it may not be the food of the gods, but it would be made by an angel.

Yeah, he would eat sweet Annie's meat loaf, then maybe he'd watch a little television with Jason or play some cards.

Then after the boy was in bed, he'd get Annie on the sofa—maybe do a little necking—let this crazy yearning grow....

Grow into what?

For the first time in his life, that question didn't scare him. "Eddy, my boy," he murmured to himself, "maybe you really are falling in love."

"Okay—here we are." The raspy sound of Hank's voice cut into the thought. "Manager is a broad named Madison—Ann Madison."

Eddy squeezed his eyes shut, his mind slamming like the door of a cell. He took a deep breath, held it for several heartbeats, then opened his eyes. "Run that by me again, Hank," he said carefully.

"Ann Madison. Been manager there for two years last October." Hank grunted. "Some coincidence, huh? The Northcott Inn started going downhill about that time."

"You're sure?"

"Sure I'm sure. Holiday season is usually their best, but that Christmas they—"

"No, no." Eddy squeezed his eyes shut again, and shook his head. "I mean are you sure she's the manager? Are you sure she's not the chauffeur?"

"Chauffeur? Nah, that's a guy named Max. Been there forever. You must remember him from when you were there as a kid."

"Max?" Eddy repeated blankly.

"Yeah, Max Harper. Used to be concierge in the golden days, now he does just about anything they need him to do—including ferry guests back and forth to the airport."

Eddy's stomach churned. He remembered Max, all right. An image of the short, round man he'd seen in the office with Annie the night before shot across his mind. The guy he'd mistaken for the elusive manager.

"Listen, Hank, I have to go. Do what you can to stall them this afternoon. I'll get something to you as soon as I can."

Eddy hung up the phone quickly before Hank could ask any more questions. He pulled on jeans and a shirt and thrust his feet into boots, grabbed his jacket just in case, then headed to the lobby.

A young man, thin, with rumpled brown hair and wire-rimmed glasses inching slowly down his nose, sat at the computer in the office behind the registration desk, intently studying something on the computer screen, oblivious to Eddy standing there.

After a moment, Eddy cleared his throat and the man jumped to his feet, pushing his glasses higher with a practiced finger.

"Oh, sorry. Didn't see you there. Can I, uh, help you?"

The man shuffled out of the office as he spoke, and Eddy thought he looked incapable of helping anybody with anything. His name tag said Austin—the desk clerk Eddy had talked to on the phone yesterday.

"I'm expecting an express package," he explained. "Would you check on it for me?"

"Oh, of course—"

Eddy opened his mouth, but before he could say anything, Austin shuffled to the office and disappeared around the corner. Eddy heard him rummaging back there, then his rumpled head poked around the doorway.

"Uh . . . sorry. I forgot to ask—"

"My name," Eddy finished for him. "Edmund Winters. I'm staying in the penthouse."

Austin started to walk away again, then did a double take, staring at Eddy through the smudged lenses of his glasses. "Really?" he finally croaked.

Eddy didn't have the time or patience for this. So far, every person he'd talked to at the inn had asked him the same question. "No," he barked. "I haven't seen the ghosts."

It seemed to take Austin a moment to comprehend. Then he gave a weak smile and pushed at his glasses again. "Oh, well, I suppose everyone asks you that."

"Just about," Eddy said grimly. When Austin went on standing there, staring, Eddy prompted, "My express?"

"Oh—right."

After what seemed like long moments, Austin came back with a large, thick envelope and handed it to Eddy. Eddy muttered his thanks and turned away just in time to see Jason heading across the lobby toward him.

"Hey, Eddy!"

"Hey, good morning, sport." Eddy felt guilty, though he'd done nothing but pick up an express package. He glanced quickly at the envelope. Crazy—the kid didn't have X-ray eyes. And if he did, all he'd see was a list of the inn's employees. Would his mother's name be at the top?

Jason patted his stomach. " I just had *two* stacks of pancakes."

Despite what he had on his mind, Eddy grinned. The boy's enthusiasm was definitely contagious. "With chocolate milk, right?" he asked.

Jason nodded energetically. "Right! You goin' in for breakfast?"

Eddy shook his head. "Not just yet." He glanced toward the café. "Where's your mom this morning?"

"Aw, she's busy talkin' to housekeeping about something."

Eddy was tempted, very tempted to ask Jason a question or two. But looking at him, at his wide, trusting eyes, his nose scrunched up just like his mother was fond of doing, Eddy couldn't bring himself to do it. Besides, there had to be some reasonable explanation for the whole thing.

Maybe Hank had it all wrong. Maybe Annie was just the assistant manager, which would put her farther down on the list of suspects.

Eddy squeezed his eyes shut. *Suspects?* He hadn't even found anything yet. There was no suspect because there was no crime—not yet, anyway. And if there was and if there had to be—well, there was no way it was going to be Annie.

"Hey, Eddy, wanna walk me to school?"

Eddy looked at the envelope in his hand. He should go upstairs and tear it open, see what there was to be seen and get down to work. Then he saw the hopeful look on Jason's face. What difference would a few more minutes make?

"Sure, Jase. Why not?"

"All right!"

Outside the air was crisp, not too cold. The sun still shone on the snow, and winter birds fluttered and chirped around the trees planted along the street. Eddy tucked the envelope under his arm and tried not to think of anything but the winter sun on his face and the chatter of the boy at his side.

"Do you know how to play ice hockey, Eddy?" Jason asked.

Eddy shook his head. "Never learned. What about you?"

Jason scuffed up some snow with his foot before answering. "Nah—my dad always promised, but..." His words trailed off and he bent his head low.

Eddy looked at Jason's mahogany head and knew exactly what the kid was feeling. "Well, dads get busy sometimes," he said. "Mine didn't spend a lot of time with me, either."

Jason nodded, then brightened. "He played in college. I've still got his hockey stick. I'm always askin' him to come visit in winter so we can see a game together, but... well, I guess he's got a lot of stuff to do in California."

Yeah, thought Eddy. Stuff that was a lot more important than taking his son to a hockey game. Eddy could relate to that—definitely. Old Nathan, Jr., had always been too busy, too. But at least Eddy had had Hank. Who did Jason have?

The kid had gotten interested in a branch he'd picked up off the sidewalk, scraping patterns with it in the snow as he walked, maybe forgetting all about those games his father never took him to.

But probably not, Eddy knew. Probably not.

"Look, Jase, if there's a home game while I'm here and we can still get tickets, how would you like to see a game with me?"

Jason swung around, sending the branch sailing into a front yard. "No kidding?"

Eddy laughed. "No kidding."

"Awesome!"

Eddy never saw it coming, but Jason suddenly flung himself into Eddy's arms, giving him a hug that ended almost as quickly as it had begun, then running ahead to leap up and bat the low-hanging, snow-covered branch of a tree with his hand, sending a shower all around his shoulders.

Eddy's pace slowed. How surprising, he thought, that the kid would hug him like that—right out on the street.

But the really surprising thing was the way it made Eddy feel.

It made him feel special. Warm.

And it made him want Annie not to be the manager of the inn more than ever.

They rounded a corner. Jason's school was just ahead.

Jason started running, then turned, his feet still taking him toward the redbrick building. "You still comin' for supper tonight, Eddy?"

"Sure, sport," Eddy said with a wave. "See you then."

Eddy took his time walking back to the inn. He knew he was stalling, trying to postpone the moment when he had to open the envelope. Which was crazy. When and where he opened it wouldn't change the outcome of what was inside.

He turned into the block the inn was on and stopped dead in his tracks. The sight of it got to him every time. He just couldn't imagine it not being there. Sure, he'd avoided it for years, but he'd always known it was there.

"Knock it off, Eddy," he muttered to himself as he started walking again. "You're getting soft."

Yeah, well maybe he was. But he couldn't help but think he was the only one who could really save the place—if he wanted to. And if he could find a way to live with the strings that came with it.

He bounded up the wide stone steps and pushed through the door. Annie was standing in the lobby talking to Austin.

"That's okay, Austin," she was saying. "We all make mistakes." She patted him on the shoulder. He smiled shyly, pushed up his glasses and shuffled to the office.

Then Annie turned and saw him. And the smile on her lips made him wonder if those strings wouldn't be such a bad thing, after all.

HOW LONG had he been watching her? She felt heat start to creep into her cheeks and willed it to stop. "Hi," she said, as casually as she could. "Cold out?"

He shook his head, his long, streaked hair streaming away from his face, the diamond in his ear glittering with the same kind of light that shone in his ice-blue eyes. It came to Ann that he would have looked more at home on the ropes of a tall ship than in the slightly shabby lobby of the Northcott Inn, this Viking pirate who was striding toward her, making her heart shoot into overdrive.

"I just walked your son to school," he said.

Nothing out of his sexy mouth could have enchanted her more.

She grinned. "You've got a big fan there, you know."

Eddy shrugged a shoulder, but he looked pleased at the thought.

"I don't have much experience with kids."

"Maybe not, but you do remarkably well."

"He's a great kid, Annie. I think you're the one who's done remarkably well."

Now she really did blush. "Thanks."

"Oh, by the way. Do you know where I can get hockey tickets?"

"Hockey? You a fan?"

"Not really. But Jason is."

She was silent for a moment, trying to digest what she thought she'd just heard. "You're taking Jason to a hockey game?"

"Do you mind? I guess I should have asked you first, huh?"

She shook her head. "No—no. Of course not. He'll love it. His father always promised, but—"

"I know. He told me. I had one of those fathers, too."

She cocked her head. "You're really sweet, you know that? You don't have any idea how much this is going to mean to him."

"I think I do." He looked away from her. "My parents were divorced when I was not much older than Jason. I know what it's like. I had stepfathers and stepmothers." His gaze fell back on her. "And they all had one thing in common. No time for me."

She needed to reach out to him, so she touched his arm, feeling how tense the muscle was beneath the leather of his jacket. "I know what you mean," she told him. "I worry about Jason not having a father. I try to make up for it—" She gave a little shake of her head. "But it's not the same." She smiled. "It's no fun going to a hockey game with your mom. Especially when that mom doesn't know a bat from a puck."

He grinned and touched her nose with a finger. "It's a stick, Annie. In hockey it's a stick."

She raised a brow. "See?" Then she sobered. "If his grandfather were still alive..." She let the words trail off, then finished, "And my mother lives down in Florida now."

She felt his arm relax under her hand. "He's got you, Annie," he said softly. "I think that makes him a pretty lucky kid."

She rubbed his arm, feeling emotion rise in her throat. And it wasn't just Jason she was feeling for. She was feeling for the boy Eddy once had been—the boy nobody had time for.

Behind her Austin announced that she had a telephone call. "I've got to get back to work. See you tonight?"

"Yeah, Annie. Tonight."

He watched her walk away, wondering if she would think he was so sweet if she knew the real reason he was staying at the inn.

He waited until she'd gone into the office, then he strode to the elevator. After the doors had closed, he punched his floor number. At last he was alone with the envelope. No more reason to stall. He ripped it open and drew out the files. Her name was at the top of the list.

Ann Madison. Thirty-six. Divorced. One dependant. Hired as general manager of the Northcott Inn in October—over two years ago.

He fanned through the first few pages. No assistant manager. Move sweet Annie to the head of the class.

The elevator stopped and he strode out. When he let himself into the penthouse, the first thing he noticed was that the scent of lilacs was back again—and the room wasn't empty.

"What the hell are you doing here?" Eddy demanded.

The squat man turned. "Oh...uh, Mr. Winters. Sorry—I was just—"

With the door still open, Eddy took a few steps toward Maxwell Harper. "You were just what?" he asked.

"I was just, uh..." The old guy flushed, a ruddy color mottling his sagging face. "Okay, you caught me," he finally said. "It's me who's been doing it all along."

Eddy's eyes narrowed. "You who's been doing what?" he asked carefully.

Max started to take something from his uniform jacket pocket, and Eddy's training caused him to brace himself, his body ready to lunge.

But it wasn't a weapon Max pulled out of his pocket. It was a can of air freshener.

"I been visitin' the penthouse and sprayin' it with this stuff for years now."

Eddy relaxed his body and held out his hand. Max placed the can in it. "Lilacs," he said, after reading the label. "Just like Hattie wore."

Max looked at him sharply. "How did you know?"

Aware that he was precariously close to blowing his cover with the old man, Eddy turned away from those sharp eyes. "Uh—Annie, Mrs. Madison told me when I commented on them in the portrait the night I checked in."

"Oh," the old man said, moving over to the mantel. "Yeah, she wore them as often as she could. Her husband had them shipped in from down south some place."

"You must have liked her a lot to want to keep the penthouse smelling as though she were still alive."

"Oh, I more 'an liked her." The old man chuckled softly. "But I guess everyone who knew her was part in love with her. She had a way about her..."

Max turned away from the portrait, and Eddy bent his head slightly, hoping Max wouldn't see the resemblance to the two people he'd just been staring at.

"Well, like I said, I'm sorry. I shouldn't have come in with you stayin' here."

"Don't worry about it, Max," Eddy said, handing the can to him. "No harm done."

"Thank you, sir," Max said on his way toward the door. "That's mighty kind of you."

Eddy turned away again until he'd heard the door shut.

"Close one, Winters," he muttered to himself.

Eddy shrugged out of his jacket, threw it on a chair and strode to the kitchen. He needed coffee. Hot and strong. For one quick moment, he thought he'd had something—something that would keep him from having to investigate Annie. But Max had only been trying to keep a memory alive—and Annie was back to the top of the list.

He slammed through the old-fashioned wooden cupboards, pushing around their contents. Then he remembered. Hattie always kept the coffee in the refrigerator.

Sure enough, there it was. The coffeemaker was new, though, and he blessed whoever had had the foresight to install it in the penthouse.

While he waited for it to perk, he wondered. Was Annie the manager also Annie the embezzler?

He didn't want to believe it. But she had lied to him. She was no more a chauffeur than he was a cabdriver. And who was in a better position to falsify records?

Lara had access to the computer. And then there was Austin, who looked like maybe he didn't even have access to his own brain. Besides, according to the housekeeper, Austin's hours were short and erratic, his duties light.

Despite the fact that he had yet to see one piece of evidence, Annie was still the most likely suspect. But why would Annie want to ruin the Northcott Inn?

"Why else?" he muttered. "Money."

But something didn't fit. Her car belonged in a junkyard. Her kid worked on the hotel's computer because, according to Jason, they couldn't afford to buy him one. She shopped discount. She rented the bottom half of a bungalow in a neighborhood that had seen better days.

If sweet Annie was ripping off the Northcott Inn, what was she doing with the money?

The coffee had perked, so he poured himself a cup and took it into the sitting room, snatching the personnel list off the table and flipping through it. It was inflated, all right. A regular hot-air balloon.

Where *were* these people? How were they still showing up on the payroll?

"Come on, Eddy," he muttered, "you know how. Simple. The simplest one you've come up against yet." Sweet Annie was firing people but leaving them on the payroll. But that would only work if Annie herself did the payroll. Easily checked—and as soon as his computer arrived, that's exactly what he'd do.

But he had the feeling he knew what he was going to find.

He was going to find that the woman he'd been dreaming about ever since he first saw that fiery confusion of hair tumble out from under her hood was firing personnel and collecting their paychecks.

But what was she doing with the checks?

He blinked and braced himself against the mantel. "Forgery," he said under his breath.

Annie an embezzler? Annie a forger? Sweet Annie? *His* sweet Annie?

The coffee cup clattered as he set it on the mantel. Thrusting his hands into his hair, he paced the room.

"No," he said out loud. "Not Annie."

Then who?

He turned to the portrait above the fireplace. "Come on, Hattie. If you really do haunt, help me out here. Who's doing this to your beloved inn—and why?"

The portrait stayed silent—the only thing haunting was the lilac scent put there by a man who lived in the past.

He was going to have to confront Annie about her lies—that was the first thing he should do. But he couldn't—not yet. As soon as his laptop arrived, he'd gain access to all the inn's files. God, he hoped he'd find something—anything—that pointed away from Annie.

DUSK WAS APPROACHING. Max was laying a fire in the fireplace in the lobby. Ann wandered around, plumping pillows and turning on lamps.

"Max, what would you think of the Northcott Inn serving an afternoon tea?"

Max straightened and turned to her, brushing down the sleeves of his jacket. "Tea?"

"Well, tea and coffee and maybe hot chocolate in the winter, iced drinks in the summer—"

"If we're still here in the summer," Max grumbled, picking up an ancient bellows to blow the sparks in the kindling to flame.

"—and little sandwiches," Ann went on, pretending she hadn't heard him. She didn't want anyone to dampen the enthusiasm she was working up for the idea. "And cakes and cookies, too," she went on.

Max grunted.

Ann put her hands on her hips. "Max, come on. Show a little enthusiasm here. I'm trying to figure out a way we can all keep our jobs."

Max shook his head sadly. "New York'll never go for it."

"Why not? A tea could bring in people visiting the galleries and shops in the area, or skaters from Cathedral Square. Then those people could start telling their friends about how charming the place is. It could help business, Max."

Max held out a hand, his fingers short and stubby and worn—like the rest of him. "Don't get me wrong, Ann. I'm not knockin' your idea. It's a good one. But how are you going to get New York to agree? Won't you need some money to start it off?"

Ann sank down on the arm of the sofa and stared into the infant fire trying to take hold. Max was right. She couldn't do it without some start-up funds. She looked around. And the lobby could use some sprucing up. Nothing much. Maybe new throw pillows, some cut flowers. That would do for now. With the fire in the grate, the place looked welcoming enough. And the drafts were barely noticeable.

If the place was hers, she'd—

If the place was hers. How often over the past months had she thought those very words? One of these days, she'd have enough in her savings account to approach the bank. Yeah, one of these days—probably in the year 2001. Whenever, the way things were going, the place would be dust—or a parking lot—before any bank was going to seriously consider making a loan to her to buy the thing.

What was the matter with that grandson, anyway? Didn't he realize what he was throwing away? The place was warm and alive—not only a home for the weary traveler or a little piece of paradise for a romantic couple, but it could be, *should* be, a home for a family. How often she'd pictured her and Jason upstairs in the penthouse. How often she'd thought of what it would be like taking the elevator down to work every day. Heck, every night. She'd be willing to work twenty-four hours a day, if that's what it took.

And that globe-trotting, irresponsible grandson was throwing it all away.

She was still staring into the fire when she heard the fax machine in the office kick in. Her gaze swung to the office and she sighed. Faxes these days meant nothing but bad news. Might as well get it over with. Taking one last look at the fire and the dreams dancing in it, she made her way to the office.

The fax was from New York. Groaning, she ripped it off the fax machine. The home office was turning down her requisition for new bedspreads. She threw the fax down next to the one she'd received two days ago denying her request to reinstate valet parking for the winter months, at least.

What the heck did they expect from her out here? How could she help make the place turn a profit when she was shot down at every turn?

"Well, that kills the tea, for sure," she muttered. If they weren't willing to replace moth-eaten bedspreads, they sure weren't going to spring for tea cakes and scones.

She picked up a pencil and tapped it against her lower lip. On the other hand . . .

Throwing down the pencil, she pulled out her desk chair and sat, bringing up the company letterhead on the computer. What would it hurt to just write and ask? She'd lay the plans out in detail—and in writing, since that was how New York always wanted things done.

She grabbed the fax again and looked at the initials. C.N. Was that the elusive grandson? No, he was a Nathan, too. The third. Well, heck with C.N., whoever he was. She was sending this little missive to Nathan III. And while she was at it, she just might ask for more than tea cakes. She just might ask him why he didn't do the right thing and come and claim his inheritance before everything his grandparents had wanted him to have was gone forever.

She didn't know how long she sat there, engrossed in trying to find the right words to plead her case, but when next she looked up, Eddy Winters was leaning in the doorway, just watching her.

Almost involuntarily, she started to smile, but the look on his face wasn't anything to smile about.

Chapter Seven

"You lied to me, sugar," Eddy said, his voice a deep, lazy intrusion on her well-being.

She wrinkled her brow. "What?"

"Why did you lie to me?" The words were low, strangely monotone, but the emotion missing in their inflection was shooting like fire from his eyes. He looked a little dangerous, standing there so still, his lips the only thing moving as they said those surprising words.

She shook her head, stunned by the question, trying to search her mind for any plausible reason for his accusation.

There was none.

She tried to smile again, but she knew it wasn't turning out to be much of one. "I didn't lie to you, Eddy. We really are having meat loaf."

She'd meant it as a joke, meant it to lighten the mood. The Viking pirate wasn't finding it funny.

"You told me you were the chauffeur here. But you're not, are you?"

She wrinkled her nose in confusion. "*I* told you I was—oh, you mean at the airport? My tongue was in my cheek, Eddy. I only meant I was the chauffeur for that night—under special circumstances. I told you, remember? The limo wouldn't start. Mine was the only car in the lot that would.

I couldn't very well let Max drive the thing. I mean, you've seen it—"

Still, he didn't budge, his face like stone. But she knew him, didn't she? She knew the sexy, funny Eddy Winters she'd taken shopping. This was the man who'd taught her to skate. The man who'd walked her home with the snow falling and his mouth doing crazy things to her insides.

Ann stood and walked from behind the desk to stand a short distance from him.

"What's wrong, Eddy?" she softly asked.

Not a muscle moved on his brooding face, just his icy eyes had followed her, and were now looking at her like he'd never seen her before. And maybe he hadn't. Maybe a kiss in the middle of T. J. Maxx was meaningless to a guy like him. Maybe a walk in the snow and a kiss good-night accompanied by murmured words of astonishment were nothing more than payment to the chauffeur for services rendered.

"Is that why you asked me to take you shopping yesterday?" she asked him flatly. "Because you thought I was the chauffeur?"

"Why else?" he said carelessly, moving his head impatiently to fling the hair from his face.

"And last night?" she asked him carefully. "The ice skating, the—" But she couldn't bring herself to mention the good-night kiss.

"Jason's idea, as I recall."

"Then you recall wrong," she told him bluntly.

She thought there might be a tiny spark of the old humor in his eyes when he said, "Do I?"

She bit down hard on her lower lip, willing herself to remain immune to his charm if he was deciding that now was the time to start using it. "I'll tell you what, *Mr. Winters,*" she finally said, with as much venom in her voice as she could muster, considering that she'd still rather be in his arms. "Next time you need someone to take you for a ride, try hiring a professional. You'll find one hanging around a lamppost somewhere in the vicinity of Twenty-seventh Street."

Something besides amusement flickered in his eyes, and he reached for her, but she was too quick. She whirled around and flounced to her desk, grateful that the phone was ringing. A perfect exit.

"Northcott Inn," she said crisply into the receiver. "Sorry, night auditor's not in yet. Try back around nine. Sure. Good night."

She slammed the phone down and turned to pull the desk chair closer so she could get back to work. The chair wouldn't budge. She looked up and found Eddy standing behind it, hard hands gripping its back.

Too bad she didn't have a cup of hot—very hot—coffee handy.

"I'm sorry, Mr. Winters," she stated primly, "but guests are not allowed in the office."

"Does the night auditor do all the bookkeeping?" he asked.

Again, his question surprised her, and she could only stare at him for a moment.

"On the phone just now," he prodded, "someone asked for the night auditor. That'd be Lara, wouldn't it?"

Confused, Ann merely nodded.

"And does Lara do all the bookkeeping?"

Ann shook her head. "There's a payroll service that—" She stopped. Why would a guest want to know these things?

If he was just a guest.

She gave him what she hoped was a quelling look. "Looking for a bookkeeper, Mr. Winters? One who will work for a kiss?"

She intended to flounce out of the office and leave him standing there, but he blocked her, and for one brief, sweet moment, her body came up against his. The scent of the after-shave she'd chosen for him stung her. Woodsy, secret.

She remembered that fairy-tale hour when the scent of it had mingled with their shared body heat.

"Annie," he said with a soft harshness. "I didn't mean—"

She pulled away from him. "Didn't mean what? The kisses? Put them out of your mind, Mr. Winters. I have."

He brought his hand up to touch her face, forcing her eyes to meet his with his thumb under her chin. "I don't believe you, Annie," he murmured.

She thrust her chin up, trying to free herself from his hold. It didn't work. He merely thrust his hand into her hair, his thumb doing strange, luscious things to the whorls of her ear.

"That's the second time today you've called me a liar," she said, proud at how steady her voice sounded. Because she wasn't steady—not steady at all. "And you were wrong on both counts."

"Was I?" he asked so softly that if she hadn't been practically standing on his toes she might not have heard him.

"Come on, Eddy. Why would I want to hide the fact that I'm manager here? Unless, of course, you think the news that you have a thing for chauffeurs of the female persuasion preceded your arrival and you figure I'm just another predatory female out to trap the magnificent Edmund Winters."

He laughed then, softly, dangerously. "Okay, I might be willing to believe that you didn't mean to lie to me then. But you *are* lying now. You remember those kisses—and so do I." His gaze, burning now where before it had been ice, moved over her face. "So do I," he murmured again, before bringing his mouth down to cover hers.

She was angry. She should push him away. But just at that moment, with his warm lips softly covering hers, she couldn't quite remember why she was angry at him. So instead of pushing him away, she started to run her palms smoothly up his chest, her fingers aching to delve into his tangled hair and pull him closer.

Then she remembered why she was angry. She twisted her mouth away from his, pushing against his chest with the same palms that were dying to caress him.

"Just a darn minute, Mr. Winters. You've asked *your* questions—now I have a few of my own."

"Questions about what?" he asked absently, bending to nuzzle the hair at her temple.

She jerked her head away. "Well..." Gosh, it was hard to stay on track with him so close. "Well, like who are you?"

He laughed softly. "Who am I? I'm Eddy Winters, Annie."

She pushed away from him, successfully this time. "You know that's not what I meant."

He sat on the edge of her desk, watching her pace around the office. A pitifully short trip, given its dimensions. "Then what do you mean?" he asked, and she could have sworn there was caution in the question.

She glanced at him out of the corner of her eye, but he looked perfectly relaxed. "Well, you've been spending time with my son, you're supposed to be coming to my house for dinner tonight, you want to take Jason to a hockey game—"

"Yes, go on."

Why was he being so reasonable now after accusing her of lying just minutes ago? "And, well, I don't really know who you are or what you're doing here. I mean," she said, feigning interest in a stack of papers on top of the filing cabinet, "maybe you're not the kind of man I should be letting spend time with my son."

To her surprise, he laughed softly again. "Do you really think that?" he asked.

Before she could answer, he'd come up behind her, placing his hands lightly on her shoulders, leaning close enough or her to feel the warmth of his breath at her ear as he asked, "You wouldn't be trying to get out of feeding me that meat loaf, would you?"

The phone started ringing again. She gave a start at the sound and he chuckled and, hands still on her shoulders, turned her toward the phone, snagged the receiver and handed it to her.

"Um..." His lips were in her hair and her mouth went dry. "Uh, Northcott Inn."

"Hey, Mom! What's the matter? You sound funny."

"Uh..." Now his mouth was at her ear, his teeth gnawing lightly on her lobe. "Uh, hi, Jase. I'm, uh, fine. What's up?"

"I'm puttin' the meat loaf in now and I set the table."

"You, uh, you set the table?" she asked, trying to ignore the heat of the pirate's lips nuzzling her neck.

"Yeah!" her son exclaimed proudly. "Is Eddy still coming for supper?"

"Uh, he's right here. I'll, uh, ask him."

She turned around and looked into his glittering blue eyes. They still looked dangerous, but for other, much more agreeable reasons.

"Jason wants to know if you're still coming for supper," she whispered, a catch to her voice.

He kissed her nose. "Do you still want me to?"

She grinned. "No."

He grinned back. "Liar. Tell Jason yes, I'm still coming for supper."

She hesitated a moment, but who was she kidding? She had no intention whatsoever of disappointing Jason—or herself. "He said yes, Jase," she said into the phone. "We'll be there soon."

After she said goodbye, Eddy took the receiver from her and hung it up, then grabbed her coat from the coat tree. "Come on, Annie. Jason's waiting. Let's go eat that meat loaf."

THE DAMN CAR was too small. He could smell the perfume in her hair. He could feel the warmth of her body only inches from his own. He had gone to her office to confront her about her lies and ended up taking her into his arms and losing himself in her mouth.

Nice work, Eddy. You're a real tough guy, aren't you?

Well, could he help it if she was the sweetest damn thing he ever held in his arms?

He inched his arm along the back of the front seat so he could tangle his fingers in her hair. Silk. He wondered if the rest of her felt as good.

She gave him a quick glance, her lips smiling softly. If it was spring, he thought, he'd take her parking. Somewhere the moon could shine down on them and the breeze could fan the fire that would build between them. He'd have a blanket in the trunk, and—

Eddy, boy, you're doing it again. You're here on a mission and all you can do is think of how you'd like to get your hands on the lady suspect. He should be using this opportunity to garner information.

"How long have you been divorced?" he asked, trying to ease into a line of questioning that might be fruitful.

"Almost four years."

"Must be rough raising a kid all on your own."

She shrugged one shoulder. "We manage."

Eddy knew from countless part-time jobs in the family business that hotel work didn't pay a lot. Well, Annie didn't look like she had a lot. "Ex send you child support?" he asked as casually as possible.

"When he remembers to. I don't count on it." She looked at him sharply, adding, "And Jason doesn't know that, so I'd appreciate it if you wouldn't say anything about it in front of him. He's been hurt enough."

The words seemed to trail off with the passing headlights, but she was worrying her lower lip over it. The temptation was there to use his fingers to soothe her suddenly troubled mouth. "Listen, Annie, I wouldn't do anything to hurt Jase. You should know that."

Her tongue came out to caress where her teeth had been, and she seemed to relax. "I'm sorry, Eddy. It's just that every once in a while it occurs to me I know absolutely nothing about you." They braked for a red light, and she sat back and looked at him. "I don't even know where you come from, or why you're here, or how long you're staying..." She paused, her gaze going over him rather thoroughly. "And I sure don't know what a guy like you is doing in my car on the way to my house so you can eat my meat loaf."

He laughed softly and she continued to stare at him. For so long he realized she was serious about what she'd said.

"Annie," he said softly, twirling a thick strand of her hair around his finger, "I'm not sure myself what I'm doing here, but I don't think there's any place I'd rather be right now."

She stared at him, her lips parting, her eyes wide, her quirky brows full of question. At that moment, he wanted her so much, he almost groaned with desire.

Behind them, a car honked. The light had changed. It broke whatever spell lay between them, and she looked away and stepped on the gas.

A few minutes more and she was pulling the car to the curb in front of her bungalow. Silently, she got out of the car. He followed, cursing himself for a naive fool when he took her hand as they went up the walk. Instead of garnering information, all he'd managed on the drive over was to fall a little harder for her. They climbed the porch steps together, pausing under the light while she fit her key into the lock.

In the glow of the porch light, he studied her profile. What was she capable of? Could she heartlessly dispose of people's jobs and then pocket the money that came from

New York to pay them? And if she could, what was she doing with the money?

For all he knew, behind the door she was still trying to open might be thousands of dollars in electronic equipment or jewelry and furs. He'd seen it before. People spent the money right away so it wouldn't be found, unaccounted for, in their checking or savings accounts. And they spent it on things that were easily tucked into their lives or just as easily sold. Things that appreciated in value—jewelry, camera equipment, artwork, antiques. Maybe Annie did, too.

The door swung open and Eddy followed her inside, bracing himself for what he might find.

"Hey, Eddy!"

Jason held up his hand for a high five, and Eddy met his palm with his own for a slap. "Hey, Jason! Something smells good. Are you the cook?"

"Nah, but I put it in the oven and set the table," he said proudly. "Are ya hungry? Did you bring dessert, Mom?"

"Oh, Jason, I'm sorry—I forgot."

"Aw—I thought we were gonna have chocolate cake."

"Tell you what, I'll run to the bakery for French bread and dessert. You can keep Eddy company."

"Cool! Come on, Eddy. I'll show you my room."

Annie left, and Eddy followed her son through the living room into a small hallway that led to two bedrooms. Jason had the larger.

The walls were covered in posters. The bed was neatly made. Planks of wood lay over old, red bricks to form shelves that held books, games and a small black-and-white television. There was an electronic game, complete with joysticks, sitting on the floor in front of it. Not the latest model—or the most expensive.

"Wanna play?" Jason asked hopefully.

"Sure." Eddy folded himself onto the floor and prepared to try to rescue Princess Zelda from the evil forces.

When it was Jason's turn he maneuvered through the labyrinth with a smoothness that spoke of hours of practice, easily besting Eddy's respectable score.

"That's it for me," Eddy said, throwing up his hands. "I know when I'm outranked."

Jason laughed but Eddy could see the pride and pleasure in his eyes. This boy could never be the son of an embezzler and forger. He was too ingenuous. Too genuine. If his mother was a crook, something, somehow would have rubbed off on the boy. Besides, Eddy thought, look at this room. It was clean, comfortable, painted brightly, the furnishings showing more style than money. If Annie was embezzling, she sure wasn't spending the money on her son.

Jason had already forgotten the game and was enthusiastically describing the movie he'd borrowed from a neighborhood kid. When he found out that Eddy hadn't seen the first Mighty Ducks film, he decided to go next door to his friend Danny's and borrow that one, too.

Eddy heard the front door slam and willed himself to stay sitting, cross-legged, on Jason's bedroom floor. But it was too good an opportunity to miss. And, after all, wasn't that what he was here for in the first place? Not to find evidence against Annie, because he was having trouble getting his mind to seriously consider that she might be guilty. But he could take a look around and rule her out completely. Then he could tell Hank with a clear conscience that they had to look beyond the manager.

He got to his feet and left Jason's room.

It was something he'd done a thousand times before, first as the adventurous jewel thief he'd fancied himself at the tender age of seventeen, and then with Hank's buddy who'd taught him the ropes of being a private investigator.

What he did for a living required him to snoop into other people's lives, but in all the years he'd been doing it, he'd never felt like the rat he was feeling like now. And he'd never hoped to fail like he was hoping to now. Whatever secrets

Annie was hiding in her small flat, he hoped they stayed hidden.

The living room held nothing of apparent value. At least nothing of apparent monetary value. But there was something rich here, something worth having. This was a home. Simple as that. Annie had taken a small, old flat and given it the same quality Hattie had given the penthouse.

The furniture was good, but not expensive. Annie had played on the cottagelike atmosphere of the small bungalow, putting simple white tab-top café curtains in the windows, flowered pillows on a blue and white checked sofa and a yellow afghan over the back of a white wood rocker.

Eddy thought about the homes he'd known as a kid. No—not homes. Houses. Dwellings. Furniture you couldn't sit on, rugs you shouldn't walk on, noise you were never, ever supposed to make.

How different summers had been.

He went over to the rocker and put his hand on the yellow afghan, causing the rocker to stir and creak. It was a good sound, a homey sound. The afghan was soft, warm. He wondered if Annie had crocheted it herself.

He smiled. This was getting nowhere. Reluctantly, he turned away from the rocker.

On the same kind of shelves she'd rigged up in Jason's room, the bricks painted white this time, there was a small color television and a bottom-of-the-line VCR. No stereo— no cable box.

He went down the hall and slipped into the smaller bedroom.

He could smell her scent as he stood in the darkness.

But he couldn't stand there forever, wishing he had his face buried in the fragrance of her hair instead of making sure there was nothing here to point to Annie as an embezzler. Jason would be back any minute.

His eyes were growing accustomed to the dark, and he found a small yellow lamp on a table near the single bed. He flipped it on.

Flowers. A field of them on the comforter covering the bed. More at the narrow window. Still more on the silky robe hanging on a hook outside the closet door. He moved toward it, touching it lightly with his fingertips. Real silk. But what did that mean? He already knew she was the Power Ranger of shopping, adept at finding values. The fact that Annie owned a silk robe meant nothing at all.

Quietly as possible, he opened the closet door. No fur coats. No expensive shoes. No jewelry boxes piled on the overhead shelf—just lots of books and magazines, stacked neatly.

Something did catch his eye, though. Something creamy and silky. He reached out to touch it, and it slithered off the hanger. Quickly, he bent to pick it up and his hand brushed something solid at the back of the shallow closet, behind the rod of hanging clothes. He parted the clothes to see what it was.

Computer equipment. Boxes of it. He stood still for a moment, listening for the sounds of someone's return, then hunkered down to get a closer look. It was the good stuff. And she'd paid for it in cash. There was a receipt taped to one of the boxes. A receipt for over four thousand dollars.

He squeezed his eyes shut and gave a little shake of his head. "Annie, Annie," he murmured to himself, "where did you get the money?"

He examined the boxes. A computer with a mini tower and a CD ROM. Powerful, too. There was a color laser printer and a set of joysticks along with a box of software. Games. Encyclopedias. Hundreds of dollars worth of software.

"Aw, Annie," he groaned, before standing up and replacing the cream silk shirt that had dropped and straight-

ening the hangers so they looked like no one had disturbed
them.

He closed the closet door and found himself staring at the
robe again. Lord, she would look beautiful in it—the yellow flowers against the warm flame of her hair, the flowing
material draping her full breasts and the luscious curve of
her hips. He brought it to his face and breathed in.

Annie. It smelled just like Annie.

"Something I can do for you?"

He dropped the robe from his face and turned around.
Annie was standing in the doorway, anger flashing in her
brandy eyes.

Yeah, he thought, *there's something you can do for me.
Take off your clothes, Annie. Put on your robe. Lie on the
field of flowers covering your narrow bed. And let me make
love to you. Let me lose myself for a little while. Make me
forget what I just found hidden in your closet.*

"What are you doing in my bedroom?" she asked, a wary
tone to her voice.

He tried for a smile, knew it was crooked at best. "Guess
I took a wrong turn."

She eyed him doubtfully, shifting the bag she was holding to her other arm, then turned and headed for the
kitchen, leaving him standing there.

He let out his breath and shot his gaze to the ceiling. How
the hell had he missed hearing her come in? His eyes slid to
the silk robe. Easy. He'd had his face buried in it, his mind
on Annie's body—and the cache of goods he'd found in her
closet.

But did it mean anything? Did it have to? For all he knew,
she'd been saving for years to buy Jason a computer.

He followed her into the kitchen. He couldn't stop himself from scanning the place like there was a garage sale going on. The appliances were nothing to write home about.
The wooden table was old and scarred, painted bright yellow, as were the mismatched wooden chairs. She'd sten-

ciled a border on the cupboards, and there was a shelf full of old crockery above the gingham-draped windows. Like the rest of the house, it showed more finesse at fixing up and making do than at having money.

He leaned a hip against the counter. "You own this house?" he asked her casually.

"No—landlady lives upstairs." She turned from the sink where she'd been filling a pan with water. "Why?"

He shrugged. "Just curious."

"We had a house, but it went during the divorce. There wasn't much equity. My share went to pay my lawyer, but that's all it paid. My ex had thoughtfully taken out charge accounts in my name and left me holding the bag."

Lots of motive here, Eddy thought, to add to means and opportunity. But the only fruits of her crime—if there was a crime—were a few boxes of computer equipment. When he got his modem set up at the penthouse, he could easily do a credit check on her, maybe delve deep enough to check out her bank records.

"Excuse me."

Annie brushed against him to get something out of a cupboard, her back to him, her sweet behind pressing briefly against him, and he realized there was something far more crucial than checking her bank records. There was the need to get her into his arms again. He slid his hands around her waist and pulled her against him. Whatever she'd been holding in her hands clattered to the floor.

Ann whirled to face him.

"Did I scare you?" he asked, his ice-blue eyes alight with amusement.

"I—I didn't expect it, that's all."

Head tilted to the side, he bent closer to her. "I didn't expect it, either, but I have this unaccountable need to touch you every time I get within reach."

SHE RAISED A BROW, outwardly fighting against all that charm while her insides were melting and her heart was tripping like it was running a marathon. "Then maybe you better stay out of reach," she managed to say coolly enough to do herself proud.

He laughed softly, then bent to retrieve the green enameled colander where it had clattered to the floor. He made a mocking little bow as he handed it to her.

Why did he have to look so damned good? She'd made a mental pact with herself when she'd come home to find him in her bedroom that she was going to keep her distance until she'd had a chance to ask a few questions herself. But the man was darn near irresistible. His hair flowed to his shoulders, moving slightly against the stark planes of his cheekbones when he moved his head. He was wearing the sweater she'd found for him, the soft cream color making his skin glow darkly, the deep V of the neck allowing an unsettling glimpse of all that smooth, tan skin covering his chest. Wasn't he supposed to be spending the evening with Jason—not standing around making her hotter than the water boiling in the pot?

"Where is Jason, anyway?" she asked, taking the colander from him and letting it clatter into the sink before going over to the stove. The more distance she had from him, the better.

"He went next door to borrow another movie."

"Oh." She dumped angel hair pasta into the boiling water, not missing the amusement in his voice.

"I thought we were having meat loaf."

"We are. I serve it with pasta." She turned from the stove and crossed her arms. "Have you got a problem with that?"

His mouth quirked slightly, and he pushed himself from the counter where he'd been leaning rather elegantly and started slowly toward her. "No, Annie," he said softly, his mouth twisting. "I don't have a problem with that. Do you have a problem with me?"

He was standing only inches from her again, and she had plenty of problems with him. "Damn right I do, Mr. Winters. For starters, I don't know who the hell you are or what the hell you're doing here."

"I thought I was invited for supper," he said.

His grin was doing its best to disarm her. Her temper fought against it like an alley cat. "You know darn well that isn't what I meant!" she said, sounding like a petulant kitten. "What is this *research* you're supposed to be involved in? And why do you ask so many questions about the inn? And what were you doing snooping in my bedroom?" She narrowed her eyes. "Just who are you, Edmund Winters?"

"I know who he is!"

They both turned to look at Jason standing in the kitchen doorway, a videocassette under his arm, a huge smile on his face.

Chapter Eight

Eddy and Annie looked at each other, then at Jason.

"You do?' they asked in unison.

Jason shrugged. "Well, yeah. I figured it out right away. He's working undercover, Mom, that's why he couldn't tell us."

Eddy groaned and shook his head, backing off from Annie and thrusting his hands into his pockets, a worried, resigned look on his face.

Aha, she thought. Outsmarted by a ten-year-old boy! "So don't keep me in suspense, Jason," she said, unable to keep the triumph from her voice. "Who is he?"

"He's a ghost buster!"

"A—a what?" she sputtered.

"A ghost buster," Jason repeated.

Her gaze shot to Eddy's face. She could have sworn he was trying to keep from laughing.

"Close, Jason. Very close," she watched him say through twitching lips.

"I knew it! You're here to find out about Nathan and Hattie, aren't you? You're here to find out if they put a curse on the inn and that's why nobody stays there anymore!"

She watched Eddy grin at her son. "You're too smart for me, Jason."

Jason whooped and jumped, shooting a fist into the air. "I knew it! I told Danny I was right! Wait until he hears!"

Eddy walked over to him, putting a hand on her son's shoulder. Man to man, he said, "Uh, Jason, I think you better keep this theory of yours to yourself for now. Okay?"

Jason's face quickly sobered, but his eyes were still shining. "Oh, sure. I get it. You can count on me, Eddy."

Ann was furious. So furious she could barely speak. "Why don't you go set the movie up, Jason?" she managed to say through a tight jaw.

Once he'd run out of the room she turned to Eddy. "Ghost buster, huh?"

"Well, I didn't actually say—"

She poked him in the chest with an accusing finger. "He believes you, you know. He doesn't know what an operator you are."

"Operator? Who, me?" he asked with just enough innocence to let her see what a handful he must have been when he was Jason's age.

In an effort to hold on to her irritation, she poked him with her finger again. "Yes, you! He doesn't know how you use your charm to get what you want from people."

Eddy covered her mouth with two fingers. "Does that mean I'm going to get what I want from you?" he asked, his voice low and loaded with dangerous innuendo.

She swatted his hand away. "I can hold my own against you, Eddy Winters, but Jason is an impressionable kid, for heaven's sake. How could you let him think—"

His face sobered as he sighed. "Look, Annie, I didn't actually *say* I was a ghost buster. I simply said that he was close to the truth. When the time comes—and it will very soon now—you'll be the first to know what I'm really doing here. And then it will be up to you to decide what you tell your son."

She put her hands on her hips. "And that's it? That's all you're going to tell me?"

"That's it. That's all I'm going to tell you," he conceded. "Now I think I'd rather take my chances with a movie about kids playing hockey than with that flashing temper I see in your brandy eyes."

"Smart move," she said to his retreating back. "Very smart move."

"THIS HAS GOT TO BE the best meat loaf I've ever tasted."

"I told ya!" Jason said.

"It's the oregano and basil," Annie explained, looking at him like she was wondering if he'd ever eaten meat loaf at all. True, he didn't remember ever having done so, but he was sure Annie's was the best to be had anywhere.

"My mom's good at cooking everything," Jason mumbled through a mouthful of pasta.

Eddy watched Annie lick some sauce from the corner of her mouth. "That doesn't surprise me."

"Yeah—you should taste her chocolate chip cookies. 'Course, I eat so much of the dough while she's makin' 'em that there's not much left to bake."

Eddy laughed. That was something he'd never done—eat cookie dough while his mother, or anyone else, for that matter, baked. When he was a child, cookies miraculously appeared on plates, and he never gave much thought as to how they got there.

"What else does she make that you like?" Eddy asked Jason.

The boy launched into a funny monologue of all the things he liked to eat—and there were plenty of them. Annie joined in to embellish stories of messes they'd made in the kitchen together.

"Hey, Mom, you remember when you tried to make fudge that time and it never got hard?"

Grinning, Annie shook her head. "How could I forget. I thought my arm would fall off from beating it."

Jason howled. "We ended up puttin' it on ice cream. But, hey, it was good!"

Eddy leaned back in his chair and listened and watched—and relaxed. These two were quite a pair. They might not have much money, but it seemed they always had fun.

Money—that was a subject he just didn't want to think about now. Nor did he want to think about the computer equipment stashed in the back of Annie's closet, or what he was going to tell Hank tomorrow. Annie's home cooking had relaxed him more than the finest wine ever had, and he wasn't going to waste this night with her and her son by thinking about tomorrow.

"Tell us about your job," Jason said suddenly.

Abruptly, Annie stood and started to clear the table. "No. He's not going to tell us about his job. That subject is off-limits."

"Aw—"

Pushing back his chair, Eddy got to his feet. "Come on, Jason, let's help your mom with the dishes, then we can all watch the second movie together."

Annie washed while Eddy dried and Jason put away. The kitchen was warm and cozy, fragrant with the earthy smells of herbs and spices. The window above the sink was steamed over with the heat, shutting out the cold night, making Eddy feel like they were in a pocket of time, far removed from what was going on in the outside world. It was a feeling he wouldn't have minded hanging on to. But for how long? He was still determined to go back to New York, wasn't he? Wasn't that where he belonged?

Maybe he just wasn't sure where he belonged anymore. The steam from the hot water had put a flush on Annie's face and a few tendrils of curls clinging to her cheeks. She lifted a hand to push them off her face, her breast rising with the movement. She was so damned beautiful, so sweet, so funny. *So real.* She was more real than any woman he'd ever been involved with. And he thought at that moment that he wanted her more than any woman he'd ever known.

And that, Eddy realized, whether he was going back to New York or not, was going to pose a problem. He'd only known Annie for a few days, but he thought he knew her well enough to know that letting things between them go too far before he'd established her innocence would be a mistake. He could just imagine the fury in her brandy eyes when she found out who he really was and what he was really doing at the Northcott Inn. Those kind of secrets between them would be shaky footing to build a relationship on.

His hand slowed on the plate he was drying. Is that what he wanted with her—a relationship? Sitting between mother and son at dinner tonight, it came to him that not only did he like being with them, but he liked himself when he was with them. He liked the new possibilities they seemed to be opening up in his life. How far did he want those possibilities to go—and where did the Northcott Inn fit into it all?

"Anyone for cake?" Annie asked, taking the dish towel from him to dry her hands.

"You bet!" Jason yelled.

"Me, too," Eddy answered. "Me, too."

ANN SAT ON THE SOFA, her attention not really on the movie. She couldn't seem to keep her eyes off Eddy and her son, lying side by side on the rug, howling together, jabbing each other with elbows, high-fiving it and in general acting like a couple of kids together. It warmed her heart to see Jason relating to a man again. It'd been a long time.

It'd been a long time for her, too. Looking at Eddy now, his long legs spread out on her living room rug, the sleeves of his sweater pushed up on his hard, muscular arms, she wished things could be as simple and uncomplicated as they'd seemed under the twinkling fairy lights out on the ice. She watched the flicker of the light from the television playing in the silver streaks of his hair, aching to run her hands through it.

She was so lost in erotic thought she didn't notice Jason had fallen asleep until Eddy rose and joined her on the sofa.

"I can't believe he fell asleep during *The Mighty Ducks*," he said. "He's so crazy about hockey."

"You wore him out with all that roughhousing. You're really good with him."

He raised his brows. "Am I?"

Some sort of emotion flickered across his face. "You sound surprised."

"I guess I am, a little." He stared at Jason for a long moment. "I guess I never thought a kid could make me feel the way he does."

She touched his arm. "And how is that?"

He turned to her. His lips parted as if he would answer, but he didn't. Instead, he raised his hand and laid it softly against the side of her face. "Aw, Annie, why do things have to become so complicated?"

She almost held her breath, wondering what the complications were and how soon they would take Eddy out of her and Jason's life. "Are they?" she finally murmured. "Are they complicated, Eddy?"

But she knew he wasn't going to answer her.

He caressed her face for a moment more, then withdrew his hand. Her cheek felt cold without his flesh touching hers.

"Would you like me to carry him to bed?"

She stared into his ice-blue eyes before answering softly, "Yes."

She watched him effortlessly lift Jason into his arms, then led him to Jason's room, turning back the covers. Eddy laid her son down gently, then drew the covers up to his chin, bending to kiss his forehead.

Her heart rising in her throat made it hard to catch her breath. Despite the complications he didn't want to speak of, he felt something for her son. There was no mistaking that. And the way he touched her, the way he kissed her, made her think he felt something for her, too.

He stood looking down at Jason for several seconds before leaving the room. She bent to kiss her son, then followed him.

He was already putting on his jacket.

"You're leaving," she stated.

"It's best if I do."

He was out the door in a flash. She brazenly followed.

"Why?" she demanded. "Why is it best?"

He stopped at the top of the porch stairs and turned to look at her. She swore she saw some sort of torment in his eyes, some sort of hesitation on his face. Her gaze settled on his mouth, and she knew she wanted to feel it against hers once more. Even if she was the one who had to do the kissing.

She started toward him.

"Annie, don't," he murmured harshly.

She stopped several inches from him. "Don't what?" she asked.

"Don't come after me. In the kitchen earlier you told me to stay out of reach. I think you were right. We should slow this down a little."

She lifted a hand to his chest, pressing it there. "I didn't think you were the kind of man who took anything slow," she said, surprised at the throaty sound of her voice.

His eyes were riveted on her, need and desire at war in their depths. It gave her courage. She skimmed her hand up his chest and into his hair, delving her fingers into the silvery strands. She pulled his mouth down to hers and took it, thrusting her tongue between his reluctant lips, pressing her body against his until she felt him respond.

"Annie," he murmured into her neck when he'd pulled his mouth away, "you don't know what you're doing. Soon

I'll be out of your life. You're not the kind of woman who—"

"Maybe I don't care, Eddy. Maybe I am that kind of woman. And I do know what I'm doing. I'm trying to get you to want me."

He laughed softly, and she felt the rumble of it in his chest pressed close to hers. "That's not the problem here, Annie. Don't you know that?"

"Then what is the problem?"

He pulled back, staring at her for a long, heart-stopping moment before he answered. "I can't answer that, Annie. Not yet. All I can do is ask you to trust me."

"I don't want to trust you, Eddy," she whispered, suddenly knowing it to be true. She didn't know who he really was, why he was really there, but with the taste of him lingering on her mouth, it didn't seem to matter. "I don't want to trust you, Eddy," she repeated. "I want to make love to you."

For a second neither of them moved. He told himself to turn around, to go, to do the right thing. But there was only so much he could take. She took a tentative step closer, and something in him broke. He grabbed her roughly and hauled her up against him, taking her mouth with a hot, violent urgency. The soft warmth of her felt damn good in his arms. The night with her and her son, with her meat loaf and her homemade curtains, with her warmth and her laughter, had all played a part in seducing him. Yet he'd meant to leave, to wait to have her until no secrets stood between them.

But she'd done the unexpected. She'd come after him.

He broke the kiss, staring at her parted lips, at her sweet, erotically charged face. He put his hands at her waist and lifted her, taking her farther into the shadow of the front porch, pressing her against the wall of the house with his body. She groaned, wound her arms around his neck and covered his mouth with her own.

And he let himself get lost in it, sliding his hands up to her breasts, finding her nipples beneath the silk of her shirt, brushing them alive with his thumbs. She pulled her mouth away and gasped. "Eddy—"

Why had he thought he could resist her? He ate at her neck with his mouth, buried his lips again and again in her hair, all the while his hands learning her body, sinking into her sweet flesh.

"Say it," she whispered harshly. "Tell me you want me."

He looked into her face, knowing he had to give in to her demand. It was only the truth. "I want you," he moaned, looking squarely into her eyes.

Her full smile of triumph made her more beautiful than he'd ever seen her before.

And then, suddenly, there was light sweeping the porch. Eddy looked over his shoulder, squinting into it. A car's headlights spotlighted them as it drove into the driveway.

Swearing softly, he let her body slide down till her feet touched the porch floor, then put his arm around her waist and turned, leaning next to her against the wall of the house, trying to catch his breath.

"It's my landlady," she whispered. Then louder, "Estelle! You're out late."

"Oh, Ann! I wondered who was out here necking on my front porch. I thought maybe you had a baby-sitter, but it's you! And, oh, my, who's your handsome man?"

Ann introduced them, explaining to Eddy that Estelle helped take care of Jason when Ann had to work late.

"Oh, by the way," Estelle said, "I saw you in that brand new BMW yesterday. A perfect color for you."

Annie grinned. "You think so?"

"My, yes. Will that be the one, do you think?"

"Heavens, no. At least, not until I've tried the Lexus."

Estelle's peal of laughter split the crisp night air.

"Well, guess I'll let you two get back to it," she said then disappeared through a doorway and up the stairs.

Annie shivered and wrapped her arms around herself. Eddy resisted taking her into his.

"You're looking for a new car?" he asked her carefully.

She laughed. "Don't you think it's about time?"

But a BMW? he wanted to ask. A Lexus? Pricey stuff for a lady who lived the way she did. Unless the lady had a private stash of money someplace that she suddenly thought it might be a good idea to spend.

"Is something wrong?" she asked, a quizzical look in her brandy eyes.

After a moment, he shook his head. "No... I've got to go."

"Go? But I thought—"

"I've got work to do."

"Eddy, wait—"

But he didn't wait. He trotted down the steps and jogged down the sidewalk where he started to run like there was a demon at his heels.

"I *want* anything with her name on it, Hank. Requisitions, invoices, correspondence. Anything the corporate office has gotten from her in the past two years. And I want copies of canceled payroll checks—front *and* back."

"So you think this Madison broad is the one?" Hank asked.

Eddy squeezed his eyes shut, pressing a thumb and finger to his forehead. He'd barely slept all night, trying to figure this thing out. It couldn't be her, but he had to prove it. Because once this thing got rolling, it wasn't going to look good for her. Buying a computer didn't make her guilty. But it looked damn suspicious. Hadn't she just told him she was in debt? Hadn't she said she rarely got child support? He knew how much she made at the inn. According to the personnel records it was barely enough for essentials, let alone top-of-the-line computer equipment, paid for in cash. He didn't even want to think about what it would look like if she showed up driving a BMW or a Lexus.

"No," he finally answered, "I don't think she's guilty. I'm just trying to eliminate her as a suspect so I can move on."

"Okay, pal, I'll get them to you first thing tomorrow."

"No—today."

"Today? Same-day air?"

"Yeah, Hank. This can't wait."

"Want I should fax it?"

"No. I want the originals." He paused before asking, "How did things go with the board yesterday?"

"Stalemate. I pleaded my case, but someone's gotten to them."

"Who?"

"I don't know, pal. But they're hot to close the place down."

"All of them?"

"Enough to matter. We're meeting again this afternoon. I'll do my best, but without something to back up your contention—"

"I know, Hank. I'm working on it."

Eddy hung up the phone. He'd finally gotten his modem up and running. A credit check he'd run on Annie proved nothing. A credit card company had turned an account over to a collection agency around the time of her divorce. He suspected, from what she'd told him the night before, that this was one of the debts her ex-husband had dumped on her. Apparently, she'd made arrangements to make small monthly payments—which she did, on time. There was nothing else. She was in debt, but handling it. And those debts weren't exactly for the luxuries in life, either. Dentists, auto repairs. Nothing suspicious there.

He'd check her out against the other databases he had access to. And he also planned to check out Lara. Because it wasn't Annie. It couldn't be. And Lara was the next most likely person to be involved in any scam at the inn.

He had his laptop set up on Hattie's small writing desk in the sitting room. He sat before it, his fingers flying on the keys, but he couldn't keep his mind on what was showing up on the screen. Instead, he kept remembering the taste of Annie's mouth, the feel of her skin, the softness of her body. He kept remembering the evening spent with her son, and the warmth of her home. Remembering how much he wanted her. How hard he was falling for her.

And how mad she was going to be when she found out what he was up to. He figured the only way to keep from losing her completely was to clear her name *before* she found out her name even needed to be cleared.

He scanned the records on the computer screen. Lara's life looked about as exciting as any twenty-two-year-old's. She was past due on her American Express. Her VISA was maxed. His fingers moved over the keys, and the screen cleared and changed. She had an outstanding speeding ticket. Other than that, she looked clean.

This was getting him nowhere. Technology had its place, but it only got you so far. He needed to get out of the penthouse and look for anything that might put him on the right track—the track leading away from Annie.

Maybe he'd see if he could run into the housekeeper again, get her talking some more. He'd done his best to lay the groundwork with her and the waitress in the café by overtipping, pouring on the charm, making friendly chatter. In this business it always surprised him what a little niceness could do to loosen tongues, especially when the workers were discontented. He let himself out of the penthouse and headed for the elevator.

He found the housekeeper on the second floor loading clean towels onto her cart.

"Good morning, Doris. How's it going?"

"Mr. Winters," Doris said, her deeply lined face creasing into a big smile. "It's goin' slow as usual. This keeps up, I'm gonna have to get a second job."

Eddy leaned against the wall. "You said yesterday it wasn't always like this?"

"I been here ten years, and it's never been this slow." She shook her head. "I remember the days we had a maid for every floor. Now, even with my arthritis, I can handle it all by myself."

Eddy shook his head sadly. "That's quite a change. And when did you say it all started?"

Doris picked up a bundle of snowy white towels, smoothing the top one with her hand as she wrinkled her brow. "Well, I'd say it's been a couple years that it's been this bad. 'Course, business was falling off right along, I guess." She shrugged. "Otherwise, why would they have let so many people go? And why," she added more emphatically, "wouldn't I be able to get new bedspreads?"

"Bedspreads?"

"I been trying to get the bedspreads replaced for months now. Can't expect people to pay good money to sleep in a bed where the spreads are falling apart," Doris muttered.

"No, I guess not," Eddy sympathized, then changed the subject. "The blond girl—Lara, is it? How long has she been here?"

A cagey gleam suddenly appeared in Doris's eyes. "You interested?"

Eddy gave what he hoped was an enigmatic smile. "She worked here long?"

"Let's see now..." Doris tapped a finger against her thin lips. "Almost as long as Ms. Madison, I recollect." Then her lips pursed. "She's kind of flighty, though, Mr. Winters. I'd watch it with her if I was you."

"Flighty?" he asked innocently.

"Well, all you got to do is count the earrings in the girl's ears to know somethin' ain't right there." Doris shook her head as she made her way into the room with her stack of towels. "It's a mystery to me how they can trust her with the books."

Eddy watched her leave, wondering if maybe he finally had something.

Right. What he had was a housekeeper who didn't trust young women with multiple holes in their earlobes. Wearing too many earrings had to fall somewhere below buying computer equipment in the suspicious-behavior department.

He headed to the elevator.

Marie in the restaurant had much the same thing to say. Things weren't the same and, even though she enjoyed working at the inn, she was thinking of leaving. But she remembered things a little differently than Doris. She remembered business falling off *because* so many people were let go.

"You can't expect people to wait over a half hour to be served. Not if you're going to get any lunch trade from the streets. People have to get back to work. Coffee shop up on Wisconsin Avenue guarantees to serve you in ten minutes or lunch is free. Can't compete with that."

When Eddy asked, she told him she didn't know why Ann had fired so many people. She assumed orders had come from the home office, like they always did.

Damian, the chef, was fed up—and quite dramatically so. He liked Miz Madison, as he called her, but, he wondered plaintively, why didn't she fight New York and get him some decent food? He had studied in Paris! How could he be expected to put up with such things?

When Eddy left the café and crossed the lobby, he was surprised to see Lara behind the desk.

"Ann in yet?" he asked her.

"No," she croaked, then sneezed into a wad of pink tissues. "Better step back, Mr. Winters, I think I caught a flu bug."

Eddy made a few sympathetic noises. "Don't tell me Ann's out with it, too?"

Lara shook her head then sneezed again. "She'll be in. She's just running a little la—ah-ah-ah-*choo!*"

"Bless you," Eddy said, then headed out to the street, making his way toward Wisconsin Avenue and Schwartz's bookstore. He kept trying to convince himself as he walked that the information Hank was sending him was going to prove Annie innocent.

Yeah. And maybe the snow around him would melt instantly and he'd find himself in Tahiti, keeping his luggage company on the beach. Too bad the airline hadn't lost him somewhere out in the Pacific, too.

Everything seemed to be heading back to Annie.

Annie fired people, Annie cut services, Annie didn't get the goods or improvements needed to keep the place up.

Half an hour later, he was striding to the hotel, a sackful of books on ghosts under his arm. He'd decided that Jason's idea made for a good cover. He'd scatter the books around the sitting room, maybe carry one under his arm. Making like he was there to study a possible haunting by the prior owners would provide a good excuse to ask questions about the inn.

When he reached the Northcott Inn, he stood across the street and stared up at it. The idea of ghosts and hauntings suddenly didn't seem so fanciful. Icicles dripped from the gables and glinted in the sun like magic crystals. Snow, blown from the roof by the wind, swirled around the turret. It looked like a place that could carry secrets, alter destiny.

Well, it was altering his, anyway. In the few short days he'd been in residence, he'd started to think thoughts he'd never had before, started to feel feelings he thought were beyond him, started to imagine possibilities that he'd wanted no part of in the past. And right now what he was imagining was Annie in flowing white ermine, sweeping down the wide stone stairway toward him, her arms welcoming, her smile enough to melt the ice around the most cynical man's heart.

While he stood there like a foolish schoolboy, fantasizing about the woman he should be investigating, Annie did materialize. Only she wasn't wearing white ermine. She was driving it.

Or, to be more precise, she had just pulled up in front of the Northcott Inn behind the wheel of a brand-new white Lexus.

Eddy watched her get out and run into the hotel.

First a top-of-the-line computer—then a luxury car. Where was the money coming from all of a sudden?

Or maybe not all of a sudden. Maybe she just decided it was time to spend a little. Maybe she felt a little heat breathing down her neck.

And maybe Eddy had been watching too much *NYPD Blue.*

He trotted across the street just as Annie and Lara came out the front door. Quickly, he ducked behind an evergreen bush, out of sight.

"Isn't it gorgeous?" Annie was asking.

Lara sneezed. "Yeah—real hot, Ann. But I like the Mercedes better."

Eddy's brow furrowed. Mercedes?

"The red convertible?" he heard Annie ask.

Lara sneezed again. "Yeah, that's the one I'd pick."

"Maybe," Annie said, obviously considering. "But this one gets much better mileage on the highway."

Lara noisily blew her nose.

"Hey," Annie said, her voice full of concern, "you better get inside. If I'd known how sick you were I never would have been late this morning. Get on home, now. Take care of yourself and give me a call later to let me know how you're doing."

Eddy listened to them say goodbye, listened to the sweetness trickle from Annie's gorgeous mouth. He flattened himself against the prickly needles of the bush as she walked past it and got into the car. She took off like a bat out of hell in the direction of the parking lot, and Eddy found himself thinking that, yeah, bats had wings, too—just like angels.

Annie the angel—Annie the thief. Was she out shopping around for her getaway car? One that got good mileage?

Eddy squeezed his eyes shut and shook his head. He had a feeling he was going to be talking about this one when he was old and retired. Yup, the boys at the bar would get a kick out of this one. Very amusing. Eddy Winters, who'd managed to keep from being caught by any woman, falling for the chick he'd come here to cage.

So why wasn't he laughing?

Chapter Nine

"Special delivery, ma'am."

Holding the receiver of the phone in the crook of her neck, Ann mouthed silently, "I'll be right with you." Then, into the receiver, "Yes, Mr. Williams, we'll have your usual room ready for you—no problem at all."

The delivery man heaved a theatrical sigh. "Lady—just sign, okay?"

"Certainly, Mr. Williams," she said while taking the pen thrust in her face and signing the clipboard where the man indicated. He slapped a large envelope on the desk, along with a receipt, and left.

"We'll look forward to it, Mr. Williams," she said, then managed to finally hang up. She would have liked to have told Emmet Williams that there'd be absolutely no problem guaranteeing him his favorite room on the night in question, over a month from now, because so far there was exactly one other reservation for that date. Emmet Williams could have any damn room he pleased. Several, in fact.

She picked up the envelope, wondering if the home office was finally responding to some of her requests and suggestions.

"Oh, Lord," she muttered after reading the shipping label. Edmund Winters. Same-day air, no less. And she was alone.

Max was en route to the airport. Austin wouldn't be in until later. She had two choices. Ring Eddy's room and tell him to pick the envelope up at the desk—or deliver it in person.

She hadn't seen him since he'd bolted from her front porch the night before, seemingly scared off by her lusty behavior.

She supposed she had acted a little brazen. After all, she had told him that she wanted to make love to him.

And he had run.

Hardly flattering.

But he'd also responded. There was no mistaking that. He'd wanted her, all right. But something had scared him away.

She bit her lip, thinking ruefully, *And why not?* To a guy like him, she probably had *respectability* and *responsibility* tattooed on her forehead and *trap* written on her nose. Her old white bungalow didn't have a picket fence around it, but it might as well have.

And Eddy Winters's theme song was probably "Don't Fence Me In."

But Ann had no intention of trying to fence him in.

Well, okay. Maybe if she had a choice, she'd choose for him to stick around and fall madly in love with her. But life wasn't a multiple choice quiz. She understood that she had no choice. She'd settle for a couple of steamy nights, a few sunny days, a few thousand bytes of memory to boot up occasionally after he left.

But, aside from throwing herself at him—which she'd pretty much already done—she had absolutely no idea how to go about it.

She picked up the envelope. The thing was weighty in her hand, looking self-important with its same-day air sticker.

Looking too important to just let it sit here and vegetate until Eddy decided to show his face again. He was probably busy with that work he was so mysterious about. Why make him come all the way down here to pick it up when she wasn't doing anything at all? Besides, maybe he'd open the envelope in front of her and she would reap a few clues as to just who Edmund Winters was and what he was doing at the Northcott Inn.

"Okay, Ann," she murmured to herself, as she came out from behind the registration desk, "you talked me into it."

In the elevator, she tried to push her independent hair into some semblance of order. Her heart was hammering. This was so unlike her—going after a man. Because that's what she was doing—going after him. Last night, on her front porch, she'd made it clear to him what she wanted. And what had he done? He'd said they should slow down and then he'd taken off into the night like he was afraid she might try to catch him and drag him back. And now, here she was, making an excuse to see him again. But, heck, she didn't want to slow down. How many chances did a girl have to be with a Viking pirate? She didn't know how long he was in town for, but she didn't feel like wasting any of it.

The elevator stopped at the fifth floor. The doors swooshed open. She stepped out, walked to his door and knocked. Her heart started to run a race with her pulse to see which one would explode into the silence of the hallway first. She knocked again, then heard movement behind the heavy wood.

The door swung open.

He looked rumpled, his shirt open and hanging out of his jeans, his hair looking as though he'd run his fingers through it half the night. He just stood there staring at her, his face closed and forbidding. It should have put her off, but in the days she'd known the pirate she seemed to have taken on some absolutely brazen qualities.

"Hi," she said in a stroke of brilliance. "You got a delivery." She held out the packet. "It looked important so I thought I better bring it right up."

He looked at her sharply before taking the packet from her hands. "Who signed for this?" he asked abruptly.

She gulped, feeling her newly brazen skin start to shed. "Uh—I did."

He frowned mightily. "It should have needed my signature."

This was crazy. He had the thing right in his hand. What difference did it make who signed for it? She stood up straighter and shrugged. "Guess the man made a mistake." She watched Eddy, still frowning, turn the package over in his hands and examine it.

"Unharmed," she pointed out, trying for a little levity. "Still sealed. Untouched by any human hands but my own and several dozen postal workers."

He was still turning the package over in his hands, so she took the opportunity to glide past him into the penthouse.

Ann always thought the title incongruous. The word *penthouse* conjured something elegant, cold, worldly. The Northcott Inn's penthouse, as furnished by Hattie Northcott when she was a bride, was homey, friendly. The chintz sofas bloomed with big cabbage roses. The chairs were covered in yellow stripes, to match the wallpaper. But the room was saved from being too feminine by the gleam of cherry wood in the tables and brass in the lamps and andirons flanking the pink marble fireplace. The green and white lattice-patterned rug was bordered with yellow daffodils and the lilacs that everyone said were Hattie's favorite. Legend had it that Nathan had the rug made somewhere in Europe especially for his wife.

"I think this must be one of the most beautiful rooms in the world," she murmured, wandering over to the fireplace to gaze at the portrait above. "Do you think it's true?" she asked softly.

"Do I think what's true?" he asked, in a voice that made it obvious he was still not ready to roll out the welcome mat.

Taking in a breath of courage, she turned to face him, giving a slightly nervous laugh. "So they haunt? Have you seen them?"

"Look, Annie, I have to get back to work—"

Ann suddenly noticed the laptop computer, the books and papers strewn about the coffee table and floor.

"Where did all this come from?" she asked. "Did your luggage finally get here?"

"No," he answered abruptly.

"Oh," she exclaimed, struggling to remain undaunted by his tone. "What are you working on?" she asked, starting to go around him, but he stepped in front of her, neatly blocking her way—and her view.

"But—" she began, intending to give him a hard time about his work again, intending to push the issue until he stopped being so mysterious about what he was doing at the Northcott Inn. But now that she was close to him again, maybe she didn't really care what he was doing here. Maybe all she really cared about was being in his arms again. His solid chest, only inches away, drew her hand like it was seeking its home. Reaching out, she touched a button on his shirt, fingering it while letting her thumb brush his bare chest peeking from beneath his shirt, feeling the hardness of the muscle under the warm, smooth flesh.

"You left in an awful hurry last night." She looked at him from under her lashes, tempted to bat them if she thought it would get her somewhere. "I hope I didn't scare you off," she purred. Or at least she hoped it sounded like a purr. Having never done it before, she wasn't sure.

His lips twitched for a moment, and the old light of amusement started to rise in his eyes. Then he seemed to catch himself, fighting it down, firming his lips into a grim line. "Don't be coy."

She dropped the act, putting her fists to her hips. "Well, brazen sure doesn't work!" She held out her hands. "Look, Eddy. No rope. No handcuffs. I'm not trying to tie you up or tie you down."

"WHAT ARE YOU trying to do?" he asked her, a sparkling hint of speculation in his ice-blue eyes.

She thrust her chin up. "I thought I made that pretty clear last night."

Her hands were fists on the luscious curve of her hips. Her brandy eyes were blazing, her pale skin flushed with temper and underlying desire. If not for the packet snugly held under his arm, and what it might contain, he'd be tempted to take up her challenge. He'd love her well and long. And he'd enjoy every minute of it.

And then what? Then they could open the envelope together and he could explain to her that he'd sent for anything the home office had pertaining to her because he was here to investigate her for embezzlement. Should make for fine after-loving conversation. And then when he tried to defend himself by saying that he thought he was falling in love with her, she could spit in his eye.

And give him an earful. Oh, yes, he could just imagine the tongue-lashing the blazing-haired wench would dish out to him.

And maybe he wouldn't even mind that. What he would mind was the hurt that would be behind the fire in her eyes. What he would mind was the fact that he would have been the one to put it there.

He stepped away from her, moving his shoulders impatiently. "Look, Annie, I've got work to do." He gestured toward the still open door. "Do you mind?"

Everything on her face changed, and he saw the hurt he'd been trying to avoid start to creep into her eyes before she spun away from him and headed for the door.

He couldn't let her go. Not like this.

Moving quickly, he reached the door at the same time she did, putting out his palm to slam it shut.

She whirled around, her soft breasts ramming into him, he was that close.

"I thought you threw me out, Mr. Winters."

He could feel her breath against his chest. He made himself fix his eyes on hers and prayed for the strength to resist her.

"I don't want you to go away mad," he began, his gaze shifting sideways as his hand—as though propelled by some outer force, because it sure couldn't have been his doing—rose and his fingers tangled in her hair.

The corner of her mouth lifted a little. "Just go away, huh?"

Now his eyes had decided to rebel along with his hand and fingers. They fixed on her mouth—a definite danger zone. "Maybe—just for now," he said softly to the lips he'd rather be kissing.

Now she did grin, and what it did to his heart was as unfair as it could get. He stepped back a pace from her.

She started to leave again, and he remembered something. "Oh, I almost forgot. I got Admiral tickets, but they're for tonight. Any chance Jason's mother will let him go with me?"

That grin was going to kill him, because it just got bigger.

"You really know how to get to a girl, don't you?"

Eddy touched the side of that grin with his thumb. "Then he can go?" he asked, surprised at the disappointment that waited should she give the wrong answer. She let him suffer a couple of heart thuds worth.

Then she nodded. "Yes. He can go."

He grinned, his breath easing out. "Good. Have him meet me in the lobby at seven." Because he just couldn't help it, he bent and kissed her nose. "Now get out of here, sugar, and let me get to work."

She closed the door behind her and he went up to it, listening until he heard the elevator start its downward journey. Then he ripped open the packet.

The first thing he pulled out was a sheaf of requisitions held together with a paper clip. At the top of the small stack was a requisition for the bedspreads Doris had complained about, along with a notation from the New York office of the date the check to cover them had been sent—over eight months ago.

He shuffled through the rest of the stack. According to what he held in his hand, the lobby had been recently wall-papered—with imported stock, no less. The staircase had been newly carpeted, and the plumbing was in the process of an overhaul. You didn't have to be much of a detective to know that the work orders and invoices were bogus as hell.

The requisitions were another matter. They looked solid. And they were all signed by Annie.

Walking over to the coffee table, he tipped the rest of the contents out. Payroll updates, giving employees raises—employees that didn't exist, at least not at the Northcott Inn. Canceled payroll checks made out to different people that all looked like they were endorsed by the same hand. And more. Every sheet of paper he picked up added to the pile of evidence.

Who else but Annie would have access to everything needed to pull something like this off? Lara? Maybe. But no one else he could think of. And Lara hadn't just spent a great deal of money on computer equipment. And Lara wasn't the one trying out luxury cars.

Eddy sank his fingers into his hair and flopped back on the sofa. What was going on here?

His gaze swung to the portrait above the mantel. "Hattie, my old love," he murmured, "give me a clue. Could I possibly be wrong about her?"

Hattie only gazed back with laughing eyes, her sense of humor eternally intact.

Yeah. And he figured the joke was on him. Because he'd met a woman, the one woman who could possibly make him change his mind about the inn. And what a coincidence, because she also happened to be the woman who was ruining it.

He stared again at the mess on the table before him. He should call Hank. Hank could take the information that someone was running a scam to the board meeting that afternoon. The Northcott Inn wasn't making any money as a direct result of that scam. Surely the board wouldn't act on trying to nullify the trust until they got to the bottom of the crime.

But he'd have to do it while keeping Annie's name out of it. Because, despite the evidence before him, despite the computer equipment and the luxury cars, he still wasn't convinced that the woman he was falling in love with was a thief.

He picked up the phone.

"HEY, MOM, what time is it now?" Jason asked for the hundredth time.

Ann looked at her watch, but it wasn't really necessary. She already knew he was late. "It's ten after seven, Jase. Just hold on, he'll be down any minute."

Yeah, right. Was she nuts? What was she thinking of, letting her son get close to a man who ran as hot and cold as the Viking pirate did? She looked at Jason slouching in a wing chair, his head bent and resting on his hand, a worried frown on his young brow. How could he do this to Jason?

She gathered the papers she'd been working on in an untidy pile, rapping them on the desk sharply a couple of times. Hell—he wasn't going to do this to Jason.

She put the papers down and marched toward the elevators.

"Where you goin', Mom?"

"I'm going up to see why Eddy's running late," she said over her shoulder.

"Wait, I'll come with."

She turned. "No, you stay here. Answer the phone for me if it rings, okay?"

For the first time in the last half hour, Jason grinned. "Cool!" he pronounced, and she waited to close the elevator doors until she saw he was happily ensconced behind the registration desk.

Once she'd reached the fifth floor, she swept up to the penthouse door, rapping sharply with her knuckles. "Come on, Eddy, I know you're in there," she muttered to herself. If he thought he was going to make promises to her son and then—

The door opened, and she forgot what she was thinking. In fact, she just about forgot to breathe.

His shirt wasn't just open, this time. It was completely off, and she found herself staring into his smooth, tan, well-developed chest.

No, amended Ann in her mind. *Make that a fabulously developed chest.*

How did he keep it so tan in the winter? She got a mental flash of him skiing naked in the snow, his smooth, bronzed chest glowing in the sun, his strong, hard thighs—

Well, right now, his strong, hard thighs were covered with tight, black unsnapped jeans. Oh, my. And his feet were bare. She let her gaze travel back up, slowly, enjoying the scenery, until it reached his face.

And that's when she remembered why she was there.

"What do you think you're doing?" she demanded.

"Annie, I—"

She poked him in the chest. "Don't you Annie me! My son is downstairs right now, waiting patiently for Eddy Winters to show up to take him to a hockey game. Do you know how many times that kid waited for his father to show up?"

"Annie, I'm not—"

"Get dressed, Mr. Winters. You're going to a hockey game tonight."

"Annie, I have every intention of taking Jason to that game. I'm just waiting for a call."

But she didn't want explanations. She wanted her son happy. And what would make him happy right now was to be at that hockey game with this man. "You listen to me, Eddy Winters. You can run hot and cold with me, but you can't with my son. That kid has been disappointed by men enough in his young life. You're taking him to that game tonight and then you can go to hell for all I care."

Dramatically, she looked at her watch. "We'll expect you downstairs by seven-thirty, Mr. Winters. Be there."

He meant to keep her there, to try to explain, but she whirled around so fast, slamming the door behind her, that he didn't get the chance. Maybe it was just as well. How could he tell her that the call he was waiting for could be far more important to her son than a hockey game?

Hell—what was he going to do? He stared at the phone, willing it to ring. Then he thought of the young boy, sitting in the lobby, waiting. Annie said that Jason had been through it before. Well, so had Eddy. As a boy, he'd had parents to spare, but he'd been left waiting more times than he could count.

He grabbed his shirt and threw it on then went to find his boots. Damn, why didn't Hank call back?

He was on his knees, fishing for a boot from under the bed, when the phone rang.

He practically crawled to reach it.

"Listen, pal, it's too late."

"What do you mean, it's too late?"

"The board acted this afternoon. The lawyer has already filed papers with the court."

Eddy squeezed his eyes shut. "You told them what I found?"

"Yeah, pal, but they say without a suspect it don't mean a thing. If I'd have had a name to give 'em, Eddy—"

"No—no names. Not yet." He bit hard on his lower lip. "Let me think this thing through." His watch read seven twenty-five. Hell. "Okay, Hank, tell 'em I'm going over their heads. I'm doing what I should have done a long time ago."

"Eddy, listen to me. It's too late for that. The ball is rolling. The only thing you can do is countersue. And if you don't move fast, it'll be too late even for that."

Eddy stuck the phone in the crook of his neck and struggled to put on his boots. "Okay, what if I gave them a suspect? What if I could prove that New York had mismanaged this all along by letting it go on for so long and not checking into it? Surely a judge would listen—"

"He might."

"Okay. Then let's do it. Get to him first thing tomorrow. Tell him I think someone is deliberately trying to ruin the inn. Get him to give me some time."

"Time for what?" Hank asked, a tired, weary edge to his voice.

"I don't know, Hank. I just don't know. But right now, I gotta go to a hockey game."

"What are ya talking about, Eddy? Are you nuts?"

"Yeah, Hank. Nuts." Nuts about a kid, he thought as he hung up the phone. And nuts about his mother.

THE AIR WAS COLD when they hit the streets. But it just pushed their elation up another notch to break out from the heat of the bodies pouring out of the arena. The Admirals had won, and Jason was delirious.

"Man, I can't believe it! What a game!"

Eddy laughed while the boy ran ahead, imaginary hockey stick in hand to swish an imaginary puck through the crowds on the sidewalk.

"Hey, Jase—wait up!" he called, jogging to catch up.

"So, I guess your first hockey game was a success?"

"Awesome! I'm gonna see if I can take lessons. Join a team."

"Sounds good," Eddy said, but privately he was thinking about the future. A future that at the moment was very uncertain.

Sitting in the crowded, noisy arena with Jason had provided a wonderful respite from the mess at the inn. He wanted to hang on to that for at least as long as it took him to walk Jason to the inn.

They replayed the game as they walked, Eddy providing commentary while Jason managed to play all positions on both teams.

Finally winded, he slowed his walk, leaning close enough to Eddy to put his head against Eddy's arm. Eddy opened it up and drew the boy in.

It seemed so natural to be walking home in the cold night with this boy tucked close to his side.

"Eddy?"

"Yeah, Jase?"

"My mom says you're leaving soon. Are you?"

The question cut into his heart a little. "I don't know, Jase. Maybe."

The boy yawned, then settled a little closer to Eddy. "I wish you didn't have to. I wish you could stay forever."

His heart swelled and the cut sank even deeper. "So do I, Jason," he answered, knowing it was finally true. "So do I."

They'd almost reached the inn when Jason suddenly stopped near a parcel of empty land. "Hey, I think this is where they might build the new stadium."

"Really?" Eddy asked absently.

"Yeah. It'd be cool, too, 'cause we could walk to baseball games."

"Sounds good," Eddy agreed, but the closer they got to the inn the more distracted he became.

He had to find some way of proving that Annie had nothing to do with those forged checks. Or the work orders. But how? Getting a sample of her handwriting might do it. With any luck, it would be as simple as that.

Of course, he'd still have to come up with a suspect. But if he could prove that Annie didn't sign those checks, then at least he could hand over the whole packet of papers as evidence, and the authorities could be called in.

He was almost relieved that there was no sign of Annie in the lobby when they'd reached the inn. Austin sat in the office, his nose in a book. He looked up when they entered, pushing his glasses up his nose.

"Ms. Madison said you could leave Jason with me, Mr. Winters."

"He's pretty tired," Eddy said, sitting the boy in a chair, where his head lolled back and his eyes half closed.

"She'll be right back. Then I think she's going off duty so she can take him home."

Eddy hunkered down next to Jason's chair. "Okay, sport. Your mom will be here to take you home in a minute."

Jason nodded, a small, sleepy but very satisfied smile moving on his lips. "Thanks for the game, Eddy."

"My pleasure, sport," Eddy murmured as the boy's eyes drifted closed. He hesitated for only a moment before he leaned forward and kissed Jason's forehead. Then he straightened, smoothed the boy's hair out of his eyes and headed for the elevator.

IT SEEMED TO EDDY that since he'd checked into the Northcott Inn he'd been spending an awful lot of time on the staircase.

This time he was barefoot, the worn rose carpeting doing its best to muffle the sound of his footfalls. Still, there were creaks and groans enough for him to occasionally stop dead and listen. Except for the restless January wind beating against the old walls, everyone seemed to be tucked in tight.

When he reached the final landing, Eddy leaned over the banister. No sign of Lara. The fire was dying in the grate, the last embers glowing through thick, gray ash. Wall sconces, still lit on either side of the mantel, provided enough light to see that the sofas and chairs in the lobby were unoccupied.

A small brass desk lamp glowed at the registration desk, but the tiny office behind was dark—and wide open.

Eddy descended the last few stairs, then became still and listened.

When he was satisfied he crossed the lobby, moving quickly, then ducked behind the desk and waited.

After a minute, he slipped silently into the office and gently closed the door.

He pulled a small metal flashlight from his pocket and switched it on. The desk was neat. Lara must have finished her work for the night. The drawers were unlocked, and he quickly went through them, looking for anything with Annie's signature on it. He found plenty. He chose a few documents—things he thought wouldn't be missed—folded them as small as possible and stuffed them into the back pocket of his jeans.

He wondered if he'd have time to fire up the computer, decided against it. If Lara, as he suspected, was in the café's kitchen raiding the larder, she wouldn't be gone long.

Still, he couldn't pass up the chance to check out the office—see if he could find anything at all he could use to back up his claim with a judge. He went through the drawers of the desk systematically, finding nothing of value. He was just about to move to the file cabinet when he heard it.

Someone was coming.

Quickly, soundlessly, he closed the drawer, switched off the flashlight, flattened himself against the wall behind the door and held his breath.

The door opened. Lara came in.

Eddy tried to slip out the door before the lights came on, but Lara must have forgotten something because she turned and ran smack into him. Something wet and hot splashed over his chest, and Eddy gritted his teeth to bite back a yowl. Before he had time to worry about his flesh being seared, he heard the sudden intake of breath, as if the woman would scream, and he quickly pulled her around so she couldn't see his face, snaked a hand around her waist to hold her against him and clamped his other hand over her mouth.

It wasn't Lara.

"Annie?" he whispered.

But he already knew it was her. Aside from the fact that no other woman he knew was so fond of hurling coffee at him, he recognized the feel of her against him, the scent of her. What the hell was she doing here? She was supposed to be home in bed.

"It's Eddy, Annie," he murmured in her ear. "I'm going to take my hand away from your mouth, but don't scream, okay?"

She nodded and her hair moved against his cheek, like strands of silk brushing him in the dark. He gentled his hand over her mouth but he didn't take it away. Instead, he spread the fingers of the hand at her waist until he was touching the soft underside of her breast. He felt her suck in her breath, felt her body sink back against his, and his own body quickened, his blood rushing and pounding.

It was worse than madness, but he couldn't resist the demand of his body urging him on. Slowly, he swept his hand upward until his palm was molded to her breast. Nudging her hair aside with his chin, he found her neck with his lips and buried them there against her fragrant flesh while he brushed the flat of his hand over her breast. Her breathing quickened as she strained against him, her breast leaping to life in his palm.

Groaning, he sank his teeth into his lower lip, telling himself it was time to stop. Stilling his hand on her round, soft flesh, he was making the effort to pull away—and then she touched him. Flattening her palm against his hip, she glided it up and down, the shy, tentative touch playing hell with logic, coming closer with every movement to the hard heat that throbbed in his groin.

When he groaned again, she flung her head away from his hand, freeing her mouth from his hold. Thrusting her other hand into his hair, she pulled his mouth down to hers.

The kiss was hot, wet—wild. Her breasts heaved, and he used his newly freed hand to cover her other one, cupping their fullness, working the nipples until she had to pull her mouth away to gasp.

He spun her then, turned her around and flattened her against the door so it closed with a bang, sending them stumbling against it. And then her mouth was on his again. He wanted more. The pounding in his veins demanded more. He slid his hand over her hip, caressed her belly, then slid lower, cupping the heat between her thighs, pressing his fingers against her. She cried out, and the sound tore through him like wildfire.

He'd never wanted anyone as much as he wanted Annie.

Not in his whole damn life.

He felt her hands at his zipper, felt it give, and then she was stroking him, and he had to tear his mouth from hers and bury his face in her hair to keep from crying out.

"Annie...Annie—" The words came from his gut, from the very soul of him. He felt a rush of such need he thought the ache of it just might kill him. "Baby—stop," he gasped. "We'd better stop now."

She shook her head, the wild silk of her hair calling to his fingers until he'd pulled her mouth to his and plundered.

And all the while, her hands made love to him.

He had to grit his teeth to keep from losing control. Somewhere, in the thick fog of his mind, he wondered why.

Why not let go? Why not let it happen? Why not lay her soft, willing body down and take what he wanted so badly?

Sweet Annie, moaning and moving against him, wanted it as much as he did.

And then he remembered.

Roughly, he pulled away. Turning his back to her, he zipped his jeans, then thrust his hands into his hair, trying to still his heart before it burst into a million pieces.

"Eddy?" she gasped. "What—why?" she murmured, bewilderment making her voice breathless.

What could he tell her? *I draw the line at having sex with women I might have to turn in to the police?*

No—not having sex. Making love. Because that's what it would have been. Despite what she might have done, despite what he might have to do, he was falling in love with her, and losing his body in hers would have been more than just sexual release.

And that's why he couldn't do it.

He took a deep breath before he turned to face her. Already, the bewilderment he'd heard in her voice had turned to anger.

"Well, you got me again, didn't you, Eddy?"

"Annie—"

"Oh, just shut up! Honestly, I must need my head examined. How many times does a girl have to be rejected before she—"

"Annie, I'm not rejecting you. It's just that—"

"Save it, Mr. Winters. And get out of here so I can get back to work."

He plowed his hand through his hair, trying to get his body, still needy, still aching for her, under control. "What are you doing here, anyway? Where's Lara?"

"Lara was too sick to come in. I'm covering for her."

Eddy looked around. "Jason?"

"Estelle has him for the night." Then her eyes narrowed. "Wait just a minute. I'm the one who should be asking the questions. What are you doing here, Mr. Winters? What—

did you come down here to give Lara a shot of the famous Edmund Winters rejection, too?"

"Annie, come on." He reached out for her but she quickly stepped out of reach.

"Keep your distance, Winters. I don't want any more misunderstandings. See, for some funny reason, when you start to make love to me, I always think you mean it."

"And what if I said I did?" he asked softly.

She stared at him for a moment. "Are you married?" she blurted out.

He couldn't help but grin. "No, Annie. I'm not married. I just wish it were that simple."

"I think you'd better go," she said, eyeing him levelly.

"I think you're right," he agreed. If he didn't go—and soon—he was going to take her in his arms again. And he didn't think he'd be able to stop a second time.

Chapter Ten

She barely waited for his backside to clear the door before she slammed it shut. The reverberating sound was satisfying, giving voice to her anger.

Of course, truth to tell, it was more herself she was angry at than him. One of these times, she was going to be the one to reject him. Yeah, she'd get him wound up then she'd spit him out and watch him squirm.

The only problem was, anytime she got within touching distance of him, the last thing she wanted to do was spit him out. Swallow him whole was more like it.

She slumped into her desk chair, wondering what she was going to do about Jason. Her son had a serious case of hero-worship, and Eddy Winters was coming up a little short in the hero department.

Still, he did take Jase to a hockey game—even if he practically had to be threatened to go through with it. But Jason had had a great time. Fought sleep all the way home to talk about it over and over again. Eddy this, Eddy that—

She just hoped that Eddy didn't manage to break her son's heart before his business, whatever it was, in Milwaukee was over. Her own heart was in similar danger, but she'd suffer a broken heart a hundred times over rather than see her son suffer.

Needing a cup of coffee to replace the one Edmund Winters was now wearing, she stood up, intending to go to the café's kitchen again. That's when she noticed that a fax had come in.

She went to the machine, wondering how long it had been waiting there and who it was for.

"My, my," she muttered. "If it isn't for Edmund Winters." She looked over her shoulder, even though she knew no one was there. Dare she? Dare she read it? Why not? He was full of questions and curiously devoid of answers. Maybe whatever was in the fax would give her some.

She tore it off and sat on the edge of her desk.

"Swell," she muttered after reading it. The damn thing was just as cryptic as the Viking pirate himself. Someone named Hank had talked to the judge, who'd luckily turned out to be someone Hank knew. He might be able to give them some time. Hank was expecting a call from Eddy as soon as possible.

"Well, that tears it," Ann said out loud. "I suppose, now to add insult to injury, I'm supposed to trot up to the penthouse to deliver a fax to the pirate."

Or she could just let it sit here until he decided to come down for breakfast in the morning.

But what if it really was important? Just because he was a jerk didn't mean that she had to be one. Besides, she'd love to see his reaction to the thing. Maybe he'd slip up and clue her in on the big Eddy Winters mystery.

The elevator doors opened and Annie stepped out. It was so quiet. Maybe he was already asleep.

If he was, she thought testily, he didn't deserve to be. Not after what he'd just done to her. She knew the little episode between them would keep her tossing and turning for many a night. Serve him right if she woke him up.

She rapped firmly on the door.

When he didn't answer, she turned the knob. It was unlocked. The door creaked open.

He was standing at the fireplace, his back to the door, naked from the waist up, his arms stretched out in front of him, hands braced on the mantel. His shirt, ruined with the stain of coffee, lay in a heap on the floor. The firelight gleamed on the taut muscles of his back, danced off the twisted muscles in his upper arms. There was something stirring in his stance—as though he was holding a visceral power in check.

She started to say his name again when he spoke in a harsh, low growl.

"You shouldn't have come up here."

"You got a fax. I thought . . ."

He turned suddenly and strode toward her, slamming the door shut behind her, ripping the fax from her hands and tossing it away. Then he swept her into his arms.

"Eddy! Wha—what are you doing?"

"I've tried my damnedest to resist you, but if you didn't know enough to stay away from me for the rest of this endless night then you're going to be made love to."

"Really?" she asked ingenuously.

He threw back his head and laughed. "Really." He strode to the bedroom, kicked open the door and threw her onto the bed. Then he came to her, placing a hand on either side of her head and bending down, his eyes like ice and fire on hers. "This shouldn't happen, Annie," he muttered roughly. "But it's going to happen unless you tell me no. You can still stop it if you want to, but I won't." He took a breath. "Not anymore."

For answer, she reached out and ran her palms down his smooth, dark chest. His flesh was hard, taut with power as she moved her hands lower until they came to the snap on his jeans.

When she undid it, it was the only sound in the room.

His zipper soon followed.

Coming alive after a wary stillness, he grinned. "I take it that's a yes?"

"Yes," she whispered and then pulled him down to her.

They rolled until she was on top. Pulling her shirt from the waistband of her trousers, he impatiently whipped open the buttons.

She shrugged out of it and he rolled her again, him on top this time, while he unzipped her trousers and slipped them down her legs, tossing them over his shoulder.

And then she was his. The Viking pirate could do what he wanted with her because her flesh and bone had turned to something molten, melting and soft and quivering for his touch. All she could do was lie there and long for him when he hopped off the bed to struggle out of his jeans.

And then he was with her again, his hands and mouth gliding over her skin, doing away with the lacy scrap of her bra and her silk panties like there was magic in his fingers.

And there was—oh, yes, there was.

And in his voice . . .

"You're beautiful," he said, caressing her breasts, lightly teasing with his fingers, then taking with his mouth while she moaned and writhed. While she turned into something she had never before been.

Where she had been the aggressor before, now she could do nothing but want and need and ache.

And then he was touching her where she wanted him most of all.

"So soft and slick and warm. I need to be here," he whispered against her throat while his fingers stroked her hot, wet center, "inside of you."

"Yes," she cried. "Yes!"

And then he was over her, bracing himself above her, his silver hair flowing around his shoulders, his eyes of ice melting. His mouth softened as he looked at her, and then he closed his eyes and thrust into her.

It was more than she could have dreamed of, this fierce, urgent coupling. Their bodies moved in synchronicity, giving and taking equally, until she couldn't hold back, could no longer do anything to prolong the divine thing that was happening to her. She cried out and hung for a moment, suspended in time. And then he caught her so she didn't fall but exploded in his arms, and she felt his body finally give in to the same madness.

"IT'S SNOWING AGAIN," Eddy murmured.

Ann stirred under the covers, her limbs weak, her body finally satiated. After they'd finished loving for a third time, Eddy had climbed out of bed and gone to the window where he'd been standing for the past five minutes.

She had the feeling that he was already regretting what had happened between them.

But she wasn't. And she never would.

She slipped out of bed, picked up the soft, cream sweater she'd picked out for him from a chair and slipped it on. Then she went to join him at the window.

"Winter wonderland," she whispered, kissing his shoulder lightly. "Outside and in."

He stirred, his tangled hair moving on his shoulders. "Annie," he whispered, and she thought she heard pain.

"Eddy, I meant what I said before. No strings." She laid her cheek against his arm and waited for his brooding to pass, for him to come to the same kind of peace she felt. When he didn't, she pulled at his arm. "Come on. The sun's not up yet—our night isn't over. We don't have to go back to our real lives for at least another hour."

She pushed him down onto the window seat and joined him, half sitting on something in the process. Pulling it out from under her, she asked, "What's this?"

"Just something I found the other day. A journal."

"Yours?"

He shook his head.

She laughed softly. "I didn't think you were the type."

"Come closer," he murmured, settling his back against the wall adjacent to the window, bending his knees and pulling her against him so she was sitting between his thighs on the window seat, her back cradled against his chest. He felt solid and warm. And real. But Viking pirates weren't real, she reminded herself. They were a dream, a fantasy. But the fantasy wasn't over—not quite yet. She pulled his arm around her middle and sighed.

The sky was beginning to lighten to a morning gray. Clouds of smoke billowed from chimneys. Below them, a boy pulled a sled full of newspapers across the brick-cobbled street.

"Hattie and Nathan must have seen nearly the same thing from this window all those years ago," she murmured.

She opened the journal, randomly paging through it, stopping to read a line or two here and there. "Oh, my goodness—this is Hattie's journal." Now she really was in heaven. With the feel of her head tucked under Eddy's chin, his hand stroking her hair, she settled in to read the words of the woman she'd imagined so many times.

A familiar name caught her eye, and she stopped to read a page.

"Eddy! Listen to this. 'I think Nathan should fire Max but he won't hear of it. Max hasn't done anything, hasn't even said anything, really. But I'll never forget how he raged at me when he heard I'd accepted Nathan's proposal. I'd never known sweet Maxwell to raise his voice before or since. I don't know why he continues to work here, for I keep thinking that he feels all this—and I—could have been his if only I'd chosen him over Nathan.'"

She heard Eddy's quiet laughter. "So the little old guy was in love with her," he murmured against her hair.

"Who would have thought it? I mean, looking at Max it's hard to believe that he ever harbored an epic passion for anyone." She turned her head until she could see into Eddy's face. "Do you think he's still in love with her?"

"Maybe. You know, the other day I caught him in here spraying lilac air freshener."

"So it's been Max all along," she mused, turning to the journal, fluttering the pages with her thumb, stopping to read again.

"She loved her Nathan so much," she murmured. "Listen to this: 'I am happier than I've ever been in my life. Father's wedding present to us was more than I had hoped for. I've always loved this old inn and often wished I'd been alive when my great-grandmother came to it as a bride. Now, I come to it as a bride. The inn will be our home, Nathan's and mine.'

"I know how she felt," she murmured, running the tips of her fingers over the words written so long ago. "It's how I feel about this place. There's something magical about it. Something you can't help but fall in love with."

Behind her, Eddy stirred, his arm tightening around her middle. "You really feel that way about the inn?" he asked, a soft urgency in his voice.

She nodded. "I've often fantasized about what it would be like to live here in the penthouse. In fact, it's my secret dream to own it someday." She laughed softly. "Impossible as it may seem."

He seemed so still behind her, and then she felt his lips in her hair, pressing there with the same urgency she'd heard in his voice earlier. She looked at the journal again.

"'I share Nathan's dream of turning the inn into something fine and prosperous. I share his dream of proving to my father that Nathan can become a success. Father still believes Nathan married me for my money. I know that's why he's cut me from his will. The inn is failing, losing money. He may have meant the gift of it to be an insult, but I see it as a test. When he sees how hard we will work...'"

She gasped softly. "Did you hear that, Eddy? It's almost as if history is repeating itself. The inn is failing now, too. Except there's nobody left in the family to feel about the place the way Hattie felt. If only her grandson—" she began, irritation edging into her voice.

Eddy moved suddenly behind her. "That's enough, Annie. Let's not waste our last moments together reading this thing." He tried to take the journal from her hands.

"Wait," she said, then continued reading. "'When he sees how hard we will work, then he'll have to admit that Nathaniel Edmund Winters is the kind of son-in-law he can be proud of.'"

Ann's heart seemed to stop for a moment, her mouth dropping open as the journal slid from her suddenly bone-less hands to thump to the floor. "Nathaniel," she murmured. "Edmund," she said, louder this time. Then, "Winters!" She shot off the window seat to her feet as she yelled.

Through a tangle of hair, she stared at him. "Winters? Hattie and Nathan's last name was Winters? I thought—"

Eddy shook his head and stood. "Northcott was her family name," he said, putting out a hand toward her.

She stepped back a pace.

"Annie, I can explain—"

She tossed the hair out of her eyes. "Explain? Explain what? That it's just a coincidence that you happen to have the same last name—oh, and Edmund. Let's not forget that your name is the same as his middle name. Your real first name wouldn't really by any chance be—"

"Nathaniel. My first name would be Nathaniel. But it's not what—"

"Oh, please—don't say it's not what I think. That would just turn this whole thing into an even bigger cliché."

"Cliché? Annie, this isn't a cliché—this is you and me."

"No, this is you *using* me!"

"Using you? Annie, I—" He came toward her.

She put out her hand. "No, just stay where you are. You're the grandson, aren't you? You're the grandson who wants no part of the inn. And you've been systematically trying to destroy it so they'll shut the place down."

"No, Annie," he interrupted, the calm in his voice making her feel like hitting him. "That's not how it is."

She thrust her chin up. "Then how is it?"

"Someone's trying to destroy this place, but it isn't me. I'm more than just the grandson, Annie. I'm a private investigator and I'm here to—"

She glared at him through narrowed eyes. "Go on," she demanded, "here to what?"

"I'm here to investigate who's been embezzling money."

She stared at him for a moment, feeling more than bewildered. "But, if that's true, why didn't you just tell me? I could have helped you. We could have—"

"Annie," he interrupted softly, "don't you know?" He stopped.

She crossed her arms. "Don't I know what?"

At first, she thought he might not answer. Then he sighed deeply, and asked, "Don't you know that all the evidence points to you? You're the chief suspect, Annie."

It took her a long moment to react. When she did, she bent and retrieved the journal and threw it at him. "You...you rat! You despicable—"

"Annie, please—"

"Don't you Annie me, you pond scum!" She started gathering up her clothes, tossed all over the bedroom. "To think I fell for all that studied charm! When all you were doing was getting close to me so you could investigate me! To think I slept with you!"

"Now wait a minute, Annie. That's got nothing to do with this."

She stopped, her arms laden with clothes. "Nothing to do with this? You just slept with me to get information out of me, didn't you?"

"No, of course not! I made love to you because I've wanted you since I first laid eyes on you."

She dropped her clothes and started to struggle into them. "Don't make me laugh!"

He put out a hand. "Annie, let me—"

"Just shut up, Nathaniel Edmund Winters III! Okay? I've let you do too much already."

"I tried to stay away from you, Annie. You know that. You wanted what happened here tonight."

"Oh," she said, struggling into her bra, "and you were trying to be so noble while I kept throwing myself at you! You poor thing." She pulled her silk shirt over her bra. She had no idea where her panties were so she yanked her trousers on without them.

"Annie, I'd intended to stay away from you until—"

She was too furious to let him finish. "Until what? Until you knew for sure you wouldn't be sleeping with a crook?"

She turned, ready to run, to stomp out of there and not look back. But she was too hungry for answers, so she turned toward him again, her hair swinging violently into her face. She tossed her head to be rid of it.

"Do you plan on sleeping with all the suspects, or am I somehow special?"

He started toward her again. "Annie," he said softly, "right now you're the only suspect."

Fear started to creep in alongside the fury. "You're not serious?"

"Everything points to you, Annie."

While she stood with her mouth open, he closed the rest of the distance between them. He was spectacularly naked, his muscles shadowed in the pale winter morning light, his limbs long and powerful, his hair in a tangle from the night of love. When he reached out to touch her cheek, she didn't flinch—she wanted it too much.

She took a deep breath and shook her head shortly, as if to clear her ears after a bubble bath. "Embezzlement." She managed to croak the word.

He nodded. "That's right."

"And you think I've been the one trying to ruin this place—that I've been taking money—"

"I don't want to think that, Annie, but there's evidence—"

She didn't let him finish. "And you've been looking into my life—checking me out, sneaking around..." She heard her own voice rising with each word, becoming clearer and crisper. "And last night, when I caught you in the office, what were you doing?" she practically yelled.

"I was looking for samples of your signature so I could compare them to the checks that were forged."

"Forged? *Forged!*" She thrust her hands into her trouser pockets and started to pace a short, fast trail, building up a fine head of steam. "Let's see, Eddy," she began with calm sarcasm. "I'm an embezzler and a forger and a seductress." She stopped pacing and faced him. "Anything else you'd like to add? How about murderess, Eddy? Because if I don't get out of here right now, I'm going to kill you!"

She flung around and headed for the door, not caring that she was barefoot, that her panties were lost somewhere in the ruins of their passion. She just had to get out.

But he was there before her, stepping in front of her, blocking her way.

"Let me out of here," she said through clenched teeth into his spectacular chest.

He thrust an envelope at her. "Look at these first, Annie. Take a look at what's in here and then tell me what I'm supposed to think."

Careful not to touch him, she took the envelope between two fingers, backed to the sofa and sank into it. She dumped the contents of the envelope onto the coffee table, then shuffled through the papers.

"I didn't authorize these work orders," she stated emphatically.

"They have your name on them."

"And I didn't sign these checks."

He moved his head impatiently. "It's your signature, Annie."

She met his eyes with a steady gaze. "Then someone's setting me up."

"Who?"

She thrust her hands into her hair. "I don't know who!"

"And why?" he went on relentlessly. "Why would anyone want to do that to you?"

She looked at the papers, her mind reaching for answers, skimming possibilities. Why? But the only thing she could come up with was, *Why not?* That was the only possible explanation. "Why, Eddy? Maybe because they can." She set the papers aside and rose. "Think about it, Eddy. If someone wanted to embezzle money from this place, or...or if someone just wanted to ruin it, close it down, who would be the likely person to pin it on? The manager, who else?"

He shook his head, and she could see he wasn't buying it. "Then where did the money come from?" he asked.

She wrinkled her nose. "What money?"

"The computer for Jason."

"Oh, that. That was money I was saving up to—" She stopped, narrowing her eyes on him. "Tell me, *Nathaniel*, did you go through my underwear drawer, too?"

He ignored her comment. "Finish what you were going to say. Money you were saving up to what?"

She looked away from him, knowing how lame it was going to sound. "To buy the inn," she finally stated. She peered at him. "I hoped that I could save it."

He was quiet for a moment, and she thought maybe she'd reached him. But it turned out he was just having trouble closing his mouth—his jaw had dropped so far.

"Come on, Annie," he finally said, "a single mother working in a little place like this? I know how much you make, Annie. And you told me yourself you had debts. You expect me to believe that you actually thought you could save enough money to buy the inn and turn it around?"

"Well," she drawled defensively, "no one in New York seemed to care about it. The grandson—" She stopped. *He* was that grandson! "*You* didn't want it! I thought maybe if I had a down payment I could get a government loan or something. I thought that if Northcott Enterprises wanted to close the inn anyway, maybe I could get the price down..."

She let the words trail off. The plan sounded desperately futile even to her own ears.

"Damn it, Eddy, don't you think I know how crazy it all sounds? Why do you think I decided to spend some of the money on Jason? He's a bright kid—he should have a computer. But I'd be the last one who would want to ruin the inn. I love it! I wanted to buy it so I could make it what I knew it could be—what it once was!"

He ran restless fingers through his hair. "But don't you see, Annie? That just makes it look worse for you. You embezzle money for the down payment and get a good price in the bargain 'cause the place is in such bad shape."

She clenched her fists at her sides. "Ooh, that is the most ridiculous thing I've ever heard! And you are the most maddening... the most—"

She stormed about the room, searching for something.

"What are you looking for, Annie?"

"A cup of coffee so I can hurl it in your face!" she answered, then she stomped into the bedroom, discovered her shoes tangled in the comforter, slipped them on and started for the door.

When she got to the door, she yanked it open. Max was standing on the other side of it, a suitcase in each hand.

Italian leather, if she knew anything about it.

She tossed her head and gave Eddy a look over her shoulder. "Your luggage has been recovered, Nathaniel Edmund Winters III," she advised him haughtily. "The masquerade is over."

Making a sweeping, arrogant exit, she nearly knocked poor Max off his feet.

When Max recovered, he stared at Eddy for a long minute. Then his gaze moved to the portrait over the mantel.

"Well, I'll be damned."

"You and me both," Eddy muttered, sauntering to the bedroom to pull on his jeans. Max was still standing with his mouth open, a suitcase hanging from each arm, when he got back to the sitting room.

"I remember you as a boy. Summers. You were the apple of Hattie's eye."

"That's me," Eddy muttered, taking the suitcases from Max and setting them down.

"I should've known it was you—I mean, the name and all." Max moved slowly to the mantel to stare up at the portrait. "I always thought of her as Hattie Northcott." Then he turned to stare at Eddy again. "You been a long time getting here, boy."

"Too long," Eddy agreed. "But I'm here now."

Max shook his head sadly. "Too late," he mumbled as he ambled toward the door. "Way too late."

"WHERE IS SHE?"

Max jumped from the computer, thumping the flat of his hand to his chest. "Whoa, you just took ten years off my life. You always were one to jump out at a person. I remember a time when you were about six—"

Eddy wasn't in the mood to take a trip down memory lane. "Where's Annie?" he asked.

The old man's eyes twinkled. "And good morning to you, too."

Eddy thrust his hands into his hair. "Look, I don't have time for this. I need to find Annie. Now, either you tell me where she is or—"

Max patted the air with his hand. "Now, now—just calm down." The old man chuckled. "You're as excitable as your granny was."

Eddy squeezed his eyes shut and pinched the bridge of his nose. "Look, Max, I'll be happy to reminisce with you sometime." He opened his eyes. "Just not now."

Max chuckled again. "And as determined as your grandfather."

"Where is she?" Eddy repeated, cutting the old man off.

Max shook his head, a bemused little smile playing at his mouth, apparently still trotting down memory lane. "She went home to see that son of hers off to school," he finally answered.

Eddy slammed his hand against the door frame. "Thanks, Max," he said, then turned, thundered around the registration desk and sprinted across the lobby.

"She'll be back soon," Max called after him.

Eddy waved a hand, not bothering to turn around. "This won't wait."

Outside, the snow was still falling. Eddy turned up his coat collar, glad of the extra warmth his long black cashmere coat offered. The quick trip to Tahiti didn't seem to have done it any harm. He gazed at the steel sky as he walked. How differently this morning had begun . . . Annie in his arms, her mass of hair brushing his chest, the snow falling gently outside.

"Aw, Annie, Annie," he murmured, "what am I going to do about you?"

But he already knew what he was going to do about her. Whatever he had to do to get her out of this mess.

In the time it had taken him to shower, shave and unpack a few of his wayward clothes, he'd made up his mind. He was going to do whatever he had to do to prove that Annie was innocent. Because he was in love with her. He was in the kind of love he'd never wanted. The kind that tied a man down and tore him up. The only kind, he was finding out, that was really worth anything.

He started to run, his footfalls sounding loud in the hush of the snowfall as they hit the sidewalk. When he reached her flat, he sprinted up the stairs, the cloud of his breath mingling with the falling snow as he tried to catch his breath.

He rang the bell and waited.

When the door opened it wasn't Annie who stood there but Jason.

Finally—a piece of luck.

"Hey, Jason!" he said between pants. "How's it goin'?"

"Hey, Eddy! You here for breakfast?" The kid held the door wide. "Come on in—Mom's makin' pancakes."

"Thanks." Eddy followed Jason to the kitchen, stopping dead in the doorway.

A radio was playing a soft rock tune. The ceiling light held the gloom of the snowy morning at bay. The air had the welcoming warmth and aroma of home cooking. In the center of it all was Annie, standing at the stove wearing the silk robe he'd held in his hands the other night. He knew how it would feel against her skin, because he'd felt it against his own.

"Hey, Mom, look who's here for breakfast! Way cool, huh?"

Annie turned from the stove. The moment she saw him, her brandy eyes flashed with heat. She opened her mouth, glanced at Jason, closed it, then turned back to the stove.

"Just terrific, Jason," she muttered, her back to him.

The sarcasm wasn't lost on Eddy, even if it was on Jason. He'd been hoping as he'd run over that Jason would still be home, banking on the kind of mother Annie was to allow him in and maybe hear him out.

"Jason says you're making pancakes."

"Yeah—Mom makes great pancakes!"

Eddy pulled out a chair and sat down. Without a word, Annie marched over to the cupboard, took down a plate and slammed the door shut.

At the stove, she plopped, none too gently, a stack of pancakes on the plate and set them in front of him with force enough to send a rattle echoing for several seconds.

Eddy tried not to grin. He poured the syrup that Jason passed him and dug in. Jason was right, Annie made great pancakes.

While he chewed, he watched her move about the kitchen, doing dishes, putting things away. Her hair, still damp from her shower, lay on her shoulders. Her hips moved against the silk. Her breasts swayed a little.

Finally, he had to stop watching her. Because all he could remember was the feel of her on his fingers, the scent of her in his nostrils, her absolute abandon of the night before. And he had to stop remembering if he was going to clear his head and find a way out of this mess for both of them.

"Jason, don't forget the time. Better get a move on."

Jason gulped the last of his milk, wiped his mouth on his sleeve and pushed back his chair.

"Hey, Eddy, wanna walk me to school again?"

Annie's mouth curved into a big, fake smile. "What a great idea, Jason," she said, her voice soaring with enthusiasm. "Why don't you do that, Eddy?" Her smile fled and her voice flattened. *"Take a walk."*

He threw a grin at her, and the fire in her eyes flashed hotter. "Sorry, Jason," he said mildly. "Another time. I've got something to talk over with your mother."

"Are you gonna stay for supper again?"

"We'll see," Eddy answered.

"No!" Annie said at the same time.

"Aw—why can't he, Mom?"

"We'll talk about it later. Now, take your books and get going. You'll be late."

Jason grabbed the books Annie held out to him, allowed her a hug and kiss, then, much to Eddy's surprise and pleasure, stopped at Eddy's chair and gave him a quick hug, too.

Neither of them spoke until they heard the front door slam.

"How does it feel to be hugged by the son of the woman you want to send to jail?" Annie asked.

Chapter Eleven

Eddy got up and started to go to her. "Annie—"

"Better watch it, Eddy," she said. "I've got coffee now." She picked up the pot from the burner. "A whole pot of it. You wouldn't want me to mess up your fine clothes, would you?" she asked him sweetly, waving the pot for emphasis.

Eddy laughed. "Listen, sugar—"

"Don't call me sugar, you swine, you rat, you—you..."

Eddy's grin deepened. "Last night you called me your Viking pirate."

She jerked her chin up. "Nonsense."

"You did. The third time, I think. Just before we—"

"Don't remind me," she cut in.

He raised a brow. "I bet I don't have to."

She put her hands on her hips. "You're insufferable, you know that? You get to know me under false pretenses—get me to take you shopping for bargains. I mean, look at you! The cost of that outfit you're wearing would feed a family of four for a month."

Eddy looked at his raw silk sweater and tailored wool trousers. "Two," he said.

She almost smiled. Almost. "Yeah, but I would never pay full price!"

He laughed. "No, you wouldn't, Annie."

"And what about the car? You told me you couldn't afford your own car!"

He shook his head. "I told you I never owned a car. And neither do most people who live in Manhattan."

"So you lied—"

Eddy shook his head and thrust his hands into his trouser pockets. "I didn't lie. I evaded."

"Evaded," she repeated. "And what do you call getting my son to like you? Pretending to like him?"

"No pretense there, Annie. I do like your son."

"Then you sleep with me to find out if I'm a crook, and now you stand here in my kitchen and try to charm me—"

"That's not why I slept with you, Annie," he cut in softly.

Her eyes sparked. "Oh, shut up!" She flounced over to the sink and started washing dishes again, suds flying, water splashing.

"Help me, Annie," he said in a voice that was too low and sexy for comfort. A voice that was far too close to keep her mind on dirty dishes.

"Help you?" she asked, hating the breathless quality in the words. "Help you do what?"

"Help me prove that you're innocent."

Sudsy water dripping from her hands, she turned around to face him. "I'd rather crawl into bed with a rat."

"That can be arranged," he told her, and pulled her into his arms.

"Let me go!" she yelled, pummeling his chest with her wet, soapy hands, trying to twist out of his arms. But the more she struggled, the worse it got. Her traitorous body was reminding her of all the things they'd done together the night before—and responding like it wanted to do them all over again.

She gave up struggling and stood still—not that it helped much.

His hard, lean thighs were pressing into hers. Beneath her wet hands, splayed against his chest, she could feel the heat of his blood through his damn raw silk sweater. But his eyes, his eyes were the worst. They were amused—damn them. Glittering, dangerous, laughing.

She supposed he'd laugh at her all the way to jail.

"Is the bounty hunter amused?" she asked scathingly.

"Private investigator."

She cocked a brow. "Private investigator, huh?"

He nodded. "That's right."

"Who also just happens to be the heir to the throne. The prodigal grandson, Nathaniel Edmund Winters III."

"Not heir to the throne, Annie. Just heir to the Northcott Inn."

"And has it occurred to you that if you'd done what your grandparents wanted and claimed your inheritance, there'd be absolutely no reason for us to be having this conversation?"

That seemed to catch him off guard and she twisted out of his arms, sparing a second to give him her best glare before she picked up the milk from the table, intending to put it in the fridge. But she stopped mid move. "You know, Eddy, I don't get it. If you don't want the inn, what do you care what happens to it? If the place is losing money, why didn't you just tell them to shut it down?"

He took the milk from her and put it away. "But the place shouldn't be losing money, Annie. Someone's been deliberately setting out to destroy it. New York has sent a lot of money for repairs and equipment. Repairs that were never done. Equipment that never arrived. And everyone you fired since you came on is still on the payroll, Annie. Some of them with recent raises. And someone's been cashing their checks."

"But—" she grabbed the bottle of maple syrup from the table "—not—" she went to stick it in the fridge but Eddy was still standing there so she shoved it at him to punctuate the last word "—me!"

He grabbed the sticky bottle before it hit the floor and stuck it on the shelf next to the milk. "The endorsements on every one of those checks look suspiciously alike, Annie. And they look like you could have made them."

"What—are you some kind of handwriting expert now, too? Let's see." She started ticking off points on her fingers. "Ghost buster, private investigator, handwriting expert..."

He studied her for a moment. "You're not taking this seriously at all, are you?"

"Are *you?*" she asked. "Don't tell me you really think I'm guilty?"

His mouth was set in a firm line while he seemed to be thinking it over. She was just about to start yelling again when he opened his mouth and said, "No, Annie, I don't think you're guilty. But don't you see how bad it looks for you? Those checks look like you signed them. Those requisitions and work orders all have your signature on them. You've just spent a great deal of money—"

"I told you where the money came from for the computer—I saved it!"

"And the car, Annie? What about the luxury car you've been shopping for? How do you think it's going to look when a single mother living on your salary buys a BMW?"

She gave a dismissive little shrug. "Don't be ridiculous. A single mother on my salary could never afford a BMW."

"Exactly. Yet you've been shopping around for a very expensive car. There are witnesses."

She wrinkled her nose. "Witnesses?"

"Your landlady. Lara. I saw you myself, Annie, with that nice white Lexus."

She stared at him. "What were you doing, hiding behind a tree?"

He didn't actually blush, but he might as well have.

"You were spying on me? You're an even bigger rat than I thought!"

"Come on, Annie. Don't you see how this all looks?"

She dragged her hands through her hair. "This is crazy. I never intended to buy any of those cars. It's just something I do—I try out cars I could never afford."

He was looking at her strangely.

"Look, I've got an old high school friend who works at a dealership. We've got this running joke. Once a week I go in there, act like I'm loaded, and she lets me take a car for a few hours." He just kept staring at her. "Don't you believe me?"

"Sure, Annie. Sure, you could get me to believe almost anything. But," he added, moving toward her, "a judge might say I'm biased toward the suspect, having held her in my arms half the night."

And then, somehow, she was engulfed in those arms again. "Eddy! Let me go!"

"I can't," he moaned, running his hands up and down her back till her whole body was humming and heating. "Not unless you get out of this robe and into something more sensible."

"Let go of me and I will," she stated with a deceptive calm.

So he did.

"I have to get dressed for work, anyway. And while I'm doing that, you can tell me why you refused your inheritance, why you never cared about the inn."

He raised a brow, a corner of his mouth twisting. "Does that mean I'm to accompany you—help with zippers and such?"

She gave him a look, although she had to admit the idea was tempting. But she had more sense than to invite the man who was investigating her for embezzlement into her bedroom. Or, at least, she hoped she did.

"No," she told him firmly, before she could change her mind. "No zippers. No *and such*." She sailed past him, holding her robe tightly against her. "I'll leave the door open a crack so I can hear you."

She really knew how to torture a guy. He leaned against the wall next to her bedroom door and could have sworn he could hear the slither of silk as her robe hit the floor. He wished he could have seen it, too.

"Can you hear me?" he finally asked.

"Yes."

"You're wrong when you say I don't care about the inn, Annie. I've always cared about the inn."

She stuck her head out the bedroom door, her cute nose scrunched sideways, giving him a tantalizing glimpse of her bare shoulders before she disappeared again. "Then why didn't you want it?" she asked.

Eddy took a deep breath, held it till the count of three, then let it out.

"This is silly, Annie. It's not like I didn't see your luscious body over and over again last night." He grinned. "In several positions, as I recall."

The sound of rustling clothing stopped. "You think my body's luscious?"

He laughed softly. "What do you think, Annie? Why do you think I'm willing to work for the opposition, as it were, to keep it out of jail?"

"Well . . ." she drawled and he liked the sound of it, as if she was weakening, softening.

Then he heard the sound of a zipper. It definitely didn't make him soften.

"Go on," she said.

It took him a moment to figure out what she was talking about. "Oh, well, like I said, I do care about the inn. I always have. I spent summers there, Annie, and they were the best days of my childhood. Hattie and Nathan were nothing like my parents. There was so much love there," he said, his throat a little thick with the memory, "it just spilled over onto anyone who spent time with them. Those were magic days for me, Annie. Pure magic."

"Then what happened?"

He shook his head and took a breath. "Divorce happened. My parents split and I got caught in the crossfire of their bitterness. My mother forbade me to spend summers at the inn with my father's parents ever again. I only saw them a few times a year when they'd come to New York—and then never alone. The older I got, the more I started to doubt my memories of the place, started to doubt that love like I thought my grandparents had ever really existed. When Hattie and Nathan died and I found out they'd left the place in trust for me, I didn't know what to think—how to feel. Part of me, that small part that had survived the divorces and marriages and the stepparents, wanted it more than anything. I had to wait until I turned twenty-one to claim it. And that, sugar, is when I learned the kicker."

"The kicker?" she asked from behind that door.

"There were strings, Annie. In order to claim my inheritance, I had to promise to live in the penthouse—"

"So? What would be so hard about that? You've already said the summers spent here were the happiest days of your life."

"There's more. I not only had to live there, I had to be married and raise a family there. Just like Hattie and Nathan had. Trouble was, by the time I'd reached the age of twenty-one, I had promised myself, after witnessing my parents' assorted failed marriages, that I would never do that to myself—or to any child."

For a moment, there was silence from behind the door. Then, "But Eddy, how could you be sure you'd never fall in love? How could you be so sure that you'd never want a family?"

He'd been sure. Very sure. But that was before he'd met a certain brandy-eyed, wild-haired wench and her ball-of-energy son. Eddy shook his head. The joke was still on him.

He'd finally started to believe that love like he remembered Hattie and Nathan sharing really did exist. He'd finally found a woman he could picture living with in those magic rooms of his childhood. And she even had a son. A son he was fast falling for as much as he was falling for the mother. Instant family. But the way things were stacking up, Annie might be getting a new address soon—and it wasn't going to be the Northcott Inn.

It was going to be a woman's prison farm.

The bedroom door opened the rest of the way and Annie came out, buttoning the cuffs on a tailored cream silk blouse—the same one that had beckoned him as it hung in her closet the other night. Instead of her usual trousers, she wore a slim camel skirt and mahogany pumps exactly the same color as her hair.

She stopped in front of him where he still leaned against the wall outside her room. She raised her hand to touch his cheek. "I'm sorry for that little boy who was hurt all those years ago," she murmured. "I wish he had come home to the inn sooner."

Her eyes searched his for a moment, and he didn't trust his voice to speak, there was so much tenderness there. No child of Annie's would ever have lost faith as he had.

Then, just as he was pushing himself away from the wall, just as he was thinking he wanted those sweet, caring arms around him, the caress on his cheek turned into a pinch—the kind an irritating aunt might give.

"But," she said, a hunk of his cheek nipped between her fingers, "that doesn't excuse the fact that you lied to me. That you got close to me just to investigate me. And it certainly doesn't excuse the fact that you used my son to—"

His fingers encircled her wrist. "Don't say it, Annie," he said, a low, dangerous edge to his voice, "because it isn't true. I may have evaded the truth—I had to—but I got close to you for one reason only." His hold on her wrist gentled, his thumb brushing her pulse. "And it had nothing to do with me being a private investigator, Annie. Nothing at all. Don't you remember? I didn't even know you were the manager at first."

"I—I remember," she whispered, making him stare at her mouth. Lord, he wanted to kiss it again. But he had to make sure she understood something first.

"And I would never, ever use Jason. That boy means something to me, Annie. More than I ever could have thought possible."

She stared at him for a heartbeat, and he could see her mind whirling behind her eyes, eyes dark with speculation. Then she pulled her wrist away from his hold.

"I've got to get to work. You can tell me what else you think you have on me on the way over to the inn."

The snow had stopped and the sun had broken through, lighting her hair. Eddy was starting to think that someone had ordered up the sunniest winter in Wisconsin's history just so Annie's hair could drive him crazy.

"Okay," she said, as she pulled into the parking lot, "you've got some forged checks, you've got some missing employees, you've got some invoices I didn't sign and some work orders and requisitions I also didn't sign for lots of stuff that's never shown up at or been done to the inn." She swung into her parking spot and cut the engine. "Is that all?"

"Is that all? Annie, I just presented you with enough evidence to send your sweet behind away for a nice little vacation at a prison farm."

She got out. He followed. She slammed the door.

"But I didn't sign those checks!" she said over her shoulder. "I didn't send any requisitions! In fact, I've got a folder full of correspondence from the big guys in New York telling me to cut this, fire that, stop—"

He grabbed her by the shoulders and swung her around. "You've got a file of—"

She shook him off, nodded and started walking again. "I'll show it to you."

Stunned that it might be that easy to clear her, he stood rooted for a moment, watching her perky little walk as she picked her way through the snow in her pumps. Nice legs. Too nice to let them languish on a prison farm. He watched those legs as they disappeared through the door to the inn. Then he followed.

Bounding up the stone steps, he shoved open the heavy front door and crossed the lobby. Annie was already in her tiny office, crouched before a filing cabinet.

He closed the door to the office just as Annie shut the file drawer and rose—empty-handed.

For the first time, he saw real fear in her eyes. "They're gone," she murmured in bewilderment. "The file with the correspondence from New York is gone."

Eddy raised his gaze to the ceiling. He should have figured things wouldn't have been that simple.

"Maybe I put it someplace else," she said.

He leaned against the closed door and watched her while she just about tore the office apart.

"Annie," he finally said. "The file is gone."

"But there was a file! You do believe that don't you?"

He didn't answer. Suddenly, he no longer looked like a Viking pirate to her. He looked like the guy who was going to send her to jail. Okay—the *gorgeous* guy who was going to send her to jail. But suddenly, he was the enemy. And it was time she stopped thinking about her libido and started thinking about self-preservation.

"I think you better leave," she told him firmly.

"Leave? Look, Annie—"

She stepped back from him. "No, don't touch me. Just get out of here."

"Annie, I want to help. There's got to be something I can do."

"Like what? Call for the police? Watch them put on the cuffs?"

"Sugar, maybe if we work together, pool our energy, we can find out what's really going on."

"Work together? Are you nuts? For all I know, you're the one setting me up! Maybe the only reason the prodigal grandson has returned is to make sure this place is failing so he can convince the corporation to sell it so he can pocket the money."

"Annie, that's crazy."

"No—what would be crazy is if I got into bed with you—both figuratively and literally. Now get out of here and let me think."

"Sugar—"

"Eddy, if you don't leave right this minute, I'm going to start screaming." And that was exactly what she felt like doing—screaming.

She sat at her desk, keeping her eyes closed until she heard the door open and shut.

When she opened her eyes, he was gone.

She groaned and leaned back in her chair. What was she going to do? Did she need a lawyer? Could she afford a lawyer?

And even more importantly—and also scary as hell—who was doing this to her? Because somewhere inside the walls of the inn she'd come to love was someone who'd been working against her for two years. Even if she really believed that Eddy was the culprit, someone had to be working with him. Someone who could pull the strings on this end. Someone who'd been learning her signature, manufacturing false documents, seeing to it that she only saw what he wanted her to see from New York. Possibly someone she was actually very fond of.

Because she was fond of all the employees who remained at the Northcott Inn.

Lara, who despite all those holes in her ears and her weird clothes was smart and loyal and always willing. Maxwell, who'd been at the inn forever and was always ready to do whatever needed doing. Austin, who was gentle and shy and who just didn't have the brains to run any kind of scam. Doris in housekeeping, Maria in the restaurant. Neither of them would have access to what a person would need to pull something like this off. And then there was Damian. But Damian was way too fond of lean meat and fresh vegetables to intentionally deprive himself, and his diners, of them.

Only two people had the opportunity. Lara and herself.

Ann knew she was innocent.

And she could never believe that Lara was guilty.

And what about Nathaniel Edmund Winters III, she thought as she chewed her lip. He'd blown in with the blizzard, and things had been stormy ever since. And how did she know he was even telling her the truth? All that stuff about his childhood. He could have made it all up just to get her bleeding heart in his hands. For all she knew, he was bitter as the devil about only being left the lowly Northcott Inn in the will and had been plotting revenge since he turned twenty-one.

She stared at the phone. She needed to talk to someone about this—about him. She picked up the phone and started to punch out the number for the head office in New York. Then she stopped, slowly replacing the receiver in its cradle. How did she know who she could trust? Maybe it was even New York doing this to her, making her the scapegoat so they could close the place down despite the provisions in Hattie and Nathan's will.

Which left her nowhere to turn. She was alone in this— and she had absolutely no idea what to do.

"WHAT DO YOU MEAN it's going to take more time?"

Eddy held the phone against his hip and paced around the sitting room, now and then glancing at Hattie and Nathan over the fireplace. "Listen, Hank, that fax you sent last night just complicated things."

Hank sighed heavily. "Sorry, pal, but I kept calling the penthouse and there was no answer. I figured you'd want to know."

There'd been no answer because he'd been prowling around—and trying to keep his hands off Annie.

"Look, Eddy," Hank went on, "you say there're workers on the payroll who no longer exist. You say none of the work that's been contracted and paid for has been done. You tell me the place is falling apart despite the records we have of money going out, money being spent. Pal, the evidence is mounting—how many suspects could there possibly be?"

Way too few, Eddy figured. And all he'd have to do is send Hank a sample of Annie's signature and that suspect list would whittle its way down to one. Because anybody studying the documents Eddy had in his possession would come to the same conclusion. Annie had signed those checks. Annie had authorized those work orders. Annie had done it all.

But Annie said she was innocent. And Eddy believed her.

"Eddy," Hank said, the unusually stern quality to his voice putting Eddy on the alert, "you're keeping something from me, and I don't like it."

Eddy willed himself to relax, willed himself to give a soft laugh. "I never could get much by you, could I, Hank?"

"Not since I first caught you trying to play hotel burglar. But I thought I saw to your reformation myself, pal. You're not forgetting which side of the law you're playing on, are you?"

"No, Hank, I'm not forgetting."

"Listen, pal, by tomorrow this is going to be out of my hands—and yours."

That stopped Eddy's pacing cold. "What are you talking about, Hank? Your fax said you could get the judge to give us a little time."

"I can, but it may be meaningless." Hank sighed. "I just found out that Cousin Clifford is booked on an early morning flight out there."

"Clifford Northcott? On his way to Milwaukee?"

"Packing as we speak, pal."

Briefly, Eddy squeezed his eyes shut. "Cousin Clifford hates Milwaukee."

"Yeah, but he loves money. And he's a rising star out here, Eddy. He's been romancing the board for months. Has them eating out of his sweaty little palm."

"And he's the one who's been trying to convince them to go to court to nullify the will."

"Right. And once he gets there, you won't be able to protect whoever you're protecting, Eddy. Once Clifford gets his incisors into it, it's gonna be out of your hands—and mine."

Eddy gave a dull laugh. Cousin Clifford had been known as Count Clifford when they were kids in honor of the size and sharpness of his teeth. The animosity between them went way back. Count Clifford would like nothing better than to close Eddy's inn down—and have the woman Eddy loved arrested for embezzlement as a little whipped cream on the sundae.

Eddy shook his head. Eddy's Inn? What a mess. It was supposed to have been his all along. And now, when he wanted it, when he'd finally recaptured his love for the place, he was going to lose it. And was in danger of losing the one woman he wanted by his side while he ran it as part of the package.

"He'll be there first thing in the morning, Eddy. And then your time is gonna be up. Understand?"

Eddy pinched the bridge of his nose against a looming headache and nodded. "Understood. And Hank? Thanks for the warning."

Eddy hung up the phone. Count Clifford. That's all he needed. Now it was more important than ever to make Annie see reason.

"HEY, EDDY, I don't think I ever had a banana split in the middle of winter before."

Eddy watched Jason hoist an enormous spoonful of banana dripping with chocolate syrup to his mouth. "It's regulation, Jase. At least one banana split in January and one in February."

Jason hooted. "That's one regulation I'm all for!"

Watching him devour the ice cream with his usual enthusiasm, Eddy only hoped he'd be around to buy Jason his February banana split, too—and that Annie would be along for the ride.

He'd done little all day but go over everything he'd already unearthed about the inn. That, and check out Lara, who seemed the next most likely suspect. He'd unearthed nothing to tie her in, though. If he didn't come up with something by morning, Count Clifford was going to get his clammy hands on everything and come to the same conclusion anyone would when they knew what Eddy knew. Annie was the one embezzling money from the Northcott Inn. Annie was the one systematically trying to ruin the place.

Eddy still didn't believe it, but it was going to look bad for Annie. Very bad. And, if he knew his cousin, Clifford was going to do anything he could to make it look even worse. And once it got into the courts, there was little Eddy would be able to do to protect her. Which was why he needed to do everything he could to clear her before tomorrow morning. But he needed her help to do it. All he had to do was convince her to crawl into bed with a rat—figuratively, of course.

Although, he thought with a grin, literally appealed, too.

He watched Jason spoon up the last of his ice cream. "I should be getting to the inn, Eddy, or Mom will start to worry about where I am."

Eddy shook his head. "You're not going to the inn today, sport. You're going to Estelle's. That's why I picked you up after school."

Jason scrunched up his nose. "Estelle's? How come?"

"Your mom's got some stuff to take care of and it might get late. I already asked Estelle if you can spend the night with her. How does that sound, sport?"

"Cool! She's got all these old videos she lets me watch and sometimes she makes hot chocolate and toast with honey—"

"Then you're okay with it?"

Jason nodded enthusiastically. "Sure, Eddy. It'll be fun."

As Eddy helped him on with his coat so he could walk the boy to Estelle's, he only wished his night would be half as fun as Jason's was going to be. If he knew Annie, she would become more wench than damsel once he'd done what he planned to do—and he was going to be in for one long, bumpy night.

Chapter Twelve

Eddy was freezing. It was late afternoon, nearly dark, and it had started to snow. Eddy was standing out in it, shivering in the shadows near the inn's entrance.

Below, at the curb, a horse and carriage waited. The horse was as white as the carriage, the gold braided into its mane echoed in the scrollwork around the door and windows. The top-hatted driver, darkly cloaked against the weather, waited in position.

The door opened, and Eddy flattened himself against the cold stone wall.

She stepped into the halo from the light above the entrance and he lunged for her.

"Agh! Put me down! What are you doing?"

Eddy winced as she pummeled his back. He'd had an image of himself sweeping down the wide stone steps with sweet Annie in his arms—just like a real Viking pirate. But the wench was struggling too much to do it gracefully. He had no choice but to throw her over his shoulder and stagger down the steps with her like a drunken Santa carrying his pack.

He struggled to open the carriage door, threw her inside, yelled, "Drive!" to the driver, and climbed in after her.

Annie scooted over as far as she could and glared at him. "What do you think you're doing?"

"I'm holding you captive until I can make you see reason."

She arched a brow sassily. "Ever heard of the telephone?"

"You know damned well I have. I've been trying to call you all day, but you just keep hanging up on me. You've kept yourself shut into your office, Max guarding the door like a latter-day Quasimodo, refusing to let me in. You left me with no choice, sugar, but to abduct you."

"Well, you can just *un*-abduct me! I've got a son who's probably right now waiting for me in front of the inn!"

"Don't worry about Jason," he began.

"Don't tell me you abducted him, too?"

"No, Annie. I simply picked him up from school and took him to Estelle's. He's spending the night."

"How dare you!" She pounded on the carriage roof. "Stop this thing—at once!" she yelled.

Eddy laughed softly. "Won't work, wench. He's got orders to take orders only from me."

She flew at him then, grabbing the collar of his black cashmere coat. "Then tell him to stop."

"Now?" he drawled. "When I've finally gotten you back into my arms?"

Her eyes grew wide and her mouth opened, and Eddy took full advantage. He crushed her lips under his, delving into the sweet anger of her mouth with his tongue until she stopped struggling and started to kiss him back.

"That's better," he said when he'd pulled away and tucked her head under his chin. She seemed content, for the moment, to stay there.

"No, it's not," she pouted. "It's not better. I want things to go back to how they were when I first walked into the Northcott Inn. When business was good and I was hopeful that I was going to be able to build a life for me and Jason without the help of my rat of an ex-husband. Before I had to fire anyone and no one was accusing me of embezzling anything.''

He buried his hand in the lushness of her fiery hair and pulled her head back till he could look into her eyes.

''But then, sugar, you never would have met me,'' he murmured.

Her eyes flashed. ''Exactly my point,'' she huffed, shoving him away and scooting to her side of the carriage again. ''Now let me out of here!''

''Not until you promise to work with me to find out who's really behind all this—and why.''

She wrinkled her nose. ''So you're really on my side? You really don't believe that I'm guilty?''

''Sugar, every shred of evidence says you're guilty as sin, but my heart—'' He paused, reaching out his hand to touch her cheek. ''My heart tells me that it just ain't so.'' He slid over to her and lowered his head until his mouth was nearly touching hers. ''Driving me crazy, sweet Annie, is the only thing you're guilty of.''

''You mean it?'' she whispered.

''With all my heart,'' he answered and then he kissed her softly, sweetly, his lips nibbling, his tongue soothing.

Outside, the snow thickened. The carriage made its way down narrow, darkened streets, the sound of the horse's hooves like a muffled heartbeat in the snow.

Inside, things were heating up.

''I'm crazy about you, Annie,'' Eddy whispered roughly. ''What the hell am I supposed to do about that?''

''You're supposed to call the board and tell them they've got the wrong girl,'' she answered tartly, pushing him away from her.

Eddy sighed. As he'd expected, she wasn't going to be easy. ''It's not that simple, Annie. Count Clifford is on his way to town, and once he gets a hold of this it's going to look very bad for you.''

''Count Clifford?''

"My cousin, Clifford Northcott."

Annie scrunched up her nose. "He's a count?"

Eddy shook his head. "Nah—we just call him that because of his teeth."

"His teeth?"

"When you meet him you'll know what I mean. Now, how are we going to find out who's doing this to you?"

Annie was eyeing him suspiciously. "How do I know it isn't you, Nathaniel Edmund Winters III, who's trying to frame me? How do I know that you're not just out to get your hands on the money you didn't get in the will? Maybe you did it all. Maybe you're hoping that the board will nullify the will so you can claim the inn and sell it." Her eyes narrowed. "How do I know you aren't abducting me to keep me quiet for the next few hours so I can't do anything to clear my name and you can hand me over on a silver platter to Cousin Clifford in the morning?"

"That's ridiculous, Annie."

"Ridiculous or not, you better let me out of here, Mr. Winters, before I start screaming!"

"Annie," he cajoled, but she was already opening her mouth wide enough for him to see that she had excellent teeth with nearly no fillings. But before any sound could come rushing up from her lungs and over those teeth, he did the only thing he could think of to shut her up. He kissed her. Hard and long and furiously. She struggled against him, and he was beginning to feel like that Viking pirate she'd likened him to, abducting the innocent damsel and making away with her into the night.

But the Viking pirate was supposed to win this fight, wasn't he? Eddy felt rapidly like he was losing. Not to mention bruising.

"For heaven's sake, Annie," he quit kissing her long enough to mutter, "hold still!"

The whole carriage was rocking.

"Let go of me, you rat!"

"Annie, Annie—" He managed to still her long enough to hold her head, face first, against his chest. "Quit struggling and listen," he pleaded. "It's true I didn't want any part of the inn, but that was before I came back to it again. A few weeks ago, I couldn't have cared less what happened to it. In fact, when Hank sent me out here to investigate, I figured it was just another one of his ploys to get me to claim the place. But, Annie, all that's changed. I feel like I'm home again, like maybe my memories haven't deceived me. Maybe a life like Hattie and Nathan lived really is possible. But, don't you see, just when I thought I'd found it again, found whatever magic, love and contentment the place holds, it's being snatched away from me for a second time. If I don't have something to give Clifford tomorrow, some reason to give him so he'll postpone trying to convince the board to go to court to nullify the will, I'm going to lose the place forever. I need your help, Annie. We not only have to clear your name, but we have to find out who's been doing this to the inn, and why. And we have to do it by tomorrow morning."

"Tomorrow?" she asked weakly against his chest.

"Morning," he confirmed. "We've got until tomorrow morning to figure this thing out. If I know Count Clifford, once he gets here, he's going to involve the authorities, Annie, and it's going to look bad for you. I may not be able to protect you, then. Work with me now, and we might be able to keep you out of it. Now, are you going to help me?"

She nodded vigorously against his chest.

"And you believe me? You don't really think I'm the one trying to frame you?"

It took a moment, but she nodded to that, too.

"Okay, I'm going to let you go. And then we're going to go back to the inn and try to figure this thing out."

He felt her relax against him, and he took his hand away from her mouth. He expected some kind of outburst, but she was alarmingly still.

"Annie?" he whispered against her hair. "Are you all right?"

She nodded and sniffed.

"Aw, Annie, don't cry."

She sniffed again. "This—this is terrible."

"I know it is."

"Here I am in a—a carriage with a Viking pirate on a night when the—the snow is falling and—and there might not be another person in the world, and—and..."

"And what, sugar?"

"And all I want you to do is kiss me—kiss me like you really mean it. But instead, you kiss me just to shut me up. And instead of going back to the inn so you can drag me up to your room and ravish me, we're going to talk about how—about how—about how we can keep me out of jail!"

The last word was a plaintive wail tearing at his heart. He looked into her face, her big brandy eyes glistening with tears, her luscious mouth quivering. "I'll kiss you like I really mean it, Annie love," he whispered. "And I'd like nothing more than to take you to my room and ravish you, if it'll make you happy."

She felt his arms leave her long enough to shout something out the window to the driver, and then he was back, his arms gentler than before, his mouth tender on her face.

"There is no one," he whispered, "in the world, Annie my love, but you and me." His fingers at her chin urged her to look into his face. He was so close that there really was nothing else, just his ice-blue eyes and his high, tan cheekbones, his strong jaw, his flowing, sliver-streaked hair and his glinting, wicked earring.

He slid her coat from her shoulders, shrugged out of his own, whipped the fur throw from the opposite seat and blanketed them with it. And then he was kissing her again, and she felt his fingers at the buttons of her shirt, and then against her skin—tingling, heating, delving into her bra and capturing the throbbing peak of her breast until she cried out and did the same for him, her hands gliding up under his silk sweater, touching his warm, smooth flesh, finding the hard nubs of his nipples. She was rewarded with his lilting groan and his hand on her thigh, sliding under her skirt.

Of its own volition, her body bucked.

"Annie, sugar," he whispered, "is this what you want?" He touched her between her thighs, and all she could do was nod furiously and wonder if it was the horse's hooves or her heart thundering.

She bit her lip when his fingers pressed against her, stroking, teasing.

"Never, never doubt that I want you, Annie," he whispered raggedly. "Because I do—and nothing is ever going to change that."

And then she was lost. If he spoke again, she didn't hear. The thundering was too loud. The carriage rocked along with her soul. Faster—faster. And all she could do was hang on to him while he took her away, running with the wind.

And when she shattered and cried out his words were again lost to her because she had to have his mouth on hers until the storm in her body was over.

Neither of them spoke the rest of the way to the inn. When the carriage stopped, Eddy swept her up in the fur throw and carried her all the way up the stone stairs to the Viking's castle glistening with enchantment in the snow.

Mr. AND MRS. ALBERT were just on their way out for their evening walk as Eddy carried her over the threshold.

Mr. Albert looked scandalized, but Mrs. Albert blushed pinkly and smiled widely. "Oh, dear—Mrs. Madison. Have you turned your ankle or something?"

Eddy didn't stop on his way to the staircase, so Ann just called over her shoulder, "Or something."

Annie heard Mr. Albert huff, "Well, I never." Then Mrs. Albert sighed and said, "Lucky girl."

And there goes my reputation with the only steady guests the hotel had, Ann thought. At least Lara wasn't at the desk to see her in Eddy's arms. But what the hell. This might just be her last night of freedom. What better way to spend it but in the arms of a Viking pirate?

Eddy reached the staircase and started to carry her up.

"Are you crazy?" she managed finally to say.

"I think I must be," he answered.

"I mean—take the elevator. You'll break your back."

He laughed. "Not what a damsel should say to a pirate, wench."

She laughed the rest of the way for the sheer joy of it. Never, in her wildest dreams, did she imagine being carried by a Viking pirate up to his lair.

"You laugh, damsel, but I'll soon have you panting again."

"I certainly hope so," she countered.

"Hmm, methinks they don't make damsels as meek and shy as they used to."

"Shut up," she said, "and kiss me."

He did, pausing on the landing to the final floor, taking her mouth with a sweetness that left her to wonder.

"Annie—" he began.

But she stopped the words with fingers to his lips. "Don't, my Viking pirate. Not now. Give us this time, please?"

HE COULDN'T deny her. Striding up the remaining steps, he threw her over his shoulder long enough to fish the key from his pocket, causing another peal of her delightful laughter. *Give us this time,* she'd asked. As the door swung open, Eddy prayed that it wouldn't be their last.

He kicked the door shut behind him then let Annie slide down his body till her feet hit the floor. He started to move away, but she clung to him.

"Don't leave me."

He removed her hand from his shoulder and kissed it. "I just want to make a fire." He smiled gently, cupping her face. "You have your fantasies, and I have mine. I want to see you in the firelight. To make love to you with the fire in your hair and warming your soft, creamy skin. Let me have that, Annie," he beseeched in a harsh, urgent whisper.

She let him go and he went to the marble fireplace and knelt. The blaze started almost immediately, hot and high, and he gazed at the portrait. If the spirits were at work tonight, they were on his side.

He stood and slipped the fur throw from her shoulders and spread it on the floor before the fire, then held out his hand to her.

Without a word, she came to him.

"I want to undress you," he whispered.

She let him. Slowly, he slipped each piece of clothing from her body, tossing them away, until she was standing completely natural, and utterly beautiful, before him. The firelight burnished her pale skin, brought her mass of hair to life. He took his time looking at her, trying not to think that, depending on what happened in the night ahead, it might be a long time before he'd see her this way again.

Her sweet mouth curved into a gentle smile. "Now, my turn," she said.

Her hands were light, quick, shy as she undressed him. When he was standing before her naked, he felt almost virginal. *Dear God,* he thought, *have I fallen in love with a woman whose life I might have a part in ruining?*

He forced the thought from his mind. Not now. Now was for them.

He lowered himself to the throw, bringing her with him, lying on his side inches from her body. They touched each other, fingers gliding, flesh quivering, breath quickening. It was slow, sweet. They didn't kiss for a long time—not until their bodies had swollen with desire, not until he knew she was feeling the same as him, wanting the same. And then his mouth claimed hers and he rolled onto his back, bringing her along, his hands at her waist, lifting her, impaling her onto his hard, aching flesh. It was she who finally broke the kiss then, throwing back her head, her hair wild in the flames, and crying out with a sound that swelled inside of him.

And then she began to move on him, fast, furious. Through hooded eyes, he watched her in the firelight, watched the abandon on her face, the passion in her full, moist mouth. Her body quivered and shook, taking him along for the glorious ride until suddenly her body convulsed on his and she was still, as if the world had stopped. He clutched her hips with his hands and thrust high into her and felt her finally explode. And then he let go, joining her in the fire.

THE FIRE had all but died in the grate and the room was nearly dark when Eddy opened his eyes, the sound of shattering glass jolting him from a shallow sleep. He held his breath and listened. Nothing. It must have been a fragment of some dream, he thought, not surprised that he would dream about something shattering.

He looked at Annie, her head nestled in the crook of his arm. They must have drifted off after they'd made love. In sleep, she looked beautiful and peaceful, and he hated to wake her. He squinted at his watch. After seven. They couldn't afford to lose any more time.

Nuzzling her temple with his lips, he whispered, "Annie, wake up, sugar."

She stirred, the edge of the fur throw slipping from her breast, and Eddy forgot the urgency of getting up and bent to take her rosy nipple into his mouth. That's when he heard it.

His tongue out, ready to taste, he froze. There was someone else in the penthouse.

The movements were stealthy, quiet, and he listened for a moment more, thinking that it might be just the wind moaning its displeasure, might just be the ghosts of his grandmother and grandfather finally materializing, come to help solve the riddle and save their beloved inn. But Eddy knew better. The sounds were all too human—and they were coming from the bedroom.

Careful not to wake Annie, he slipped out from under the throw. If someone had broken into the penthouse, she'd be in less danger if she was unaware of what was going on. Quietly, he got to his feet, pausing for a moment for his eyes to adjust to the dark on the far side of the room. A sharp, quick sound of splintering wood cracked the hushed darkness, and he moved.

With a graceful, fluid movement, he leaped over the sofa with almost no sound, landing on the balls of his feet not two feet from the bedroom door. It was ajar. Reaching out, he pushed it open.

There was a flurry of movement, a rush that was entirely human, entirely clumsy. Then something sharp and heavy whacked him on the shoulder and he staggered, losing his balance and falling to his knees while something clattered to the floor beside him and the bulk of a human body rushed past. The next sound he heard, save for his ragged breathing, was the door of the penthouse opening and closing.

"Eddy, is that you?" came Annie's frightened whisper from the darkness near the fireplace.

Eddy grunted, trying to stagger to his feet while he rubbed his shoulder.

"Are you all right? What happened?" She was coming toward him, like a lovely specter of the night, the fur throw wrapped around her, her shoulders bare. "What happened?" she asked again, her voice a frantic whisper.

He stumbled over to the lamp on the desk and flicked it on. A crowbar lay on the floor. He picked it up. It felt cold and heavy in his hands. His foot kicked something as he moved. He bent again and retrieved a small flashlight.

"We had a visitor," he told her, trying the light to see if it still worked.

She was beside him in a heartbeat, her soft, gentle hand touching his shoulder. "My God, Eddy, are you all right? He didn't hit you with that, did he?"

"He managed to connect with my shoulder, but I think he was probably aiming for my head."

Annie gasped. "Who was it? Did you see?"

Eddy shook his head. "It was too dark and it happened too fast.'"

Annie picked up the phone on the desk.

"What are you doing?" he asked.

"Calling down to the desk. Maybe Lara saw someone."

Eddy took the receiver from her hand and replaced it. "Better not. We don't know who we can trust."

"It can't be Lara!"

Eddy touched her check. "I hope it isn't, too, baby. You stay here, I'm going to check out the bedroom."

Her hand tightened on his arm. "Oh, no, you don't—you're not leaving me alone. I'm coming, too."

He spared a slight grin for her stubbornness, then soberly pushed her behind him. "Okay, wench, I won't argue with you—just stay behind me."

So Annie crept behind him, close enough to leave her hand on his shoulder. He wasn't sure if she was reassuring him—or herself. But he liked the feel of it there.

The light from the desk in the sitting room cast enough illumination for him to easily find the lamp near the bed. He flicked it on. The only thing out of place was a small wine table upended next to a boudoir chair near the closet. The antique oil lamp it once held lay smashed next to it—obviously the crash that had jolted him from sleep.

His gaze scanned the room. His wallet lay on the dresser where he had left it. He picked it up. The bills were still folded inside. His credit cards were all there. "Watch your step," he told Annie as he skirted the shards of glass and pulled open the closet door. His clothes had been moved. A shirt still swung slightly, its hanger making a little clicking sound as it moved. He pushed the rest of the hangers aside and groped to the back of the closet, switching on the flashlight he still held in his hand.

The dim light shone on a door at the back of the closet he hadn't known existed.

"There's a door back here," he told Annie over his shoulder.

"A door to where?" she whispered.

"I don't know—I've never seen it before."

"A secret door? My goodness, Eddy—is it locked?" Annie croaked from behind him.

Eddy reached out and turned the knob.

He shook his head. "Not locked. What do you think, Annie? Do we open it?"

"Do we have a choice?" she asked him. "Whoever was here, inside the penthouse, could have something to do with what's been happening at the inn. He must have been through that door—we've got to see whatever is behind it."

He felt her hand near his and he surrounded it with his own. "Okay, damsel, keep your fingers crossed."

The door opened silently, as if its hinges had been recently oiled. Eddy ran his fingers along one. They came away slicked with oil.

He showed them to Annie. "Maintenance. Whoever's been using this door wanted to make sure he could come and go without making a sound."

He gave Annie's hand one last squeeze before he reluctantly let go, moving the light across whatever lay behind the door.

"Stairs," Annie breathed.

Eddy pointed the flashlight upward. It shone weakly on a narrow, winding staircase. "What about it, Annie? Do we climb them?"

"Yes!"

He chuckled softly. "Ah, the bold wench in you is coming out."

"I've got my pirate to protect me," she whispered against his shoulder.

Eddy took in a deep breath, then started to climb into the flashlight's faint beam, fervently hoping that there would be nothing up there he'd have to protect her from.

He heard Annie climbing steadily behind him, and he wished that the adventure was merely that—an adventure, and not something that might very well spell her freedom.

The beam hit on a door ten steps above him. "There's another door up here. When you reach me, hang on, and we'll open it together."

He felt her move up next to him, felt her hand grope for his. He grabbed it and held tight. Then he reached out and turned the knob.

A thousand stars waited for them.

He heard her gasp and pulled her up and out with him.

The snow had stopped, and the sky was a clear, deep, midnight blue. The sliver of a moon hung suspended above as if the stars were coaxing it out into the night for company.

"The turret to your castle, pirate," Annie whispered behind him, and he felt the pressure of her hand squeezing his.

The turret was open to the wind, the pillars supporting the roof cutting it so that the breeze in their faces was cold, crisp but more refreshing than freezing.

Pulling her hand from his, Annie went to the railing that circled it, raising her face to the night sky. "It's beautiful," she breathed.

He watched her for a moment, watched the moonlight playing in her hair, the winter wind blowing it about her sweet face, the starlight shining in her brandy eyes, the moonlight shimmering on her smooth, bare shoulders. "*You're* beautiful," he whispered.

She turned to him. "Thank you," she whispered back. To her, at that moment, he *was* her Viking pirate, a man come to spirit her away from her ordinary life. His silver hair glistened and shifted in the wind. Still naked, his body was hard, sculpted, strong enough to stand against the winter wind. His earring glittered, and she remembered the moment she'd first seen it—the moment she first started to fall in love.

Her eyes filled and she turned away, looking at the stars. "I couldn't have asked for a more perfect place to spend my last night with you," she said.

He was beside her in a flash, pulling her into his arms. She laid her cheek against his solid, hard chest, his heartbeat pounding in her ear.

"Don't say that," he whispered into her hair. "I'm going to get you out of this—I promise. And there will be other nights for us to share."

"Shh," she told him. "Don't talk. Just hold me."

His arms tightened. The stars seemed to sway closer to the earth, the moon seemed to shine more brightly. And Annie knew that there would never be another night like this.

It seemed like an age passed before he spoke.

"You're shivering, Annie. Let me take you down."

She shook her head. "Not yet."

"Sugar—" He tilted her chin up so she was looking into his eyes. "I'd stay here forever with you if I could, standing naked against the elements, but there's nothing here that can help us. We have to go back down and start searching for answers."

She swept a hand up his chest to his face, running her fingers over his beautiful cheekbones and into his gorgeous hair. "Kiss me first," she whispered.

"Aw, Annie..."

He bent and took her mouth with a gentleness that was almost hard to bear. She didn't want gentle. She wanted hard and crazy. She wanted the kind of kiss she'd never forget—the kind *he'd* never forget.

So she took over, learning his mouth with her tongue, biting his lips with her teeth, moving her hands restlessly over and over again on his chest and shoulders, and lower, to the hard muscles of his buttocks. As if she could memorize every muscle, as if she could imprint the feel of his naked flesh on her palms forever.

"Annie...oh, baby," he murmured, stilling her hands with his own and bringing them to his lips. "I'd like nothing better than to stay here with you and make love under the stars. But we haven't much time." He kissed her hands again. "When this is over and you're out of danger, we'll have all the time in the world to make love. But right now, we've got to go back down. We've got to keep looking for whatever someone broke into the penthouse to find. And we've got to hope that that will give us a clue as to who's behind all this."

She nodded. But she knew that no matter what happened, they wouldn't have all the time in the world. Because either she would be behind bars, or her Viking pirate would have gone back to his real life. But she wasn't going to spoil what was most surely their last night together. She looked one last time at the stars, then she let him lead her by the hand to the narrow staircase.

But, of course, she spoiled the moment anyway by tripping on her own feet.

"Oof!" She slammed against Eddy, sending the flashlight ricocheting wildly, clattering down the steps, before everything went dark. Bouncing off Eddy, she fell against the wall of the staircase. "Ouch!" Then slammed into the opposite wall with enough force that something gave way. A flurry of wings fluttered around her, brushing her face, tangling in her hair.

"Bats!" she squealed, a creepy chill shooting up he spine. Then the fluttering stopped, and she brushed a han over her hair, coming away with something crumpled in he fingers.

"Stay where you are, Annie. I'll get the light."

She held her breath, standing perfectly still, hoping a ba wasn't even at that moment eyeing her hair for its nex housing project. And then there was light. She slammed he eyes shut against it, then slowly opened them again.

Eddy stood at the foot of the stairs holding the flash light.

"What's that in your hand?" he asked her.

Expecting the worst, she slowly raised her hand an opened her fingers.

Money. A one-hundred-dollar bill.

"Eddy, get closer! Train the light at my feet!" sh squealed, then bent to scoop up whatever it was that ha fluttered around her.

When she straightened, her arms were full of cash an checks.

"Money, Eddy! Hundreds of dollars! Look, the steps ar littered with it! And checks—" She held a check to her face squinting at it. "Hey, I fired this guy a year ago!"

Eddy laughed out loud, and the sound rolled through he along with the relief.

"That's what our intruder was after, Annie," he cried coming up the stairs to join her. "The money and the check he's been squirreling away behind the paneling on these stairs. It must have made him nervous as hell to have some one staying in the penthouse again."

"But this can't be all of it!" Annie exclaimed.

"Of course not. He must have hidden checks here until h got a chance to cash them. And the money—he'd have t spend that a little at a time to avoid suspicion."

"You keep saying *he,* Eddy. Does that mean you don' think Lara could have done it?"

Eddy was still for a moment, and she wanted him to say something, anything that would show that Lara was no longer on his list of suspects.

"You know, Annie, except for you, she'd be the best choice. But there's something that makes me think it's a man. Something I can't quite put my finger on—" he shook his head "—some small piece of memory that eludes me just now."

Bending, Eddy picked up the rest of the checks and a few bills that had floated from Annie's hands. "Come on. Let's get downstairs and take a look at what we've got."

Annie followed him down. But he stopped short just outside the closet, and she nearly ran into him. "What's the matter?" she asked him, peering over his shoulder.

"Can you smell that, Annie?" he asked her.

She wrinkled her nose. "Smell what?"

"That's it!" he exclaimed, his voice triumphant. "That's why I think it's a man! Cigars, Annie. Can't you smell it?"

She sniffed. Yeah, she could smell it. But she didn't like it. Didn't like it at all. Because what she smelled was cheap cigars. Maxwell Harper's cheap cigars.

Chapter Thirteen

"I just can't believe Max would do this to me. He had to know that I'd be blamed."

"Annie, the man set you up."

She shook her head, letting the fur throw drop to the floor while she picked up her panties and slipped them on. "No," she said, despite the fact that Eddy had been trying to convince her for the past ten minutes, "I just can't believe that. It has to be someone else."

Regretfully, Eddy watched her full breasts disappear behind her lacy bra. He swallowed hard. "Uh, Annie, he's got means and opportunity. Those were definitely his cigars we smelled in the bedroom. And I just told you about the time I surprised him at the computer—after he told you he couldn't even turn one of the things on. And don't forget, I found him in here once before."

Annie found her shirt under a chair. "But you said he had a perfectly good explanation for that!"

"Yeah, he was spraying lilac scent—to remember Hattie by. Does that sound like something a seventy-year-old man would do?"

Annie stopped struggling with the buttons on her shirt long enough to glare at him. "What has age got to do with it? Max is sweet and kind—just the kind of man who would never forget the love of his life. And he cares about the inn,

Eddy," she said, trying not to remember that he'd been negative about just about everything she'd proposed to help turn the inn around. "Besides, you said a suspect needed more than means and opportunity. A suspect needs motive, Eddy. Where's Max's motive?"

"He was in love with Hattie."

Annie shot him a look before bending to pluck her skirt from behind the sofa.

"You don't think I'm going to let you finish dressing if you keep doing that, do you?"

She straightened quickly. "Quit ogling me. You're supposed to be convincing me that Max is guilty."

"And I haven't yet?" he asked, coming toward her.

She quickly moved away from the sofa before he got there. "No, you haven't. Honestly, what does being in love with Hattie have to do with it? Seems to me that would swing points to his favor."

"Not if he was nursing a grudge. Not if he had a little revenge in mind. He told me he always thought of her as Hattie Northcott."

He wasn't telling her anything she hadn't already spent some time thinking about herself. Because of Max, she'd always thought of the hotel's matriarch as Hattie Northcott, too. It was the reason Eddy had been able to keep his real identity secret.

"He could ruin the inn that Hattie and Nathan worked to make a success," Eddy went on, "and he could line his own pockets at the same time."

She gave a disbelieving little snort. "Then his pockets must be deep as the ocean. The poor man lives in a rooming house, Eddy. He doesn't own a car. And he hasn't taken a vacation in the two years I've been manager here. What's he doing with the money?"

She picked up her pantyhose, decided to stuff them in her purse for now and started to wiggle into her skirt. Eddy leaned against the back of the sofa and watched her.

She gave him a twisted grin. "Knock it off, will you?"

"Just enjoying the view."

The view she had wasn't bad, either. Eddy had put on his jeans, but his chest was bare—and as tempting as the devil. Still grinning, she shook her head and zipped up her skirt. "Where are my shoes?"

"I'm holding them hostage."

She looked up, pushing the hair from her face, to find her pumps dangling from Eddy's fingers. She crossed her arms. "Okay, what's it going to cost to keep from walking out of here barefoot?"

"Come over here and I'll show you."

He was irresistible—as usual. She uncrossed her arms and did his bidding, strolling slowly over to him, her bare feet sinking into the flowers of Hattie's plush carpet, wishing they had more time, wishing what had happened between them in front of that fireplace hadn't happened for the last time.

But she knew it had.

Because, by tomorrow, she would either be up to her neck in trouble, or if by some magic the true culprit was unmasked, Eddy would be on his way to New York where modern-day Viking pirates belonged.

When she reached him, he put his hands at her waist and lifted her, placing her on the back of the sofa, where he knelt to slip her shoes on her feet. The feel of his fingers touching the arch of her foot and his thumb brushing her instep sent a shiver of raw feeling through her. When both shoes were in place, he looked at her, running his hands slowly up her legs, taking her skirt along for the ride until her thighs were bared to his glittering gaze.

"And now for my ransom," he murmured.

"Wha—what are you going to do?" she stammered.

But he was shoving her skirt higher, his palms warm and firm against her thighs, and she forgot about the question. She knew what he was going to do.

And she wanted it.

Tenderly, he opened her thighs and bent his head. Instantly, she went weak, threading her fingers into his hair to keep from sliding to the floor. Her hands delved into the tangle of silver while his teeth pushed aside the silk she'd put on only moments ago. And then his tongue was pleasuring her—moist, hot, wicked.

It didn't take long. Nothing with this man ever would. She bit down on her lower lip and rode the crest of the pleasure he gave her, her eyes wide open to keep from losing her balance, her release slamming through her, shattering her body into a million pieces, then putting it back together again.

"Oh, Eddy... Eddy," she finally moaned when he rose and buried his face against her hair.

He pulled back, his ice-blue eyes traveling over her face slowly, tenderly. "I needed to taste you, Annie," he said, and then he pulled her roughly against him. "I'm going to get you out of this mess, baby. I promise."

"Not unless we can manage to keep our hands off each other for the rest of the night."

He laughed softly. "We do seem to have that problem, don't we?"

She pulled back to give him a smile that was a little braver than she felt. "That's one problem I don't mind having," she whispered, giving him a quick, hard kiss. "Now get the rest of your clothes on and let's go find Max so he can give us his alibi and we can get on to the next suspect."

He let go of her. "Stubborn wench, aren't you?"

"Only when I know I'm right."

He took her chin in his hand. "Annie, I hope you're right. I really do. I've been remembering Max from when I was a kid. He was one of the good guys. Always had time for a word for me. I don't want him to be guilty, Annie. I just want us to have the answer before this night is over."

"Me, too, Eddy. Now let's go."

LARA LOOKED UP as soon as the elevator doors opened.

"Ann! I didn't know you were still here."

She was looking from Ann to Eddy and back again, and Ann could feel a blush start to bloom on her cheeks.

She cleared her throat. "Uh, Lara, have you seen Max at all tonight?"

"Well, he's not supposed to be on, but..."

"But what?"

"Well, I could have sworn I saw him earlier—just a glimpse of him as he zipped into the elevator."

"Really?" Ann prompted.

"Yeah. You know, it seemed odd at the time."

"Odd how?"

"Well, *zipped* is the word." She shrugged and gave a little shake of her blond head. "I mean, I didn't even know Max could move that fast."

Ann glanced at Eddy, then at Lara. "Where did he go after he came down?"

Lara shook her head. "I didn't see him come down. I must have been in the office."

The phone started to ring, and Ann told Lara to go ahead and get it. Before she could open her mouth to say anything to Eddy, he took hold of her arm and started to haul her over to the front of the lobby.

"I told you," he said.

She rolled her eyes. "Honestly, Eddy, Lara seeing Max take the elevator when he's supposed to be off duty doesn't exactly amount to a smoking gun."

Eddy gave an impatient huff. "He was in a hurry, trying not to be seen. And Lara didn't see him come down."

She raised a brow. "So?"

"So maybe he took the stairs because he didn't want to be seen."

"Oh," Ann said. She had to admit it, things were looking worse and worse for Max. "I guess we better find him, huh?"

"And fast," Eddy said, propelling her out the door.

Max's rooming house was several blocks west of the inn so they retrieved Ann's car from the parking lot. At ten the night was still clear and traffic was light. In just minutes she was pulling the car to the curb in front of the big old mansion that had been converted to a rooming house in the sixties. A vacancy sign creaked in the winter wind where it hung from the larger sign proclaiming rooms to let.

Ann peered at the house. "Think he's home?"

"I hope so, Annie, 'cause I haven't a clue as to where to start looking for him. Do you?"

She shook her head. "No. I guess I really don't know that much about him. I mean, he could have a girlfriend someplace, or—"

"Or he could still be carrying the torch for Hattie. A torch big enough to burn the place down."

"Oh, Eddy, I hope not."

"I don't know what to hope, baby. On the one hand, I'd like the guy to be innocent. On the other hand, I'd sure like to be able to turn the real embezzler over to Count Clifford come morning."

"Well, I hope he's innocent," Ann said firmly as she got out of the car.

Eddy followed her up the walk and onto the porch. She bent to squint at the mailboxes beside the door.

"Here he is. Number seven."

She pushed the buzzer next to number seven, and they waited. Nothing happened.

"What do we do now?" Ann asked.

"The sign says vacancies. Try the super."

Ann pressed another buzzer. Immediately there was an answering buzz, and they opened the outer door, went in and started to climb the staircase that led up from a wide, ornate entrance hall.

They found it on the third and last floor.

"I guess we better knock, huh?" Annie whispered, staring at the brass number seven on the polished oak door.

"Want me to?" Eddy asked.

She shook her head, raised her hand and knocked.

They heard an unmistakable rustling sound from inside.

"Someone's home," muttered Eddy.

"Yeah? Who's there?" came Max's gruff voice from behind the door.

"Max? It's Ann Madison. Could I talk to you for a minute?"

They heard more rustling and something that sounded suspiciously like a woman's voice. Then the door opened, and Max's grizzled head peered out.

"Ann—something wrong? What are you doing here?"

"We have some questions we'd like to ask you, Max," Eddy said, reaching out to push the door wider. Max stepped back and it swung open.

There was a woman sitting on the bed. She jumped to her feet. "Oh, my," she said, clutching her prim, high-necked blouse. It was impossible for Ann not to notice that the blouse had been buttoned wrong. And fairly recently, she'd be willing to bet. "Maxwell, should I go?" the woman chirped.

"No, Daisy," Max said, patting the air reassuringly in her direction. "Sit tight. I'll be right back."

Max came into the hall and shut the door protectively behind him. "What's this all about?" he asked.

"I'm sorry we're interrupting you, Max," Ann began. "But it's important for us to know where you were tonight."

Max's forehead furrowed. "Why?"

Ann looked helplessly at Eddy. She didn't want to go into everything unless they had to.

"It's a long story, Max, and we don't want to keep you from—uh, Daisy too long," Eddy said.

Apparently, he'd hit on exactly the right excuse, because Max glanced over his shoulder at the closed door before readily answering, "I been with Daisy all evening."

Ann and Eddy looked at each other. "Uh—can she verify that, Max?" Ann asked.

Max's expression turned surly. "Does she have to?"

"Yes," Eddy answered emphatically before Ann could say anything.

Max was clearly thinking it over. "Okay, wait here."

He disappeared behind the door, reappearing a moment later with the lady in question.

"These people want to know if you were with me all evening, Daisy. Will you tell them?"

Head moving as fast as a little bird's, Daisy looked at each of them in turn. "If you think I should, Max."

Max gave a nod. "Go ahead."

"I've been with Maxwell all evening. First we had dinner, then we went for a walk, then we came back here and—"

Max put his arm around Daisy's thin shoulders. "That's enough, dear," he said, and Daisy blushed prettily and stared at her feet, which Ann noticed for the first time were bare.

She was all for leaving these two in peace. Apparently Eddy had other ideas.

"Is there anyone that can verify that?" he asked.

"Eddy!" Ann gasped.

Max drew himself up. "Don't forget, boy, I knew you when you were in short pants. You best take care before you insult any woman of mine."

"Oh, Maxwell." Daisy tittered. "So gallant. But there's no need. We were on a double date, so all you have to do is ask the other couple."

"Other couple?" Ann asked.

"My, yes. Ada and Harold Albert doubled with us. We had a coupon, you know. If we bought three dinners, we received one free. So I said to Maxwell . . ."

It was another five minutes before they could politely bid the couple good-night and leave.

"Honestly, Eddy, talk about embarrassing! And then you've got to practically intimate that Daisy might be lying!"

Eddy grinned. "It wouldn't be the first time a moll had lied for her crooked boyfriend."

"I never saw anyone who looked less like a moll than Daisy," Ann said, opening the car door and waiting for Eddy to climb in.

"I agree. But looks can be deceiving, Annie." He tweaked her nose. "Who would have thought when I was rescued by the phantom of the airport that she would turn out to be a stubborn wench who could drive me wild in bed when she—"

"Don't you dare," Ann cut in, looking around furiously as if they had an audience.

Eddy laughed. "Tell you what—I'll keep my mouth shut if you let me drive for a change."

"Oh." She pouted mockingly. "Is your masculine pride feeling ignored?"

"No," he said, nipping her nose lightly with his teeth. "I'm just tired of scooting over on the seat. You do it this time."

She dropped the keys into his waiting hand, got in and scooted over.

"Where are we going?"

"Back to the inn to talk to the Alberts."

"You still don't believe Max, even though you've talked to his alibi?"

"Corroborating witnesses, Annie. A good private eye never takes anything for granted," Eddy said as he cranked the engine.

"Okay, Dick Tracy, peel out. We're wasting time."

So he did.

"I just hope the Alberts are up and they tell us they were with Max and Daisy," Annie said as they pulled into the inn's parking lot. "I really don't want it to be Max."

"Well, I'd rather save your sweet neck, sugar, than his grizzled one."

Eddy got out of the car and held the door while Annie scooted over, her skirt riding up her bare legs in the process.

He grinned. "I knew there was a reason I wanted to drive this time."

She gave him a look while she wiggled her skirt into place. "Keep your mind on business, pirate, or the next time you see these legs they're going to be in prison stripes."

He took her hand as they started to walk to the inn. "If it comes to that, sweet Annie, I'll have to make like a real pirate and kidnap you for good." He squeezed her hand. "But it isn't going to come to that," he said firmly. "I won't let it."

They rounded the corner and Eddy slowed his walk, letting go of Annie's hand and pulling her in close to him with an arm around her waist. The inn looked more like a castle than ever. Charmed or cursed, at that moment it was hard to tell which. The sliver of moon winked in and out of scudding wisps of cloud. Bare, dry branches rattled in the wind. Snow, sparkling as fairy dust, swirled from the roof and around the turret where icicles hung like the daggers of a wizard gone mad.

"Do you think Hattie and Nathan ever made love up in that turret?" Eddy murmured.

"You're bad, you know that?"

"I know what I'd like to do to you up in that turret someday—and it wouldn't be bad at all. It would be very, *very* good."

"Hold that thought, my Viking pirate. With any luck, you'll get your wish."

When they started to mount the stairs, Annie suddenly stopped.

"What's the matter?" Eddy asked.

"I'm not comfortable walking in there with you."

"Why not?"

He felt her shrug. "It's going to be a long night, and I don't know if I want Lara to see me going up to the penthouse with you. I mean, how will that look if something happens—you know, if we can't clear me? You'd be defending a woman that everyone would know had spent the night in the penthouse with you."

Eddy thought about it a moment. He supposed it made sense. "Fair enough. What do you propose we do?"

"You go in first. Keep Lara distracted while I sneak in and take the stairs."

Eddy laughed softly. "You're pretty natural at this cloak-and-dagger stuff, damsel." He kissed her hair. "We'd make quite a pair."

Reluctantly, he let go of her halfway up the steps, gave her a wink and entered the inn.

A fire glowed in the grate and Lara was sitting in front of it, coffee cup in hand, looking at an early edition of the morning paper.

Eddy made enough noise for her to hear him come in.

"Hi, Mr. Winters. It must be cold out. Would you like some coffee?"

He shook his head. "No, thanks. But I wouldn't mind a copy of that paper if you have an extra."

"Sure. The boy always leaves five copies."

Eddy followed her over to the desk, taking a quick look over his shoulder in time to see Annie slip in the door and start for the steps.

Lara took a paper off a small stack on the registration desk.

"There you go, Mr. Winters. Anything else I can do for you?"

With the pretext of tossing the hair from his face, Eddy managed a covert look towards the open staircase. It was empty.

He turned to Lara. "No, nothing else. Thanks, Lara, and good night."

"Night," she said as he headed for the elevator.

When he reached the fifth floor, Annie stood outside the penthouse door, waiting for him.

"I haven't got a key," she told him.

"I'll have to get you one. I'm finding I like the idea of you sneaking up to my room in the dead of night."

"Yeah, well, I just wish we could spend the night together doing something a little more pleasant than trying to prove that I'm not an embezzler."

Quick enough to catch her by surprise, he pulled her around and pressed her against the door. "Something like this?" he asked, then he took her mouth with enough force to surprise them both. Her breath was hot and sweet as it rushed into his open mouth. His tongue explored, hers answered. He felt her hands thrust into his hair, holding him fast to her, and he moaned his pleasure at her immediate and visceral response.

"How am I supposed to keep my mind on business, wench," he murmured when he'd pulled his mouth away, "when you're so cooperative every time I touch you?"

Giving him a wicked little smile, she answered simply, "Don't touch me." Then she scooted sideways away from him.

"Easier said than done," he muttered, making a grab for her again.

She stepped out of reach. "Uh-uh," she said, wagging a finger at him. "Get that door open, we're wasting time. We've got to call the Alberts so they can verify Max's whereabouts. And then we have to find the *real* suspect."

Eddy didn't say anything to that. In truth, he didn't know what to hope for. If Max and Daisy were lying, which seemed farfetched, indeed, Annie's problems would be over. But to think of Max as an embezzler, to think that he would pin it on Annie—

He unlocked the door to the penthouse and went in.

"No lilacs tonight," Annie murmured as she followed him.

"Max was obviously busy with other things."

He shrugged out of his coat, tossed it on a chair and strode to the telephone.

"Wait," Annie said. "Let me do it. It'll seem more natural that way."

Without saying a word, Eddy handed her the phone, then stood and listened while she talked to Ada Albert, asking about the restaurant they had gone to that night on the pretext of wondering if she could recommend it to other guests.

"Pretty smooth," Eddy said when she'd hung up the phone. "You're a natural. What did she say?"

"She said that she and Harold were watching Jay Leno. Then she said what I thought she'd say—Max and Daisy spent the evening with her and Harold."

"And we're out of a suspect," Eddy muttered, sinking down onto the sofa and picking up the crowbar from the coffee table where he'd left it.

"Don't sound so disappointed, Eddy. I'm glad it couldn't have been Max."

"I know you are," he told her softly. And he supposed he was, too. But the fact remained that Annie was suspect number one—and Clifford would be there to stir things up in a matter of hours.

Running his hand over the cold, hard surface of the crowbar, he thought about what they should do next. "You know, maybe we're going about this the wrong way. Maybe we should forget means and opportunity and start focusing on motive."

Annie took off her coat and threw it on top of Eddy's before plopping next to him on the sofa. "I thought you said we needed all three to nab a suspect?"

"Yeah, we do. But we're forgetting that if someone has a strong enough motive, they can always find means and opportunity."

"But isn't the motive money?"

"Money makes a good motive," Eddy agreed, "and the most likely one. But what if something is behind the money motive? What if someone was really trying to ruin the inn for reasons of their own?"

She sighed. "I thought we'd been through that. First with me thinking you might be trying to settle the score for only getting the inn in the will—then with you thinking it might be Max, out for revenge."

Eddy sighed and sank deeper into the sofa, leaning his head against the back and stretching his long legs out on the coffee table. "Plenty of brick walls in this case," he agreed. "But maybe it's someone in New York—someone at Northcott Enterprises."

"Someone like Count Clifford?" Ann asked.

Eddy grunted. "Perfect choice, as far as I'm concerned. But what would he have to gain? If this place closes down, Northcott Enterprises doesn't stand to gain much. And don't forget, if someone wasn't pulling strings, the inn would probably be making money. Not as much as the luxury hotels in the corporation, of course. But it'd be viable enough that, given the terms of the will, the board would never vote to shut it down."

"So what do we do now? It's getting late and we're running out of time."

Eddy sat up, leaning forward to grab the morning paper Lara had given him downstairs—more to keep his hands busy than anything else. If Annie continued to sit close to him, if he continued to smell the flowers in her hair, he was going to have to have her in his arms again, and they couldn't afford to waste any more time. Not that Annie in his arms would ever be a waste of time. But they needed to come up with some kind of strategy to hold Clifford off once he got there, because it was getting more and more doubtful that they were going to come up with an alternative suspect to Annie to hand Cousin Clifford in the morning.

His eyes restlessly scanned the headlines while he told her, "We need stalling time, something that'll keep Clifford in the dark for a while at least until—"

He stopped. Something about the day's major headline caught him. It was something he thought he'd heard about before, but he couldn't think where.

"County Board Admits Downtown Site for New Stadium Still in the Running," he mumbled.

Annie sat up straight. "What?"

"This headline. Something about it—"

She looked over his shoulder. "Oh, that. They've been going back and forth for months on that issue. Some think they should build it next to the old stadium. Some think downtown would be better for the city as a whole. Sometimes I think—"

"Jason!" Eddy interrupted. "That's where I've heard this before."

"Jason?"

"Yeah. While we were walking home from the Bradley Center after the Admirals game. We passed this empty land and Jason said that's where they might build the new stadium."

Annie nodded. "Right. Just a matter of blocks from here."

Eddy stared at her. "It's been here all along," he said.

She shook her head. "What? What's been here all along?"

"Motive, Annie. The new stadium is our motive." He stood and started to move about the room, thinking aloud on his feet, too keyed up to remain still. "Somebody in the company knows about this. If that stadium goes up a few blocks from here, this little piece of land that holds the Northcott Inn is going to be very valuable."

"It's only got twenty-five rooms, Eddy. It'd hardly be a gold mine. Besides, why try to ruin its reputation now if you want to cash in on it later?"

"Not the inn, Annie. The land. A luxury high-rise hotel could be built on the same size parcel that holds the inn. That, Annie, with the stadium within walking distance, would be your gold mine."

Annie's mouth dropped open, and he knew she understood.

"Where are you going?" Annie asked as he made for the door.

"I'm going down to get a fax off to Hank. See if any large blocks of stock have been put into play."

"In the middle of the night?"

Eddy grinned. "Hank's fax never sleeps. Hell, Hank barely sleeps."

"And if there has been stock action?"

"Then we might just be on the verge of uncovering a hostile takeover attempt of Northcott Enterprises."

He started for the door, but her breathless voice stopped him.

"Eddy, you think this could be it?"

He turned to look at her, standing in the middle of Hattie's sitting room, looking like she belonged there as much as the daffodils on the carpet beneath her feet. She had a sweet, hopeful look on her beautiful face. "I think this could be it," he answered, then he strode toward her, thrust an arm around her waist, pulled her in for a quick, hard kiss. "Wish me luck, damsel," he whispered against her mouth.

"Good luck, pirate."

And then he was gone, leaving her standing there, uncertain whether to laugh or cry or hope or despair. She decided to do none of the above. Instead, she went to the kitchen to make coffee. She had a feeling they were going to need all the caffeine they could get to make it through the night, whatever it might hold.

Ann had always loved Hattie's kitchen. It was bright yellow and green, old-fashioned and cheery. She filled the pot with water and switched on the coffeemaker. From the cupboard she took down yellow ceramic cups. Hattie's cups, she thought as she placed them on a tray. Hattie must have done this a thousand times for her Nathan—and now Annie was doing it for Nathan III. Eddy. It was a simple pleasure, marred by the fact that their adventure together was coming to an end. What happened in these hours before dawn would determine whether she'd be spending the next days being grilled by corporate heads—and possibly the police—or whether she'd be spending it saying goodbye to Eddy.

Either way, she knew she'd be spending it nursing a broken heart. Because she loved him. And she knew with a certainty that there would never be another like him in her life. She also knew that she'd go it alone rather than settle for less.

Tomorrow, or the next day, or the next, the Viking pirate would go out of her life, leaving the sweetest, craziest memories a woman could ever want.

The coffee had brewed and she was pouring it into the cups when she heard a sound from the sitting room. Eddy was back.

She picked up the tray and carried it in.

"Eddy," she began, then stopped dead in the sitting room doorway. It wasn't Eddy. "Max! What are you—"

The man turned, and although he was wearing Max's jacket and cap, he wasn't Max.

Chapter Fourteen

"*Austin,*" she said, intending to say more. But the wind went out of her and she had no breath to speak when she looked at the crowbar he held in his hands.

"M-Ms. Madison," he stammered, obviously as surprised as she. "I—I saw Mr. Winters leave. I—I didn't know anyone was up here or I wouldn't have—"

Ann swallowed. "You wouldn't have what?" she managed to croak out of her dry throat.

He looked at the crowbar in his hands as if he wasn't sure how it had gotten there. Then he raised it and took a step toward her. "You—you just stay where you are and I—I won't hurt you. I just have to g-get something, then I'll be gone."

The crowbar was shaking in his hand. His glasses were sliding down his nose. His cheeks were mottled with scarlet, his lips bloodless and white. This was Austin, the kid who couldn't get anything right. If he'd meant to scare her, he wasn't doing that right, either—because suddenly she wasn't.

She set the tray down on the nearest table, picked up a cup of the coffee and started to move slowly toward him. "Look, Austin, I don't know what you're after, but Mr. Winters will be back any minute and then—"

He raised the crowbar higher. "Don't come any closer. I—I don't want to have to use this."

"Of course, you don't, Austin," she told him sweetly and calmly, much, she imagined, as one would talk to a mental patient. "Why don't you just put it down and have some of this coffee. We'll sit and talk this thing out. If you're in trouble, maybe I can help you. Maybe—"

Then Ann heard it. For a stunning moment, her eyes locked with Austin's, and she knew that he'd heard it, too. The elevator.

She started to move, but Austin raised the crowbar higher, a comically wild look in his eye. "Get over behind that door," he growled. Well, as much as Austin could growl. Ann was tempted to laugh but she decided it was best to play along. Still clutching the coffee cup, she scurried behind the door. Austin wedged himself in front of her, crowbar ready to strike.

"You're not actually going to use that thing, are you Austin?" she asked.

"I—I don't want to, Ms. Madison, but I don't know what else to do. If you hadn't been here I'd be gone by now. I don't want to hurt Mr. Winters, but—"

The key rattled in the lock, and Austin firmed his hold on the crowbar. She was close enough behind him to feel his thin body coiled like a spring, ready to strike. The door started to swing open.

"Look out, Eddy!" she yelled.

With a gasp of betrayal, Austin swung around, and Ann's mind flooded with the image of the crowbar about to come down on her head. Without a moment to think, she did what seemed to come naturally. She threw the hot coffee in his face.

Austin screamed. The crowbar clattered to the floor. And then Eddy was there, forcing Austin backward until he stumbled into the sofa and hit the cushions with a thud.

"Are you all right?" Eddy asked her over his shoulder while he kept a firm, hard hand on Austin's shoulder.

"I'm fine. Luckily, I was holding a cup of coffee—"

"Your weapon of choice," Eddy interrupted, as he pulled Austin's hand away from his cheek to inspect the damage. "You better get him a cold cloth or something for this burn."

"Right." Annie hurried to the kitchen and came back with a tea towel soaked in cold water. Sitting next to Austin, she pressed it to his cheek, the only area that seemed to have been damaged.

"I—I wouldn't have hit you, Ms. Madison," Austin stammered. "Honest."

Looking at his face, deathly white where the coffee hadn't scalded him, Ann tended to believe him.

"I couldn't be sure, Austin, but I'm sorry that I had to hurt you." She gave Eddy a look, hoping to convey to him that she wanted to handle this—and handle it as gently as possible. Eddy apparently got the message. He let his hand drop from Austin's shoulder and stepped back, but remained close by.

"We already know why you broke into the penthouse, Austin. We found the money and checks in the hidden staircase."

Austin groaned and closed his eyes. "Then you know it's been me," he moaned.

Ann shot Eddy a look. "Yes, Austin. We know. We just don't know why."

He shook his head. "Do you know how hard it is to get a decent scholarship, Ms. Madison? My parents' dream was always to send me to an Ivy League school, but they couldn't afford to do it on their own." He opened his eyes, focusing them intently on Ann. "I needed money—lots of it. Far more than I could make working while still going to college here. When I got turned down by the scholarship committee—" he quickly and furtively glanced at Eddy, "—my grades weren't all that good—I just couldn't tell my parents. I mean, they were counting on me. So I just waited, hoping that something would come up before I had to tell them."

"And something came up," Ann said gently when he paused.

He looked wildly from Ann to Eddy and back again. "The man said I wouldn't get in trouble because it was his idea and I was just following orders. It wasn't me, Ms. Madison—you've got to believe that. He thought of it all—I just did what he told me to. And yesterday he called and told me to get rid of anything I'd hidden here because the inn was going to close down."

Ann looked at Eddy, and she knew what he was thinking. Someone in the corporation was behind this—someone who desperately wanted the will nullified so the inn could close. "The stadium?" she mouthed silently.

Eddy nodded.

She turned to Austin. "And what else had this man asked you to do?" she asked him gently, hoping to keep him talking until they had the whole story.

And Austin did talk. He almost seemed relieved to be able to do so. He told them how he intercepted Ann's letters before they could be mailed so they could keep New York from getting anything incriminating, how he collected the payroll checks of employees Ann had been firing under false orders, and how he forged signatures to cash the checks at places that didn't ask too many questions.

"But you made the signatures look like I could have made them. How did you manage that?"

Austin's mouth twitched wryly. "That's about the only thing I'm good at, Ms. Madison. I had years of practice when I'd forge my mother's signature on excuses to get me out of gym class in high school." The slight smile fled and he looked beseechingly at Ann. "But it wasn't my idea to set you up, Ms. Madison. You've got to believe that! He made me do it!''

"He?" Eddy said, breaking his silence. "Who's *he?*"

Austin's panicked gaze shifted between them again before he bowed his head, a flush staining the cheek that hadn't been burned. "I don't know," he mumbled.

Ann saw Eddy start to react, and she stopped him with a look and a hand out, palm up, while shaking her head. She could tell by the look on his face and the coiled power of his body that the effort to hold back wasn't easy. She understood, but she also felt that it was best to handle Austin with kid gloves. If they scared him too much, he just might clam up entirely. Giving Eddy a small smile of thanks, she turned to Austin.

Ann placed a gentle hand on his shoulder and asked, "You don't know who you were working for?"

Austin shook his head.

"You're wearing Max's uniform. Does he have anything to do with this?"

"Mr. Harper?" Austin was clearly surprised by the question. "No! I just borrowed his jacket and cap in case someone saw me or something."

So Max was out of it completely. Ann was glad. "This man you're working for, how did he contact you?"

"By phone—at home." Austin gave a helpless little shrug. "I just did what he told me to do."

"And he never told you his name?"

Austin shook his head again.

"And you never met?" Ann asked him gently.

"Well, just once, right after he called me the first time. He told me to meet him in the parking garage at the Grand Avenue Mall so he could give me some money and make me sign some papers that he said would keep me quiet if I ever changed my mind." He finally looked up, his eyes wide and frightened on Ann's. "I wanted to change my mind, Ms.

Madison, as soon as I found out that you were going to get blamed for it all. But—but I couldn't. My parents—''

Ann patted his shoulder. "I understand, Austin."

"Well, I don't!" Eddy shot out, taking a menacing step toward Austin. "Do you have any idea what could have happened to Annie? She might have gone to prison. And what about Jason? Didn't you think of anyone besides yourself?"

Austin, hanging his head again, mumbled, "But he promised to set up a fake scholarship so my parents wouldn't have to find out. He said . . ."

When his speech faltered, Eddy grabbed Austin's chin in his hand and forced his head up until Austin had to meet his eyes. "He said what, Austin? Did he say his name? Who were you working for? Who was pulling your strings?"

Ann placed a restraining hand on Eddy's arm. She could feel the muscle, hard, ready for combat. "Eddy, please," she began.

He shook her off. "A name, Austin," Eddy demanded, his voice tight, dangerous.

"I—I can't give you a name, Mr. Winters. Honest."

"A face, then. Would you know him again if you saw him?"

"I—I don't know," Austin stammered. "It was dark and—"

Just then, the door to the penthouse opened. Purely on reflex, Eddy grabbed Austin by the jacket and hauled him to his feet as he turned toward the door behind him.

"That's him!" Austin croaked. "That's the man!"

Eddy let go of Austin, and he stumbled onto the sofa. Ann knew who the man was before Eddy spoke. The size and sharpness of his incisors was unmistakable.

"Well, well," Eddy said, a dangerous grin on his face. "Cousin Clifford. Been in any good parking garages lately?"

'Wow! And then what happened, Mom?''

"And then the police came—''

"And carted Count Clifford off to the slammer!'' Jason managed to shout despite a mouth full of pancakes.

"And carted Count Clifford off to the slammer,'' Ann acquiesced.

"Wow! I wish I coulda been there!''

"Well, I'm glad you weren't. And I'm glad it's over,'' she stated firmly. "Now things can get back to normal.'' But as she said the words, Ann wasn't at all sure they were true. Oh, she was glad her name was going to be cleared. But she wasn't so glad that things would be getting back to normal. Not if it meant that the Viking pirate was going to disappear into the snow. Cup of coffee in hand, she stood at her kitchen window, watching the lazy flakes drift, knowing that every snowfall for the rest of her life would make her think of the Viking pirate and the magic he brought briefly into her life.

"Can I tell Danny?'' Jason was asking.

She smiled softly, a little sadly. "Yes, you can tell Danny.''

"All right!''

Shaking her head at her son's enthusiasm, she wondered if the whole thing seemed no more real to him than a video game. That was something they were definitely going to have to talk about later. For now, she would let him have the thrill of knowing that his mother had helped solve a crime.

She put her coffee cup down and turned around. "Come over here, Jase.''

"Aw, Mom—you gotta hug me now?''

"Hey, I didn't even think of that. I just wanted to wipe the syrup off your chin. But now that you mention it—'' Pulling him into her arms, she gave him a big bear hug.

Jason didn't quickly end the hug as he usually did, but clung to her for moments more.

"Mom?'' he asked, his arms still around her waist.

"Hmm?"

"It's okay now, huh? I mean, you didn't get hurt, and neither did Eddy, right?"

"Right," she said, pulling back enough to ruffle his hair.

"Aw, Mom," he complained.

But he kissed her on the cheek before he grabbed his jacket and books and started for the door. Then he hesitated and turned back.

"Will I see Eddy today?" he asked.

There was worry on his childish brow, and Ann wondered if he'd already guessed that they were going to lose their Viking pirate.

"I don't know, Jase. We'll see," she answered. He gave a solemn little nod and headed out the door.

WHEN ANN got to the inn, the front door was locked. She fished in her purse for her key, unlocked it and went inside. Lara was just gathering up her things to leave.

"What's going on, Lara? Why was the door locked?"

"Orders from headquarters," Lara said. "After all the trouble last night and since we've got no reservations on the books for a while, guess New York just decided to close the place down."

"Mr. and Mrs. Albert?" Ann asked.

"Checked out this morning."

"Oh..." Ann felt like the wind was knocked out of her. Apparently, the board had decided to close the inn despite what they'd learned about Clifford Northcott. Maybe they were going to go along with tearing the place down anyway, and replacing it with a high-rise luxury hotel. Ann didn't even want to think about that possibility.

"Well, I'm outta here. I'll call you later to see if you've found anything out, okay? If they don't reopen the inn, I'm going to be job hunting."

"Me, too," Ann answered weakly. "Me, too."

She watched Lara leave, locking the door behind her. Then she just strolled around the lobby, wondering how it could all be coming to an end despite everything she and Eddy had found out.

Count Clifford had been engineering the whole thing, working behind the scenes with the corporation that was attempting the hostile takeover of Northcott Enterprises. Apparently, he'd been promised stock and a position with more power than he'd ever wielded at Northcott if the takeover went through. And the takeover would only go through if the company attempting it could be assured the inn could be torn down to make way for a very lucrative hotel near the new stadium.

She hadn't had time to talk to Eddy much once Clifford showed up and the police had gotten involved. And then he'd had to rush home to get Jason off to school. But Eddy had taken the time to assure her that the takeover could be halted now that they knew who was behind it. But apparently, Northcott had decided to close the inn, after all.

Ann went to her office, figuring she might as well clear out her desk. But all she had to do was open the first drawer to know she didn't have the heart for it. Glancing toward the staircase, she wondered if Eddy was still up in the penthouse. It took her less than a second to decide to find out.

The elevator took her to the fifth floor, and she got off. Pausing at the penthouse door, she wondered if Eddy would even have time for her, with everything else that he must be dealing with. Then she decided that she didn't care. She had to see him—because she didn't know how many more mornings he'd be there.

She raised her hand and knocked.

No one answered.

She tried the knob. The door was unlocked, so she went inside.

The place didn't smell like lilacs this morning. She wondered if it ever would again.

"Eddy?" she called, but he didn't answer. He wasn'
there.

She went to the mantel and gazed at the portrait of Hattie and Nathan. Now that she knew Eddy was their grand
son, she could see Nathan in Eddy's good looks, Hattie i
the twinkle in his eyes. She hoped they knew that it had beer
the boy hurt by divorce and bitterness who had rejected thei
legacy—not the little boy who'd spent his summers witl
them and who'd loved the place as much as they had.

She walked around the room, touching this and that
When she came to the bedroom doorway—

The turret. She wanted to climb up to it one last time.

The snow was light on her face when she'd climbed th
stairs and opened the door. She stood at the railing and re
membered the night before, when she'd stood there with he
Viking pirate, the man she knew she'd love for the rest of he
life. Soon, she couldn't tell if it was the snow melting on he
cheeks—or tears falling there.

"I thought I'd find you up here."

She turned, and there he was. Her Viking pirate. But no
as she'd first seen him. This morning, he was dressed in hi
fine cashmere coat, a designer suit beneath it, his hai
dragged into a ponytail. But the diamond still winked in hi
ear.

"Were you looking for me?" she asked him.

"Of course I was looking for you. When I finished at th
police station I came here and cleaned up, then went to you
house. But you were already gone."

She smiled, dashing at the wetness on her cheeks. "I cam
looking for you, but you were already gone. I—I though
maybe you'd already left for New York," she added, hop
ing he'd tell her he had no intention of going back to New
York.

"No, my flight leaves later this afternoon," he answered.

"Oh..." Her heart felt like it had dropped out of her chest. Quickly, she turned toward the railing again, hanging tightly onto it, trying to focus on the street below.

He came up behind her, placing his hands on the railing next to hers, trapping her body between his solid arms. It seemed only natural to lean back against his chest, savoring the last time she would be near him.

"So you're going," she said.

She felt him nod. "There are a lot of loose ends to tie up."

"Of course."

"I figure it won't take long—maybe to the end of the week. Then I'll be back."

She swung around, wondering if she'd heard him right. "You'll be back?"

His ice-blue eyes glittered at her. "Of course I'll be back. What did you think?"

"When I got here this morning and Lara told me the inn had been closed down, I just thought—"

His arms left the railing and came around her. "Temporary, sugar. Just until I can get things straightened out in New York and get some renovations started on the place. I'll be living in the penthouse, so it'll be easy to oversee the work myself."

Her mouth dropped open. "Living in the penthouse?"

"That's right." He grinned at her. "I'm finally claiming my inheritance."

"But—but I thought it came with strings. I thought you had to get married and raise a family in order to inherit."

"I do." His arms tightened, and he buried his face in her hair. "How about it, sugar?" he murmured into her ear. "Are you going to marry me and live in the penthouse with me?"

She pulled away from him. "Are you serious?"

His eyes sobered. "Very serious. I love you, Annie. Say yes, and we can work together to make this place what it once was."

"Eddy, you're moving too fast for me."

"You do love me? I'm not wrong about that, am I?"

The tears were starting to fall again. Dashing them away
she nodded. "Yes. Yes, I love you. But—"

"But, what?"

What was wrong with her? The Viking pirate was asking
her to marry him. Maybe it was too fast, maybe it was too
crazy, but was this the time to be practical?

She looked into his gorgeous face, at the silver hair the
wind was doing its best to pull from its confining band, a
the diamond winking wickedly from his ear. "Tell m
again," she whispered.

He touched her face. "I love you, Annie. I want to marr
you. I want the inn to be ours."

"And you'd be happy with a life like that?"

He grinned. "Oh, I might want to take a case once in
while, but, yes—I'd be happy with that."

He took her hand in his and brought it to his lips. The
felt firm and steady against her skin. "Listen, Annie," h
said, "I spent my life avoiding attachments, thinking onl
of the next adventure, looking for anything that was differ
ent than what my parents had. Then I came to the in
again." He kissed her hand again. "Then I met you. An
suddenly it was clear. This—you, the inn—is what's bee
missing from my life. I know what I want now—what I'r
finally ready for. The kind of love I'd given up believing r
ally existed and the kind of life that goes with it. I want yo
as my wife, Annie. I want this place as my home."

"And Jason?" she asked, holding her breath for the an
swer.

"I love him, Annie, and I want to help raise him. I wan
Jason as my son . . . and maybe even a sister for him some
day. Or a brother. Or both. How would you like that, An
nie? A bunch of little pirates and damsels running aroun
the penthouse?"

The tears were coming in earnest now, flowing silently own her cheeks to mix with the drops of snow. She dashed t them again, wishing she could dash away her practicality long with them. She snuffled. "You don't really know me, ddy. And I don't really know you—"

He laughed softly and shook his head. "You're going to e difficult again. I should have known." He sighed dranatically. "Okay, damsel. However long it will take is how ong I'll give you. I'm prepared to spend the rest of my life omancing you, Annie, if you promise me one thing."

She swallowed and sniffed. "What's that?"

"You'll work with me while I'm trying to sweep you off our feet. You'll help me restore this place, help me open it gain."

She closed her eyes, feeling another tear slip past her ashes. "You know I will, Eddy. You know it."

"Good—just don't make me wait too long. When the enovations are done, I want to be able to carry my bride ver the threshold." He yanked her into his arms, running is hands up and down her back, arranging her body so it nolded to his. There was enough heat between them to ren-ler the cold wind and the increasing snow harmless.

He bit gently on her lower lip. "I have a few hours until ny plane takes off," he murmured, "and I think I know just ow I want to spend them."

His mouth skimmed her jaw, his teeth nipped her ear, his ands skimmed her body—and she got the message, loud nd clear. She couldn't think of a better way to spend a nowy day.

"Um, Eddy?" she asked, despite her quickening breath nd her beating heart. "Can we have new wallpaper in the obby?"

"Yes," he murmured against her neck.

"And can I pick out the new bedspreads?"

She felt him nod as he unbuttoned her coat and slipped is hands inside.

"And—and curtains to match?" she managed to as while his hands were doing delicious things there under h coat.

He laughed softly, pulling back to look at her. "An thing else?" he asked, his pirate's eyes glittering dange ously.

She grinned. "Oh, lots. There's the carpet on the stai case and the fixtures in the bathrooms and—"

He nipped her lower lip again. "Wench."

She grinned. "Pirate."

"Shut up a moment about fixtures and carpets and ki me," he demanded in his best pirate's growl.

So she did.

AMERICAN ✦ ROMANCE®

The Randall Brothers—living out there on their Wyoming ranch with only each other, their ranch hands and the cattle for company.... Well, it could make a body yearn for female companionship! Much as they miss womenfolk, these four cowboys don't cotton to being roped and branded in matrimony! But then big brother Jake brings home four of the most beautiful "fillies."

Don't miss what happens next to

Chad—COWBOY CUPID October '96

Pete—COWBOY DADDY November '96

Brett—COWBOY GROOM January '97

Jake—COWBOY SURRENDER February '97

They give new meaning to the term "gettin' hitched"!

Everyone loves the _Holidays_...

Four sexy guys with two things in common:
the Holiday name
and humbug in the heart!

the holiday heart

by Linda Cajio

DOCTOR VALENTINE
(February)

Dr. Peter Holiday with his cool good looks and logical ways
thought he had love, that figured out. As far as he can tell,
the condition is nothing more than a chemical imbalance.
But Cupid, in the form of a feisty redhead wants to make
sure Peter gets the supreme loverboy's point...right in the
rear!

This year Cupid and his romantic cohorts are
working double—make that quadruple—time, not only
Valentine's Day but also Mother's Day, Labor Day and
Christmas—every holiday season throughout 1997.

#678 BACHELOR DADDY
(May)

#694 BOSS MAN
(September)

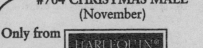

#704 CHRISTMAS MALE
(November)

Only from

FREE VALENTINE'S BROOCH! $9.95 U.S. retail value

This Valentine's Day Harlequin brings you
all the essentials—romance, chocolate
and jewelry—in:

Matchmaking chocolate-shop owner Papa Valentine
dispenses sinful desserts, mouth-watering
chocolates…and advice to the lovelorn, in this
collection of three delightfully romantic stories
by Meryl Sawyer, Kate Hoffmann and Gina Wilkins.

As our special Valentine's Day gift to you, each copy
of *Valentine Delights* will have a beautiful, filigreed,
heart-shaped brooch attached to the cover.

Make this your most delicious Valentine's Day
ever with *Valentine Delights!*

Available in February wherever
Harlequin books are sold.

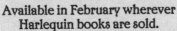

HARLEQUIN ®
®

Harlequin and Silhouette celebrate
Black History Month with seven terrific titles,
featuring the all-new *Fever Rising*
by Maggie Ferguson
(Harlequin Intrigue #408) and
A Family Wedding by Angela Benson
(Silhouette Special Edition #1085)!

Also available are:
Looks Are Deceiving by Maggie Ferguson
Crime of Passion by Maggie Ferguson
Adam and Eva by Sandra Kitt
Unforgivable by Joyce McGill
Blood Sympathy by Reginald Hill

On sale in January at your favorite
Harlequin and Silhouette retail outlet.

HARLEQUIN®

Don't miss these Harlequin favorites by some of our most
distinguished authors!
And now, you can receive a discount by ordering two or more titles!

HT#25645	THREE GROOMS AND A WIFE by JoAnn Ross	$3.25 U.S. $3.75 CAN.	☐
HT#25647	NOT THIS GUY by Glenda Sanders	$3.25 U.S. $3.75 CAN.	☐
HP#11725	THE WRONG KIND OF WIFE by Roberta Leigh	$3.25 U.S. $3.75 CAN.	☐
HP#11755	TIGER EYES by Robyn Donald	$3.25 U.S. $3.75 CAN.	☐
HR#03416	A WIFE IN WAITING by Jessica Steele	$3.25 U.S. $3.75 CAN.	☐
HR#03419	KIT AND THE COWBOY by Rebecca Winters	$3.25 U.S. $3.75 CAN.	☐
HS#70622	KIM & THE COWBOY by Margot Dalton	$3.50 U.S. $3.99 CAN.	☐
HS#70642	MONDAY'S CHILD by Janice Kaiser	$3.75 U.S. $4.25 CAN.	☐
HI#22342	BABY VS. THE BAR by M.J. Rodgers	$3.50 U.S. $3.99 CAN.	☐
HI#22382	SEE ME IN YOUR DREAMS by Patricia Rosemoor	$3.75 U.S. $4.25 CAN.	☐
HAR#16538	KISSED BY THE SEA by Rebecca Flanders	$3.50 U.S. $3.99 CAN.	☐
HAR#16603	MOMMY ON BOARD by Muriel Jensen	$3.50 U.S. $3.99 CAN.	☐
HH#28885	DESERT ROGUE by Erine Yorke	$4.50 U.S. $4.99 CAN.	☐
HH#28911	THE NORMAN'S HEART by Margaret Moore	$4.50 U.S. $4.99 CAN.	☐

(limited quantities available on certain titles)

	AMOUNT	$
DEDUCT:	**10% DISCOUNT FOR 2+ BOOKS**	$
ADD:	**POSTAGE & HANDLING**	$
	($1.00 for one book, 50¢ for each additional)	
	APPLICABLE TAXES*	$_____
	TOTAL PAYABLE	$_____
	(check or money order—please do not send cash)	

To order, complete this form and send it, along with a check or money order for the
total above, payable to Harlequin Books, to: **In the U.S.:** 3010 Walden Avenue,
P.O. Box 9047, Buffalo, NY 14269-9047; **In Canada:** P.O. Box 613, Fort Erie, Ontario,
L2A 5X3.

Name:_____

Address: _____ City: _____

State/Prov.: _____ Zip/Postal Code: _____

*New York residents remit applicable sales taxes.
 Canadian residents remit applicable GST and provincial taxes.
Look us up on-line at: http://www.romance.net

HBACK-JM4

Heartbreak RANCH

Four generations of independent women...
Four heartwarming, romantic stories of the West...
Four incredible authors...

Fern Michaels
Jill Marie Landis
Dorsey Kelley
Chelley Kitzmiller

Saddle up with Heartbreak Ranch, an outstanding
Western collection that will take you on a whirlwind
trip through four generations and the exciting,
romantic adventures of four strong women who
have inherited the ranch from Bella Duprey,
famed Barbary Coast madam.

Available in March,
wherever Harlequin books are sold.

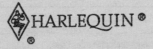

HARLEQUIN ®